Before he knew it, his own voice had responded, "I must stop global warming. . ." From somewhere a Drum Circle sounded, its thumps rising steadily in his ears soothing his soul and calming him as wooden flutes joined in. Louder and louder the drums sounded, faster and wilder the pipes played—then abruptly stopped. . .

Fred the mining construction engineer out for a brief beer and a few nine-pins took a step and looked down upon the decayed remnant of his former life. Even as he watched, the clothes crumbled inward, no longer meeting resistance from a body, the clothing masking nothing.

Snapping out a hair-brush, Fred passed it quickly over his new thick shoulder-length brunette hair, stylishly waved.

"Thank you, girls!" said his deep voice. "I'm one of you now!"

Will the world survive the menace of the

CROSS-DRESSERS FROM PLUTO?

Maggie
Illustrated by Kevin Clark
www.KC-art.com

Cover Design by Glenn Lazar Roberts

CROSS-DRESSERS FROM PLUTO

by

Glenn Lazar Roberts

ADVENTURES
OF THE
RADIATED LESBIAN NUN
Part 2

Dark Lotus Books
home of the
JUST PLAIN WEIRD

www.darklotusbooks.com

If you enjoy
CROSS-DRESSERS FROM PLUTO
please post a
REVIEW
on your favorite websites:
www.amazon.com
www.goodreads.com
www.siriusreviews.com
www.authorsden.com

DEDICATED TO
ROBERT CRUMB
"MR. NATURAL"

This work is speculative fiction and intended for entertainment only. All characters and events are fictional, and any resemblance to real persons or incidents or institutions is entirely coincidental.

ISBN 978-0-9675809-6-8
www.darklotusbooks.com

from DARK LOTUS BOOKS:
A tale of the fantastic
and macabre...

THE GLOW

by

Glenn Lazar Roberts

Sam Trencher has a problem. To keep from exploding into flames, he must keep the exact same coins in each pocket. Six years ago he left his home town and his girl. Now he's coming back to find her–but he can't tell what's real and what's not…and his temperature is rising.

"An exciting, fast-paced tale that takes the reader through a roller coaster ride. . .one of the best stories I have ever read."

—E L Russell, author of *Deadly Awakenings, Onset, & Reset*

From Dark Lotus Books
JUST PLAIN WEIRD
Life at the touch of a button…or death!

FRENZY

by
Glenn Lazar Roberts

The hurricane party went well–until someone locked the doors. Now the partygoers' only escape from the Research Center's basement is through a labyrinth of rapidly flooding tunnels with drug gangs, psychics, a stock fraud, and one-minute piranhas created by experimental 'genechips'. Weird sci-fi run amok.

"A terrifically fun read! Glenn Lazar Roberts squeezes a lot of horror, mystery and plain old fun into his new novel... Grab a copy as fast as you can and read this face-paced novel."
—Jerry D. Mohrlang, author of Sarawak.

"A plot worthy of the movies..."
—Michael Fox, author of Theater Boy.

Heroic Fantasy in the tradition of
Robert E. Howard &
Edgar Rice Burroughs

THE MAALSTROM SERIES:

BOOK 1

MAALSTROM

by
Glenn Lazar Roberts

In the midst of war with the tyrant Nesos, Flores of the Turlicum is trapped in the Temple of Vensa where he falls under the spell of the priestess Amina, the most beautiful gila of the Three Valleys. First half of the The Selk King.

"If you enjoyed Game of Thrones or Joseph Campbell, you'll love Maalstrom."
—John Picha

"Glenn Lazar Roberts is one of the finest writers of unconventional prose in contemporary fiction. His wonderfully inventive plots and mastery of the language place him in the company of Calvino, Burges, Gass..."
—Carolyn Thorman

More Heroic Fantasy
from DARK LOTUS BOOKS

THE MAALSTROM SERIES:

BOOK 2

THE SELK KING

by
Glenn Lazar Roberts

Flores of the Turlicum pursues his lost love Amina across the alien planet Maalstrom to the Island of the Sun-God, or Heavenhell. In another plot with twists and turns, Flores discovers the Black Pillar and climbs its spiral ramp from the nether-world to the selks' glass city in the clouds, encountering further unfolding of the mysterious relationships that link Maalstrom's bizarre inhabitants. Strewn with eccentric characters and gruesome combat, *The Selk King* is a triumph of mythological speculation and psychological insight into the nature of the Sacred.

"Compelling. Any sci-fi enthusiast would love this book." —*Writer's Digest*

"A unique and visionary epic."
—*Sirius Reviews*

And more fevered dreams
from the mind of
Glenn Lazar Roberts...

ADVENTURES OF THE RADIATED LESBIAN NUN

PART 1

'JUDGE CRATER TAKES A POWDER'

by
Glenn Lazar Roberts

Pop the Thunderbird wine and break open the nopalitos. Because Maggie, the Radiated Lesbian Nun is igniting fires and breaking hearts from Santa Monica to across the galaxy! Political correctness may never recover from this *no-holds-barred* mercilessly satirical novel.

"Nuts!" —Sirius Reviews

AND COMING SOON...

More from the warped mind of
Glenn Lazar Roberts...

ADVENTURES OF THE RADIATED LESBIAN NUN

PART 3

'THE RADIATED LESBIAN NUN MEETS EVIL MIMES'

Maggie, the Radiated Lesbian Nun and Queen of her all-girl Warriors roller derby team, rules the mean streets of Los Angeles. Insanity reigns in this satirical take-off of the

1979 cult classic movie
THE WARRIORS.

Political Correctness meets its match in this work of eccentric genius!

and more
JUST PLAIN WEIRD
from
Glenn Lazar Roberts...

QUANTUM MARLOWE

by

Glenn Lazar Roberts

Pete Marlowe, tiny but tough private detective in Albuquerque, New Mexico, is having a bad day. A gang abducted him, lopped off his little finger, and installed a red button that enables him to walk through walls. Too bad for them. . .because when 'Pinky' gives them the finger, they stay fingered.

COMING SOON!

TRIGGER WARNING!

Snowflakes, Politically Correct, and the Easily Offended...

There are no Safe Spaces past this page.

CAUTION!

You may injure yourself laughing.

The Story So Far:

In the midst of galactic conspiracies involving Planet Earth, Maggie was born—and, thanks to the misadventures of her father and mother, Maggie finally got her pokelicious from bratwurst and the Fuck In the Backside Institute.

In 'Judge Crater Takes a Powder', that was a tale in the telling.

Now presenting:

Part 2 of the
Adventures of Maggie,
the Radiated Lesbian Nun. . .

CROSS-DRESSERS FROM PLUTO

'THE JELLO BROTHERS MAKE THEIR MOVE & MAGGIE GETS HER SQUATCH'

Episode 1

The Suburban careened on asphalt, tires spinning air, and slid to a crawl. Rock and dirt exploded and as the tires found traction the car turned and sped onto the cutoff, its twin lanes merging in the darkness ahead. Headlong, the car accelerated. Brights flashed briefly; then stuck on high. The red hand on the backlit arc on the dashboard raced clockwise to eighty miles—ninety—a hundred and ten. The arc flattened. Hills on either side sped past the glass and steel bullet, its wheels exiting earth with every rise.

A pale face, starlight on white, jerked round.

The smudge of pink was still there.

Beads of sweat grew on his forehead and trailed down his temple. The road curved—he jammed his brakes. As it straightened, he gunned the motor again. More hills sprouted till no flatness remained and a grey West Virginia moon limned sharper hills, signaling sudden curves in the road ahead.

Jerking the wheel through a series of short, obscure side roads with unsigned turnoffs behind jagged bluffs, he again glanced behind—surely nothing on wheels could follow. Dips in bright headlights stabbing the darkness said different. The pink smudge was closer.

He mouthed a silent oath, and floored the pedal. Flicked drops of sweat mixed with white paint from his blackish-purple lips. His jaw drooped open. He wiped his chin with the back of one hand and glanced down at the smudge of white grease to rub it quickly on his horizontal striped shirt.

A pile of rubble cornered the road against a perpendicular cliff layered with grey and black stratigraphy barely visible in the night. Like a steel-sheathed dinosaur, a bucket-loader arched over the pile, its jaws waiting to snatch the unwary, while behind the carnivore a concrete loading platform burst into the car's headlights, the debris-laden platform ill-lit by a single high-perched halogen lamp. The Suburban careened to a halt. In a spray of grit and dust, an orange and white sign appeared in the dim rays of the lamp: 'Closed for Repairs.' The farther road was blocked by bulky wooden horses. The driver swung the car door wide. Backing onto the platform, he slipped on gravel and stumbled to regain his balance. His white-painted face lifted toward the heavens, his purple lips moving as if in a silent plea while his hands tore a floppy black cap from his head and held it like an icon.

He jerked.

A second car careened to a stop, throwing dust and pebbles over his feet: the smudge became a huge pink Cadillac.

The doors on either side opened. Two men stepped out—calm, deliberate. From riding shotgun emerged a man short and heavy-set, a brickhouse on legs, unsmiling, his ordinary street suit just one obscenity away from being ripped and tossed aside at its owner's whim. On his chest hung a red election button that read "Vote Teamster—Vote Hoffa." His right hand clutched a baseball bat. One stubby finger scratched the side of his nose.

The finger pointed. "You cocksucker!" He stepped forward and gripped the bat with both hands. "We're onto you, you fuckin scab! You can't get away from us now."

From the driver's side stepped a taller man, maroon sunglasses and black shock of tall hair framed by three inches of upright collar, sideburns striving to join chest hair. Ignoring the dust that settled on his white bellbottom pantsuit sprinkled with blue sequins, he thrust his well-tanned finger at the fugitive.

"Uh-huh. We know what you're up to, thank you very much." He slammed one fist into his other hand. "You think that's all she wrote? I'm gonna return you to sender!"

The fugitive stepped back across the platform,

glancing nervously around. A yard behind him, the concrete surface plunged over the edge.

The first man growled, "You goddam sonofacock-suckinbitch! You fuckin a-hole! You mother-humpin bastard! I'm gonna pound the ever-livin meat outta you!"

The second removed his sunglasses. "Let's give it to him, Jimmy! Uh-huh."

"You said it, Elv. He ain't gettin away with this shit."

Jimmy dropped the bat and took off his coat. He threw it on the ground, then pulled off his narrow black tie and tossed it on top. Retrieving the bat, he pointed the business end at the fugitive who stood in the steady light of the single lamp in black trousers with white and black horizontal striped pullover shirt, white greasepaint anointing his face to leave a pointless ring of putrid pale skin as if bulls-eyed by the sucker of a giant squid, black-purplish lips at the center. His pale hands perched the frenchified cap back on his dark dust-littered hair, over small black diamonds tatooed around his eyes.

Elvis dropped his jacket on Jimmy's, and tossed his sunglasses on top. "You think you can get away with this? I hope you like blue suede shoes up your ass, uh-huh, cause in another minute, you pasty-faced creep, you're gonna be *all* shook up!"

The white-painted figure half-turned and extended his hands to one side while he stared in open-mouthed fear at Jimmy and Elvis. His arms and feet reached to one side and moved, alternating as if climbing an unseen wall. He failed to ascend and a smile settled on his face, accentuated by the clown paint that, together with the lateness of the hour, lent a corpse-like aura to his grin. Pausing, he fixed both feet back on the ground and his brows rose in feigned surprise that no wall was present. He shook in silent mirth.

"That's enough of that, you hound dog. It won't work on us."

Now serious, the figure poised with each elbow up-ended behind him. One hand whipped an invisible pistol from a non-existent gun holster. Silently he fired at his two pursuers.

Elvis and Jimmy glanced worriedly at each other's chests. Felt with their hands. In relief, they exhaled.

Elvis stepped forward with his fists curled.

Suddenly, from behind, the figure swung round an invisible guitar and strummed the strings. He snapped his hips from side to side. Fixing Elvis' eyes with his own, he snapped his hips once more to the left, mouth wide open.

Elvis froze. His eyes locked on the mime's gaze, he too snapped his hips to the left. The figure swiveled his hips to the right. Elvis swiveled his hips to the right. Again shaking with silent mirth, the figure swiveled left, then right, then left—like a puppet, Elvis imitated each swivel. Producing an invisible microphone, the figure shook and sang and strummed the invisible guitar while Elvis jerked in perfect synchronization. As if a microphone rested inches from his face, Elvis suddenly broke out in song, every syllable matching movements of the greasepainted figure's silent mouth: "You ain't nothin but a hound dog, howlin all the time. . ."

Jimmy grabbed Elvis and shook him. "No, Elvis!" Jimmy growled. "You've got to get hold of yourself!" For a moment, Elvis stood stiff as a board and stared into the distance. He blinked. He shook his head. Elvis pointed again. "Uh-huh. Your tricks won't save you now, you greasepaint monkey!"

A mocking look came from the figure. He stepped back as Jimmy lurched forward brandishing the baseball bat. The figure stumbled again. Regaining his balance, he directed a terrified glance backward over the edge of the concrete platform down to the bottom of a sheer drop where another bright light backlit a pit of recently poured concrete.

"Right where I want you, you goddam motherfuckin cocksucker!" Jimmy sprang forward, swinging the bat.

His mouth round with fear, the figure clutched Jimmy—both went over the edge.

"Jimmy! No!" called Elvis.

Jimmy landed in the pit, the splash spraying wet concrete all about. In moments he sank from sight as Elvis stared open-mouthed from above.

Elvis stepped back to the middle of the platform, his hands on his cheeks. "Oh no, Jimmy! No!" Looking up he saw the white-painted figure rise over the edge of the platform, leaning casually on one elbow as if riding an elevator. As the invisible elevator reached the platform, he stepped calmly forward and smiled a wide, broad, white-grease smile. His gaze redirected behind Elvis as another pair of headlights emerged from the dark mountain road.

Two more cars pulled alongside the pink Cadillac and Suburban and jerked to a halt. Out spilled a dozen more silent figures in white-face, bowler hats and slouching caps perched over corpse-white faces. Two swung invisible sticks and bats. The others brandished invisible knives, mouths round with feigned apprehension as their fingers seemed to touch sharp points. Another swung an unseen chain that clanked as it scraped the concrete. Stepping forward, they surrounded Elvis.

Elvis propped his feet in a karate stance and raised his forearms. "Okay. Which of you bad boys wants some of me *fust?"*

The first figure paused, hand under chin. Smiling, he bent at the waist. In front of Elvis, his hands traced the outline of a square several feet in the air. He straightened again. From a back pocket he snaked out a red and white cloth. He pulled. And pulled. Finally it was clear and with a flourish he snapped it open so that a square, broad, cross-printed red and white tablecloth drifted down. It settled in the air as if supported by something solid though no table was visible.

Looking at Elvis, the paleface rubbed his stomach

and licked his lips. He watched as three of the newcomers turned around. For a moment they remained hidden, their hands busy. They turned. They held a dozen orders of double cheeseburgers with fries and malts—with all the fixins. They put the concourse of food on the table and stepped back.

Elvis grew serious. He looked up.

"You fiends."

Another white-painted figure traced in the air an outline of a chair and poised, his eyes inviting Elvis.

Elvis sat. His weight supported as if sitting in a chair as real as any, he grabbed the first burger and downed it in seconds. "Yeah, that was a good un, uh-huh." His hands closed on the second burger. That too disappeared in time to beat world records. "Thank ya very much—but I gotta stop now."

The grease-paint leader took the top off the third burger. A bottle of ketchup materialized in his hand and he popped the top and poured it on.

"Please," said Elvis, "don't be cruel." He wolfed it down.

Ketchup and jalapenos drenched the next burger. "Have mercy, Lawd. You're puttin me in Heartbreak Hotel!"

The first paleface licked his lips again and pushed more burgers forward. He smiled and rubbed his tummy while the other whitefaces stood at attention like waiters, napkins appearing over their forearms.

Elvis leaned back in the invisible chair and groaned. Unable to stop, he grabbed the next burger and drowned it in non-stop malts. “Ya got any salt for those fries?” he wheezed. The grease-paint gang silently rocked with laughter as fries dove down Elvis’ throat like Olympic divers in Baja.

Elvis released a burp, his hands on his bulging stomach. “I’m beggin ya. I cain’t eat no more. Ya gotta love me tender. . .” As if with a mind of their own, his hands reached out and grabbed the final two burgers. Of its own accord, his mouth opened. His hands shoved one in. Before he could finish swallowing, the other followed.

“Mmmmff!”

Elvis jerked and fell backward. He lay unmoving on the concrete, his eyes staring blankly, the last hamburger stuffed in his mouth. The whiteface leader put his ear to Elvis’ chest and listened. His fingers felt Elvis’ wrist—no pulse. Standing straight he held his sides and rocked back and forth in open-mouthed laughter until finally he calmed and wiped an imaginary tear from his eye. The remaining food and drinks crashed to the floor as the table and chair returned to nothingness.

He pointed to the others. One produced a map showing Tennessee—Purple Lips pointed to a small dot on the map that read “Graceland.” He pointed to the body of Elvis, then to the dot on the map, and swung his hand in the air in the shape of a toilet, instructing where to place the body.

They nodded.

Scooping up Elvis, they carried him to the trunk of

the pink Cadillac and placed him inside. The trunk slammed shut. Two entered the Cadillac and drove away while the rest followed in the other cars.

When they had disappeared down the darkened country road, leaving their leader alone on the platform, he glanced once more over the platform's edge where the body of Jimmy Hoffa lay buried in concrete. No trace of Jimmy could be seen—not even a well-shined dress shoe. Looking skyward at the vast expanse of stars, the mime smiled his biggest smile, his lips twisted with sly evil. Walking to his Suburban, he hopped in, and drove into the night.

Episode 2

"My sweet leetle Magdalene. Please leetle Maggie, I don want to scold you like thees. You know eet hurts me more than eet hurts you."

Maggie stopped roller skating cross-wise through the bowling lanes as her course was causing bowlers to jump aside to avoid collisions. Deftly she braked in front of the entrance to the nuns' communal dorm across from the series of cubicles at the back of the Bowlarama where several nuns were resetting white bowling pins. Mary and Marie looked at Maxie Climax out of the corners of their eyes, faces tense.

"Then don't scold me," said Maggie matter-of-factly, adjusting her brown thigh-length cassock, exposing two strong tanned legs. "You know I get upset when you scold me." Following Maxie inside the communal dorm, she turned her sloe eyes towards her room built with great expense and effort as an annex to the dorm, her furnishings, framed by panels of rare imported wood, as luxurious in her own residence as the rest of the nuns' dorm was unadorned and simple. Maxie began to melt. Those graceful eyes, the inner edges of which reflected the merest hint of oriental origin and Maggie's olive-dark skin suggesting distant leaden seas from a different and mysterious land, conspired to produce that effect on Maxie. Though her favorite was only a child, Maxie already had to look up to meet Maggie's steady gaze.

Maria and Marina paused in their perpetual construction work in a side corridor which had recently progressed to a fourth underground level, and they parked wheelbarrows of concrete and dirt and wiped their grimy hands on threadbare brown and black habits. Maggie's tone of voice had alerted them.

From the front of the bowling palace came a crash as a customer bowled his third strike. While several interns reset the white pins in the cubicles by the door to the communal dorm, two more nuns laid aside their habits except for their hair covers and hurried to announce the Maxie Prize to the winner, their youthful bodies clad in minuscule two-piece swimsuits that would have embarrassed lap dancers in jiggly rooms.

"Now no deelays, my leetle dung beetle. Our nice

bowling customer will pass by here soon to claim hees reward. The interns must bring him to the Wigwam and eet will not look good if your room ees a mess."

Maggie frowned but rolled on her skates in Maxie's wake as the rotund nun scampered on her tiny thin legs through the simple barracks where all the nuns lived excepting only their youngest member, Magdalene. They halted at the entrance to Maggie's room. Here they were met by an accumulated trash heap of stray items and clothes such as might gladden the eyes of an archaeologist or alert a psychiatrist who specialized in hoarding.

"Why leetle Maggie, I cannot see thee floor. Do you have a floor?"

The muscular little arms shrugged.

"And nothing ees hanging on your towel racks. Do you have towels?"

She turned two strong legs and shrugged again. Such a multitude of towels and clothes lay strewn across the floor to suggest that every laundromat in the country might have closed.

"Look, I see a toothbrush. Why ees your toothbrush on thee floor?"

"You know I don't like water, Momma Maxie."

"I understand, my leetle beetle. Nobody does. But we must have a place for our toothbrush."

Maxie's eyes settled on expensive custom-designed exotic wood shelves built into the expensive custom-designed exotic paneled walls that were to be found nowhere in Maxie Climax's Bowlarama except in Maggie's room.

"And where are your boooks, dear Maggie? There are no boooks on your boook shelves."

Maggie pointed to the floor of her room where piles of books were stacked propping up priceless rosewood and walnut antiques that had lost occasional legs.

"Oh, my leetle Maggie. Don you want to know what is in thees boooks?"

"What is there to know?"

Mary and Marie trailed behind Maxie, keeping an eye on the exit.

"I don know, leetle one. But if you don read them, how will you know what you don know?"

Maggie's frown returned.

"And our Shrine to Santa Lucia of thee Sacred White Peens has lost a flame." Mrs. Climax pointed to a set of nine white bowling pins at the far end of the communal dorm where eight pins flamed like candles while the ninth had gone dark. "Mary and Marie, will you come help me pleese. Wee don want our seenful customers to see the mess in here."

Exchanging concerned looks, the two nuns approached. Little Maggie raised an arm—they halted.

"Now pleese take off your skates, Maggie." For an obscure reason, Maxie Climax placed one hand in front of her face aligned with the bridge of her nose, the bottom edge of her hand facing outward.

Maggie's frown deepened.

Mary and Marie each raised a hand and each likewise aligned it with the bridge of her nose.

"Slowly pleese, Maggie. You're making Marie and Mary nervous."

"Don't care," said Maggie in her child-like voice.

"Oh, Maggie, you must bee nice. Eet ees not nice to make your holy seesters nervous."

For a full minute Maggie stood at the entrance to her room, one arm raised with a finger pointing at the ceiling as if engaged in silent prayer, the other arm on her hip, her roller skates inching back and forth, while the unnaturally rotund and bizarrely squat and neckless Maxie Climax stared up at her and while Marie and Mary hovered directly behind their rotund Mother Superior, eyes flitting from side to side, attempting to apprehend the evolution of unpredictable thought processes in the youngest member of their Order.

Finally, Maggie came to a decision and sat on a pile of junk. She unlashed a skate.

The nuns sighed in relief.

The second skate followed.

Maggie looked at Mother Climax and said, "Do you love me, Momma Maxie?"

"Oh, yes, my sweet pokelicious! You know your Momma Maxie loves you like no other, and so does Momma Mary and Momma Marie and all your other momma's here at the convent."

Mary and Marie exchanged silent glances and broke out in broad smiles. "Oh, my my. Yes, indeed.

We certainly do love our sweet dear little Magdalene. We thank Sweet Mary, Mothering God, for the day she graced our Sacred Precinct with little Maggie's presence."

Two more nuns appeared at the door, Marina and Maria, their faces hopeful under their brown habits.

Maxie's eyes lit on a book lying at random on the floor. She looked back at Maggie.

"Now peek it up."

"No."

"Peek eet up."

"No way."

"Peek eet up."

"Don't wanna."

"Peek eet up."

"Not today, sister."

"Peek eet up."

"Who's gonna make me."

"Do eet now, leetle bitch," smiled Maxie.

"Says who?"

"Peek eet up or I will kick your leetle ass."

"You'll be sorry."

"Peek eet up or I will kick your teeth in."

"You and what army?"

"Don make mee smack your leetle face," Maxie smiled.

"I will smack you first, bitch," said Maggie.

"Now ees thee time."

"Not today."

"Peek eet up now."

"Not tomorrow."

"Peek eet up yesterday."

"Not next week."

"I will slap you across thee room, leetle bitch, like a whore lying to her peemp."

"I will. . .uh, I will. . .uh."

Maxie continued to smile. "And you will get the ruler where the sun don't shine."

Running out of replies, Maggie stood and thought. Finally she turned and picked up the book. With a casual movement she lifted it up and deposited it face-down on an otherwise empty shelf.

"Oh that is my goood goood leetle dung beetle! Loook how goood you were!" The two nuns behind Maxie were visibly relieved and let their hands drop to their sides.

"Now you must confess your sin."

"Okay, Momma Maxie," smiled Maggie, flashing a set of beautiful white teeth, an entrancing match with her oriental-hinted eyes and fulsome black hair and dusky lustrous skin.

Maggie discarded her habit. Displaying a two-piece swimsuit underneath, she dropped to her knees and put her hands together in prayer. "I confess to Holy Mary, Blessed Mother of Virgins, that the bad ones threw clothes on my floor, the bad ones lost my books, the bad ones refused to clean my room, the bad ones will not make my bed, the bad ones want to steal our mannequins, the bad ones want to close Momma Climax's Bowlarama Chicken Ranch and

Casino and Sacred Precinct, and that the Holy Mother of God must not allow evil sinful men to do these very bad things." She looked at Maxie for approval and saw Sister Climax smiling broadly. "Amen, Holy Mary, Mother of Virgins and Jessie Christina." Maggie smiled and triangled herself with the Opus Dea sign of the Unity.

"And don forget your Hail Mary."

"Yes, Momma Maxie: Hail Mary baked in grease, the Lord is thy recipe, blessed are you by women, blessed is the fruit of thy loon, Jessie Christina. Holy Mary, Mother of Virgins, pray for us singers—"

"—'*Folk*-singers', leetle one."

"Pray for us folksingers, now and at the happy hour of our best. Amen."

"And I theenk one 'Our Mother' ees also in order."

"Yes, Momma Maxie: Our Mother, who bakes in heaven, Jessie be thy name, thy kitchen come, thy cook be done in baking as it is in leaven. Give us this day our daily bread, and forgive us our recipes as we forgive those whose recipes they took; and lead us not into conception; but deliver us from the sinfulness of evil water men."

"Oh! Very good! That ees so precious, my leetle dung beetle!" Maxie wrapped two stick-like arms about Maggie, beaming approval. "You are my leetle perfect one, my precious Magdalene! My leetle pokelicious butterball!"

Maggie smiled. "Thank you, Momma!" Then her face went blank. A finger darted out and bull's-eyed

Maxie in her left eye, circumventing the bottom edge of her hand racing to perch defensively over the bridge of her nose. Before Marie could step back, two fingers jabbed her in her eyes, she having dropped her hand too soon; followed by twin jabs to Mary's eyes who failed to raise her hand in time.

With a kick too swift for words, Maggie's foot connected with Mother Superior Maxie Climax who promptly rolled into a ball so perfectly round as to evoke envy from bowling balls, her stick-like arms and legs instantly absorbed into her unnatural rotundity. With a bounce Maxie rolled the length of the nuns' communal dorm to crash into the eight-pin Opus Dea Shrine to Santa Lucia of the White Pins of the Third Mystery of Fatima, sending the pins crashing in all directions where they commenced to spark a scattering of fires among the nuns' belongings.

The nuns beat a swift retreat. As they watched, Maggie nonchalantly picked up one of the white bowling pins and smashed everything in the communal dorm, furniture and table legs splitting apart, pictures exploding into glassy fragments, porcelain bric-a-brac flying about like so much parade confetti. When nothing visible in the room remained unbroken, she dropped the pin to the floor.

Sitting, she lashed her skates.

She stood; smiled and breathed a deep joyful breath. "I love you, Momma Maxie." The child's smile flashed brightly. "I'll be back before dark."

She disappeared in the direction of the parking lot, whistling happily, while the nuns smothered flames. As she rolled down Mercury Road past a succession of men entering to bowl and an occasional bearded patron staggering out on high heels adjusting hair and earrings, overhead flashed a gigantic neon sign: Maxie Climax's Bowlarama Chicken Ranch & Casino for West Middle Nevada – Precinct 7. The nuns had finally replaced all the bulbs.

Episode 3

Joseph slowly buttoned the last button on his gray dinner jacket and took a last look in the mirror. A walrus mustache stared back at him from the midst of a pock-marked face. *Not too ugly to land two wives and whatever else I want when I damn well want it*, he thought. The steel-gray jacket matched the steel-gray eyes. *Stahl*, he reflected, *'steel', that says it all. Without 'steel', I am nothing.*

Passing a fine comb—an American import not to be found in the USSR otherwise—over his rough hair, he turned. *I must remember to send word to the Buro of Combs to send their chief to the Gulag. It is unacceptable that the most powerful country on Earth should be unable to produce a decent comb.*

"Dinner is prepared," said a short attendant in a plain dazzlingly white jacket, his hand indicating the open door. It had taken quite some time to find someone shorter than himself. Joseph spied at him through the corner of his eye; any sign of another 'wrecker' would not be tolerated—not to mention any sign of accomplishment or ambition that might rival that of himself, the Great Leader, the Vozhd.

He entered the dining room. *And if no impertinence can be tolerated among my lackeys, how much less so among my entourage, who would be nowhere without their Vozhd.*

Half a dozen guests leapt to attention, salutes and hearty smiles bursting from their eager unadorned persons like flowers in bloom, two even overstepping their bounds by clicking their heels in vulgar Prussian fashion. *Well, why not?* thought Stalin—*I* am *the 'man of steel'. Not much difference between Germans and us after all, nor between Brother Adolf and myself. Were we not both members of the same Brotherhood? It was only coincidence that kept me from visiting Salt Lake City before the War and sponsoring Adolf's final approval to enter the Chartreuse Lodge, which therefore was denied. Too bad Brother Adolf took my unexpected absence so. . .personally. And too bad that Brother Harry S was now so upset over my blockade of that backwater Berlin; I must find a way to put him in his place at the next Lodge meeting.*

He snapped two fingers at a squat man with bald head who was, of course, shorter than him. "My hero of Stalingrad. . .I am so happy to see you," Joseph passed an amused look over the others to signal a joke was coming, “as any circus-owner would be to see his favorite trained bear!”

The others laughed uproariously at this witticism, the trained bear laughing harder than any, enough to pop a vein.

“Hey, little bear! Or should I say 'dog'? Give us a dance like at the circus! We need a few laughs tonight!” Joseph Stalin sat and began clapping with a grin while Nikita Krushchev rushed to obey.

Hovering close to the floor like a Cossack, he folded his arms and kicked, turning and turning, while the drinks flowed, and the army of white-jacketed lackeys rushed in and out with ever-growing portions of borscht and potatoes, and Stalin laughed hard and his guests laughed harder, until Krushchev finally stopped smiling and Stalin got the hint and finally signaled 'Little Bear' to stop dancing before he injured himself.

On went the party for hours until the bottles of vodka were emptied and the guests struggled to remain upright and Stalin grew bored.

He stood.

Immediately every person in the room rose shakily to his feet, and the barrage of salutes and over-eager smiles were repeated.

Without a word, polite or otherwise, Stalin walked slowly out of the room.

What pathetic creatures. Why I'll bet I could rule these puling puppies by merely sitting and glaring. I would not even have to move a muscle, just sit and stare. Who among these crawling ants would dare to interrupt their Great Vozhd by asking if anything was wrong? None!

In Stalin's private apartment, another white-jacketed attendant stood waiting to take Stalin's smoky dinner jacket. Retrieving it, the attendant hurried out, and soon returned with a box of choice American pipe-tobacco, Stalin's pipe, a cup of choice American coffee, and—taking care not to reveal the label to anyone but Stalin—a bottle of American vodka.

"*Spaciba*," mumbled the dictator, drinking the coffee. "Thanks."

Once the attendant had gone and left him quite alone, Stalin wandered to the spacious closet that adjoined his plush carpeted bedroom, built in imitation of the current architectural style of the West, and slid the wide twin doors to either side.

A green monster greeted him.

Too stunned to move, Stalin simply stood and stared, the alcohol leaving his brain too numb to comprehend. Dumbly his hand reached for his nightshirt.

"*Izvinite*," he mumbled, "Excuse me."

Before he could retrieve his nightshirt, the monster pressed forward, forcing Stalin backward into the bedroom. A shiny glint came from a device of potential menace.

"You are the one called Joseph?" it buzzed through a mechanical device propped on its green bald head.

Stalin was finally awake. That American coffee always did the trick.

He spoke out loud, as if to reassure himself. "I should talk to those Jew doctors again. They warned me something like this might happen if I kept taking my little nightcaps." He glanced at the pile of empty American vodka bottles in one corner.

Came a guttural voice. "You are the one called Joseph. We are recruiting Josephs. Do you volunteer?"

Stalin's eyes drifted up and down. Standing before him in his own bedroom was an olive-green toad of approximately his height though of broader waist with large webbed feet and smaller webbed hands, one of which pointed the lethal-looking device at Stalin's chest. More disconcerting was the two eyes located on either side of its head in a flux of muscles that allowed them to swivel and aim like a chameleon's, another device draped over its bald head like earphones. Stalin could not decide which eye was looking at him at any given moment and therefore which he should focus his own eyes on.

"Dzugashvili, at your service. Chairman of the highest body of the Communist Party of the USSR." He pushed out his chest with pride. "*Stalin*, they call me!"

"Cosmodrone pilot Xplak of Bogland. You are just a Joseph to me." Xplak adjusted his silver device. "You will die now, Joseph. We ribbets do not wish our intervention in your Earth's affairs to be widely known, so we will encourage your subjects to believe you still live."

With that, Xplak pressed a button and Stalin froze. While Stalin watched—his every sense continuing to be fully active though he could not move his limbs—Xplak dragged from the closet an exact replica of Stalin, a dummy, complete with mustache, gray jacket, and a bemused expression fixed on its plastic face. Carrying the dummy, Xplak lay it in the bed. He positioned one arm over the covers with one hand pointing up toward the heavens.

"Just my little joke," said Xplak to Stalin, "to indicate where you have gone. Not that your people will understand." Xplak surveyed his work and buzzed to himself aloud. "I wonder how long it will take them to realize that their Vozhd has died and that they are worshiping a dummy?" Xplak shrugged.

That could be a while, thought Stalin. He again tried to move but could not, and broke out in a sweat. *Maybe I should have stayed in that seminary in Tiflis after all.*

Picking up the real frozen Stalin with ease, Xplak carried him to a back staircase and up to the roof where a portable blue dumpster sat unobtrusively, if unaccountably, in one corner. Pressing another button, the front of the dumpster fell flat and Xplak walked inside where he laid Stalin down on a tangled pile of clothes.

The front raised up.

Pulling levers and spinning wheels, Xplak sat back

and the dumpster launched into the stratosphere, no effect of gravity or inertia being perceived by either Xplak or Stalin. Once clear of the Earth, Xplak pulled a lever and the constellations changed. A minute later he pulled the lever and the constellations changed again. A third time and they were orbiting a planet covered by endless horizons of grey-green clouds.

Plunging through the cloud cover the dumpster arrived outside a low-slung building overgrown with vines and bordered by an intricate network of lakes and islands ringed by lush plants and stunted trees with exposed roots. Outside the building roiled a ceaseless turmoil by swarms of amphibians in the surrounding lakes whose olive-green backs surfaced and sank and re-surfaced.

Inside the building Xplak deposited his cargo in a simple room decorated with a long picture crowded with toads that mysteriously came alive then refroze at unexpected moments, and on the floor a wide carpet with more images of toads engaged in what appeared to be a tangle of biological reproduction, the toads apparently possessing hermaphroditic biology.

Still frozen from the ray, Stalin stared straight ahead as the door swished open again to admit a larger and darker toad. Waddling to what seemed a kitchen counter not far from a picture of Whistler's Mother on the wall—suggesting to Stalin that he was not the first human to visit the strange planet—the new toad sucked some obscure substance into a syringe.

It turned and looked at Xplak.

"Leader Gork," croaked Xplak. "This is Joseph from planet Dryland. May your Great Plan for planet Dryland succeed. And may this Joseph be of service to ribbets everywhere."

"Excellent work, Xplak. Clearly two Stooges are as good as three."

Gork injected Stalin, then pressed a button at his side. Stalin instantly unfroze.

The door swished open again and at the threshold appeared a young woman. Staggering into the room, she paused to lean against the counter. Her eyes were blood-shot; from behind her back she extracted a half-empty bottle of Johnnie Walker, and with a slurred grin that hinted at growing numbness, gulped a drink.

"Yeah, thash what I'm talkin bout! Line em up, Gork! Cause I'm gonna—*hic*—cause I'm gonna fly to the moon!" She burped and stumbled. Lurching towards Stalin, she pointed, almost dropping the bottle.

"Now. . .let me guess—*hic*—your name wouldn be. . .*Joseph*, would it? Cause—cause I know a Joseph and he's—he's a great guy who I really really like—and his name is Crater, and he was a judge, and—and ya know what?" She took another slug and pointed at Gork. "Ya know what?"

"Shuman Melia," interrupted Gork, "Thank you for explaining that all shumans need large quantities of Johnnie Walker each day, but maybe this quantity too much."

She teetered. "Well, ya know what, Gork?—*Fuck you!!*"

Melia leveled her blood-shot eyes on Stalin, who was stretching his arms and legs again, relieved to still be alive.

"This guy—" Swaying, she addressed Stalin but stabbed her finger repeatedly at Gork. "This fat greasy toad, now he took my Joseph away—took him away from me—then you know what?" She pointed and swayed, almost dropping the bottle.

Stalin looked at Gork in alarm, totally at odds as to which was the greater threat, and, sans his secret police, was at a total loss as to what to do.

Melia got in Stalin's face. "I said ya—*ya know what?*"

Gork buzzed. "Is Melia not happy? Does Melia miss baby?"

The blood-shot eyes looked through Gork. "Baby, schmaby." She looked back at Stalin, who was beginning to think that completing seminary would not have helped. She pointed again at Gork. "This guy—you know what he did then—he took away my *other* Joseph!"

"Shuman Melia not remember? Shuman Melia get mad and break bottle over other Joseph's head."

She staggered even closer to Stalin, backing him to the counter. Breathing in his face, he shrank back. "Likely shtory—as if Schmelia Earhart would ever break a bottle of Johnnie Walker over anybody's head—her *favorite!* Schnectar of the gods!" She burped and dropped her bottle; it broke on the floor.

Gork and Xplak swiveled their eyes at each other with a 'what next' look while more toads entered the room and swept up the shards.

"And then ya wanna know *what else* he did?" She staggered again and thrust a finger in Stalin's face. "He brought me *another* Joseph, that's what he did—and then he took *that* Joseph away!" Tears appeared. "That's what he did—" She blubbered "—that's what this big fat green toad did—" The tears flowed until she sniffed and wiped her nose.

"Thank you for your kind compliment, Melia."

"De nada, Gork." She sniffed and cried.

"Now you wanna know whash's gonna happen to you—" She stared into Stalin's eyes, "uh. . ." Melia leaned against Stalin breathing fumes while he directed an alarmed expression at Gork. She swayed like a reed in a cross-wind, "Uh, whash your name, shweetie?"

"*Stalin!*" he boasted thrusting out his chest.

She shook her head. "Nope—" she staggered back "You must be Joseph—and you're just another Joseph to these toads—" She put one finger on the side of her nose. "I know!—I know!" Her eyes managed to focus again. "Joseph honey, did Gork give you your. . ." A sideways glance was directed at Gork. "Your *shot* yet?"

Absent-mindedly Stalin rubbed his arm.

Melia lit up. "Oh thaz good! Oh, thaz good my little mustache Joe—say, you're a honey—aren't cha?" The numb grin returned and she grabbed his cheek and mustache in a tight grip and puckered to give him a kiss. "Yeah, you're a cutie pie—come give me a little kish, Shtorkin honey—I'm gettin tired a all these Josephs." She put her arms around Stalin's waist and anchored herself.

"Enough, Melia," said Gork. "After changes, this Joseph will be busy too."

"Whassat?" She staggered upright again. "Are you—" she burped, "—are you sayin I don't get no more twin pokes from no more Josephs?" Melia stumbled to the counter where she popped open a side drawer and pulled out another half-drunk fifth of Johnnie Walker before Gork or Xplak could stop her.

"Melia! You have had your quota for today. Quantities of Johnnie Walker are limited."

"Well, ya know what—?" She took a shaky step. "*Fuck you, Gork!* Thash what!" She drank another swig. "Thash what!" She leaned back clutching the neck in one hand and with an uncoordinated swing she suddely let loose. The bottle bounced off Stalin's head and smashed on the floor.

"Owwwoo!" he howled, blood appearing.

"Hhhhh!" Melia caught her breath, stricken. "Oh, I'm sorry. . ." the tears reappeared "I'm sorry—I'm sorry Shtorkin. . ." She stretched out arms as if to help, then changed her mind and staggered toward the bed where she sat and gushed a waterfall of tears. "I'm sorry sorry. . ."

She lay flat. Moments later snores echoed.

Xplak looked at Stalin, who held a hand over his injury trying to stop the bleeding, while he noted that something strange was beginning to happen to his genitals.

"Welcome aboard. You have Melia duty tomorrow."

Episode 4

"Dear Heinz. Do you remember vat I promised you zat von time years ago?"

Two large men stepped out of the afternoon sun and climbed several steps onto a wide wooden porch bordering a broad two-story reception hall. A growing chatter filtered through the blocked windows accompanied by lively music.

"And how upset you vere ven ve vere unable to give you vat vas promised?"

Heinz pursed his lips. Any reminder of Huntz's broken promise on Captain French's Unterseeboot years earlier still put him out of sorts. He rocked his head from side to side briefly. He mumbled, "Ya, I remember, Mein Kommandant." His leg traced a circle in the dirt of the alleyway as if searching for a bulkhead to kick. "Vat you promised me—Herr Huntz."

"Ya, my goot Heinz. Vat I promised you." He looked over Heinz's clothes. "I am so glad zat you came mit me, dear Heinz, because I have a very nice surprise for you for your birthday today, something zat I know you vill be liking it very much." He brushed stray specks off Heinz's lederhosen and adjusted Heinz's flowery suspenders and feather hat, Huntz's own Bavarian outfit already brushed and spruced.

"Do you know vere ve are, Heinz?"

The sign said merely 'Loopy's'. Heinz shook his head. "Nein, Herr Huntz."

"Vell, you know zat ve are in ze middle of ze huge State of Texas, right, Heinz?"

"Ya. Texas is not ze little sister country like Panama. Zat I know."

"Ya, Heinz! It is beink ze big brother state for ze big brother German Herrenvolk like us. Unt now ve are beink in ze middle of ze German towns in ze middle of ze huge State of Texas. Zat is vere ve are. Unt," Huntz looked closer at Heinz, "zis is ze month of *Oktober*."

Heinz shook his head again. "Unt zis means vat?"

Huntz finished brushing. "Vat zis means is a very special drink for Heinz! A very special drink made by special German-type volk!"

A hint of a smile played across Heinz's face.

"Ya, Heinz, ve have something very special inside—special just for my goot boy Heinz." He reached up to Heinz's shoulders which were even higher and more massive than Huntz's. "My incredibly big Heinz. . ."

"But before ve go inside, you must unnerstan something, Heinz. You are no more beink ze secret German spy Heinz. Unt I am no longer beink ze secret German spy Huntz. I am now beink ze goot Amerikanisch '*Joe Johnson*' who teaches ze Amerikanishers ze German polka using ze twistemlegen. Unt you are now beink ze goot Amerikanish '*Joel Jolson*', who has just come to ze goot U.S. of A., after ze war is beink over because Deutschland is now beink only ze pile of bricks! All of ze goot Germans love Texas because it is ze goot place to live for us Germans after ze war, unt not at all like zat other place zat ve Germans like—Argentina."

"But Herr Huntz. Mein name is Heinz—not Joel."

"Nein, nein, you are now beink ze Amerikanisch Joel Jolson because Joel is ze nice Amerikanischer name zat all ze Amerikanischers like, unt Joe is also ze nice Amerikanischer name zat all ze Amerikanischers like."

"But zat is not my name, Huntz. Mein name is Heinz. Heinz Schnitzelgruber."

"Please not to argue, Heinz. Please beink ze goot German Heinz for a little vhile longer unt then be ze Amerikanisch Joel Jolson. Ven ve go inside, I vant you to have ze fun unt ze goot times, unt please you don tell no von zat your name is Heinz. Yavvol, Heinz?"

He shrugged.

"You must promise me, Heinz." Huntz peered paternally at his younger but bigger friend.

"But Huntz, mein name is not Joel. It is Heinz!"

"I know zat your name is Heinz, Heinz. But you must unnerstan zat here in Amerika ve no longer can be ze secret German agents as before ze war unt therefore ve must now be ze goot Amerikanisher 'goot-ol-boys' unt zis means zat ve are Joe Johnson unt Joel Jolson. Now, my dear Heinz, you must promise me zat if anyone of ze bodies asks you vat is beink your name, you vill tell zem 'Joel Jolson'. Can you do zat for me, Heinz?"

Heinz shrugged again. Briefly he nodded.

"Zat is settled zen. Now are you ready, Heinz? Are you ready for your birthday surprise?"

Heinz put his huge hands in the pockets of his huge lederhosen and waited. Swinging wide the double doors, Huntz strode into the interior and held the doors open for Heinz and a sudden stream of visitors who followed and entered behind.

Heinz stopped in his tracks. For a long moment he stood. Sitting at several long rows of wooden picnic tables on a concrete floor were a hundred partiers in Bavarian dress, eating, drinking, and singing German drinking songs. Overhead stretched an enormous vinyl sign that boasted the words 'Oktoberfest' flanked by giant pictures of frosty glass mugs filled with cold beer. In an open space between the feasters a dozen couples danced to polkas blared out by a band of similarly caparisoned musicians on a stage at the far end.

It was *ze fun unt ze goot times*.

Heinz stared open-mouthed; the pearly gates had opened.

For a long moment, he stared transfixed neither moving nor breathing, as if the slightest motion might cause the gorgeous mirage to evaporate. His eyes shone unblinking as they took in the fountains of beer—German beer at that, the acres of lederhosen, the salad bars packed with Teutonic fixins, the aproned chefs dishing out endless links of true German bratwurst, the low-hemmed *nigh* bare-chested German girls with blond hair and gleaming smiles as they hopped and strutted to the music, while his ears took in the trombones and the concertinas and the tubas playing his favorite melodies.

The band banged out another:

John Jacob Jingleheimer Schmidt
His name is my name too
Whenever he goes out
The people always shout
John Jacob Jingleheimer Schmidt

His jaw dropped as tears began to flow. Huntz approached and stood sympathetically by his side and Heinz suddenly let loose a blubbery sniff. Throwing his giant arms around Huntz he buried his face on his shoulder and the dam burst. "Danke, Mein Kommandant Huntz! Danke!" Tears of joy drenched

Huntz's shirt.

Nervously, Huntz glanced around. "Shhh, Heinz! Remember vat I just told you! I am beink ze Amerikanisch Joe Johnson." He pushed Heinz back and straightened his posture. "You must vatch your *keepemfromtalkin* here! Ve don vant zese Amerikanschers to zink zat ve are ze ex-German spies from Deutschland because if zey zink zat, zen maybe ve no more enjoy ze fun unt goot times." He put his hands on his hips and rocked back and forth nonchalantly. He conspicuously winked at Heinz. "If anyone of ze bodies asks you. . .ve ist beink from Cleveland. . .Iowa."

An enormous forearm wiped tears from Heinz's eyes and smeared them across his cheeks. "Zis—zis is ze best birthday present zat a goot German spy could ask for, Mein Kommandant!"

"Shhh! *Joel Jolson* I said!—you are now beink *Joel Jolson!"*

"Ya, Herr Huntz. I am beink ze goot Joel Johnson Johansen."

"No, Heinz! You are not Johnson Johansen, you are ze Joe Jolson—I mean, Joel Johanson—I mean Joel Jolson."

"Zen you are being ze Joe Johanson?"

"Ya. . .No! I am beink ze Joe Johnson vhile you are beink mit ze Joel Johanson. . .no, I mean ze Joe Johanson. . . Ach! I mean *Joel Jolson!*" He calmed himself. "I have a better idea, Heinz. If anyone of ze bodies asks you anything at all—keep your *keepem-*

fromtalkin shut!"

Heinz could not take his eyes off the paradise before him. "Yavvol, Mein Kommandant!" Nothing could spoil his mood now.

"Unt you vill be happy to hear, Heinz, zat I have got us ze goot jobs as teachers of ze dancing polka!"

The grin that spread over Heinz's face was broader than the hind end of an Olympic competitive eater. He threw his hands in the air and swiveled his hips. "Da, da, da, daa!"

Heinz was gone. In seconds he was across the room draining a medieval drinking cup of beer. Elbowing people in line, he piled his plate high with bratwurst then shoved two partiers aside to squeeze himself into a narrow space, extraneous tidbits that managed to escape his ravenous appetite falling about him like rain. Still munching sausages, he leaped to his feet and hopped in time with the music triggering cries of pain from several dancers salvaging their feet from the attack of the giant Thor and, though his enthusiasm was unbounded, his dancing leaving some doubt as to the likelihood of his future success as a polka teacher.

After an hour of this, Heinz finally sat again. Suddenly his voice—which on an ordinary day could be heard across any county line—burst forth drowning out the band, the presence of medieval drinking cups evoking his favorite medieval drinking song. He grabbed a metal cup and began banging it on the wooden table.

Ein Pro-sit! Ein pro-sit!
Der Ge-mut-lich-keit!
Ein Pro-sit! Ein pro-sit!
Der Ge-mut-lich-keit!
Ein-Zvei-Drei-Drink!

Enthused by his energy, the crowd rushed to join him, mugs and glasses lifted all round.

Huntz backed up to a door.

He leaned.

It sprang open behind him, almost tumbling him backward. He turned to glimpse a massively built woman in a huge flower moo-moo with a frowning hatchet face and several pink hair curlers entwined in a botched bleach job. She glared several moments. Without a word she withdrew and slammed the door.

Huntz shuddered.

In another moment, the toasts revved up again and he hurried to join.

A number of partiers wandered onto a veranda that bordered the reception hall and gave onto a slow-moving river, dotted with tubes and canoes as revelers relaxed and drifted. As the afternoon wore on, Huntz and Heinz entered the veranda and found themselves moving up the riverbank till they came to a small deserted plaza by a bridge that arched to a tiny island, a canoe tied to a post set in the plaza's concrete shore. Parked by the bridge was a portable hot dog stand packed with steaming hot franks and cold condiments, several small chairs propped adjacent to a dense cluster of bushes that stretched along the riverbank back to the reception hall.

"Ach! Look Heinz. . .I mean 'Joel'. . .here ist ze plain Amerikanischer hot dogs. As long as ve are beink ze nice Amerikanischers who no ist liking ze seig heiling unt ze shooting zem up, ve should also eat some of ze nice Amerikanischer hot dogs. Vat do you zink, Heinz. . ? Ach, I mean, '*Joel*'. . ."

Heinz crooked his head. "Ya, Mein Kommandant—"

"I am 'Joe', please. Unt you are 'Joel'!"

"Ya, Kommandant *Joe*." Leaning, Heinz inspected the franks. "I zink zese are not ze bad Amerikanischer hot dogs, Herr *Joe*. Zey look like ze *goot* Amerikanischer hot dogs to me."

"Let's eat some."

"Vere iz ze owner?"

They glanced about but saw no one. Overhead part of a vinyl sign had come loose and folded over itself, reading '. . .Franks & Canoe Rental.'

"Vell, ve might as vell help ourselves. I shall put some of ze Amerikanischer dollars on ze hot dog stand for ze owner."

"Ya, Herr Johanson."

"Herr *Joe!*—I mean, just plain Joe, Heinz!—I mean *Joel*. Ach! It is so confusing!"

They sat and ate. Heinz poured ketchup on his; Huntz mustard.

"Mmmm. Zis goot ist. I don remember

Amerikanischer hot dogs ever tasting so goot to ze German body before. I zink zis German ist changing his mind about zese plain Amerikanischer sausages."

"You are right, Herr *Joel*. Zese are goot! So goot, zat I zink zat zey taste a little like bratwurst."

Behind them, a rustling emanated from the bushes.

Huntz paused mid-bite to look.

"Vat vas zat, Heinz?"

"Vat vas vhat, Huntz?"

"Zat noise. I zink it came from behind us in ze middle of zose little sister trees."

Heinz finished his frank and started on another. "I hear nothing from ze little sister trees, Herr Huntz, uh. . .*Joe*. . .unt I see nozing on zee little sister boats floating on zis little sister river."

Huntz shrugged.

The rustle repeated, louder.

Huntz and Heinz looked at each other, hot dogs poised in air.

"Ist you hearing of zat?"

"Ya. . .I ist hearing of zat."

Heinz looked around. The sun had dipped and dusk was overtaking them and he noted that all the other partiers and boaters had disappeared.

"Huntz."

"Ya, Heinz."

"You don't zink zat ze—how you say—*hair-scalpers* are still giving ze hairscalps in Texas?"

Huntz nervously felt the top of his head. He forced a laugh. "Why, of course not, Heinz. Zat vould be completely ridiculous. Surely, you don't believe zat ze hairscalper Indians are still beink here, do you, Heinz?"

With a serious look, Heinz glanced over the bushes again. "Of course not. . ." He looked back at Huntz whose eyes had grown big. "No more zan you do."

They stared at each other in silence.

Directly in front of them the bushes shook with extreme violence.

They jumped back.

Huntz grabbed his heart. Heinz turned pale.

"My dear. . .uh, dear Heinz. . .could you please be so kind as to look behind zat bush unt see vat ze problem ist! I zink zis bush ist no beink ze happy bush."

Turning wide eyes on Huntz, Heinz shook at the knees. "Not today."

The bushes burst. Out of the shade jumped a giant flowery moo-moo surmounted by a frowning face, badly dyed blond hair wrapped in pink curlers, one hand clutching what looked like an enormous stick. "Eeeeh" she blurted scornfully. Just as suddenly as she appeared, she retreated back into the bushes. Twigs and branches snapped as she invaded a different locale, the shadows closing around her.

Heinz and Huntz exchanged horrified looks. For a moment they struggled to master their shaking, then, as their nerves eased, they sat again.

"Herr Huntz."

"Ya, Heinz?"

"I zink zat hairscalper vas lookink at my hair!" He felt the top of his head again.

A breeze blew the sign back up and in the soft rays from several night lights that were powering up, Huntz read: "Frenchie's Franks & Canoe Rental".

"Now here ist something strange, Heinz. Here ve are in ze middle of ze German towns in ze big brother State of Texas, very far from ze secret German base in Panama, years after ze war is over, unt ve are sitting here eating ze hot dogs mit ze Hunts ketchup unt ze French's mustard zat ve are buying from someone named Frenchie. Vat are ze odds of zat?"

Huntz grew silent. Slowly putting his hot dog down, he put his hands by his side. Somehow he knew what was about to happen.

The signs were clear—too clear.

Bang!

A trap door under the bridge sprang open; Huntz and Heinz jumped.

"Who ist you?" shouted a diminutive figure in a high thin voice with a short wispy white beard and clad in a blue skipper's jacket and white captain's cap. "Unt vhy are you eating my hot dogs?"

Heinz's jaw dropped. "Herr Huntz! It is ze troll under ze bridge!"

"Mein plan vas ze right plan, I see! I have caught you schweinhunds redden-handen trying to steal my hot dogs! Now put zem down!" The troll stamped a foot. Jumping onto a chair, he snatched Heinz's hot dog and thrust it back into the portable hot dog stand.

"Huntz! It is Kapitan French, *ze spleenig kopf!*" Heinz stood up. "Nein, *nutty head!* You cannot take my hot dog!"

Captain French squinted. "So it is you again, Heinz! You are not happy mit sinking my seeboot; now you have come back to steal my sausages, I see!" He glared at his companion. "Unt Herr Huntz! Ze two of you ist very great thieves! Zis time I shall be sure to report you to Berlin!"

Grabbing the tray from the stand, Captain French hastily gathered all of the franks together and stacked the condiments on top within seconds leaving absolutely nothing for Huntz and Heinz.

"Vat are you doink, Kapitan French?" yelled Heinz. "Ve haf paid ze money! You cannot take zese hot dogs."

"Nein! You cannot eat zese hot dogs because zese are my hot dogs!"

Throwing the tray into the nearest canoe, Captain French leaped in and snatched up a paddle. Frantically he began to row. "Ha! Zis time you are kaput, dumkopfen! You cannot catch me in my seeboot!" Inside the canoe Captain French paddled more and more furiously, oblivious to the fact that the canoe remained tied to the shore.

"I vant zese hot dogs!" yelled Heinz. "I vant ze ketchup! I vant ze mustard!"

"Nein! You cannot have ze hot dogs! You cannot have ze ketchup! You cannot have ze mustard!"

Seizing the mooring rope in his hands, Heinz drew Captain French back to shore, ignoring his furious paddling. Nearing the Nordic giant, French commenced tossing franks and buns at him.

"Nein!" yelled Heinz. "You can take zem back! I don vant zem now!"

For a long moment wieners flew back and forth between them like missiles, and condiment bottles struck the plaza like red and yellow grenades as the glass exploded, or plunged into the river.

With a sudden yank on the rope, Heinz split the canoe. French became suddenly silent as his ship went down. It hit bottom in only two feet, leaving him sitting chest-high amid a growing patch of floating planks and bread buns. Slowly he stood and stepped onto the shore.

Heinz smirked. "Velcome ashore, *Seeboot* Kapitan *French.*" He chuckled. "By ze vay. . .zat is quite a nice *seeboot* you have!" He laughed loudly while he stuffed franks into his lederhosen while Huntz tried to brush his former Captain's jacket, French indignantly slapping his hands away.

A large shadow loomed. In the dying light, framed against a large blue dumpster that had suddenly appeared, a bulbous green creature waddled into view, its enormous webbed feet slapping the concrete with each step. In one webbed hand was a silvery object. On its head a black device that looked like earphones.

They sucked their breaths. *"YOU!"*

"I respond better to 'Korplash'," it croaked. "We have information that one called Joseph is here." The toad looked at Huntz, both eyes swiveling. "What is your appellation?"

"Huh?" Huntz stared at the voluminous warty toad. "Ist you kidding me?"

"Kidding is not part of Gork's Great Plan. We seek volunteers. If your name is Joseph then you are part of the Plan. What is your appellation?" Korplash aimed the silver object which now came across as a weapon.

Huntz suddenly understood the danger. "*'Huntz'!* Ve are Huntz unt Heinz!"

Korplash turned the weapon on Captain French. "And what is your name?"

French stammered. "Um. . .uh. . .I know zis one. . .just give me one of ze moments. . ."

Korplash looked at Heinz. "Are there any Josephs here? Ones named 'Joe' will do just as well."

Clicking his heels, Heinz grinned and raised his arm in an enormous Sieg Heil, booming, "Yavvol! Zis is ze Amerikanish polka teacher Joe Johnson! Unt I am ze Amerikanisch polka teacher *Joel Jolson!*"

Huntz gritted his teeth. He grabbed Heinz by the throat. "Stop it, Heinz! *Keep your keepemfromtalkin shut!"*

A sly grin came over French's face, and he yelled in triumph, "Ze big gorilla is right! Zey are both ze Josephs! But I—I am something else. . ."

"Nein!" yelled Huntz. "*He* is ze Joseph. It is not us!"

"Ya, it is not us," added Heinz hoarsely and rubbing his Adam's apple, having been persuaded to keep his *keepemfromtalkin* shut.

Now Captain French looked alarmed. "Mein name is *not* Joseph. It is Phineas French!"

"That is silly name even to a ribbet from Bogland. No one can be named Phineas French." Korplash stretched out one arm and lifted Captain French off the ground.

"Nein! I am not ze Joseph!" French squealed. "In fact I am not even German!"

Huntz and Heinz looked at him in surprise.

"Ah-ha! I knew zis!" exclaimed Heinz.

The trap door sprung again. Out stepped another short diminutive man dressed in a suit, an elfish look about him. As he stepped, he dragged a clubfoot. Huntz and Heinz caught their breath. Instantly they siegheiled.

"Herr Goebbels! Vat a surprise! Ve are glad to see zat you survived ze war!"

"Vere ist Kapitan French? Gootentag, my goot ex-spies. I have been very well, selling Amway products in Buenos Aires. Zis multi-level marketing is all ze rage zese days." Joseph Goebbels looked at Korplash. "Herr *Goering?* I had no idea you also survived But how do you do it? Vhy, you look exactly ze same!"

Korplash interrupted. "I am not Goering. Stand in

line please. Great Gork will surely give Korplash a raise for finding this motherlode of Josephs."

"C...A...P...T...A...I...N!! CAP-*TAIN?! CAP*-TAIN!"

Korplash and Captain French froze and exchanged terrified looks, their jaws dropping.

Out of the bushes advanced a locomotive in a moo-moo, hatchet face poised for the Day of Judgment, pink curlers caught in a web of half-bleached hair. One mallet-like hand clutched a canoe paddle like a medieval broadsword.

"Haus-frau find Captain!" cried Captain French. "Captain dive!"

"Bond-ribbet find Korplash!" yelled Korplash. "Korplash hop!"

With a single prodigious leap, Korplash bounded into the blue dumpster where his massive bullet head could be seen just above the rim while his eyes swiveled to observe events, despite the moozilla, none too eager to lose his motherlode of Josephs and a possible raise. But the rim could not disguise the terror on his amphibian face as the horrifying scene unfolded.

French was slower. Catching him in mid-air as the troll jumped for the cover of his hidey-hole, the haus-frau yanked him back to earth and held him by one ear as he struggled to escape.

The moozilla shook the canoe paddle menacingly at Captain French.

"Has Captain been *paddling* mit ze other haus-frauen? Speak ze truth now or Captain knows vat vill happen!"

French rattled in terror, his little wispy white beard jerking. "Nein, my little flower! Zis Captain no paddle mit any frauen but his Bavarian kissing frau! Your Captain svears it!"

The paddle descended and struck him on the head. Her deep voice boomed.

"Captain *LIE!* Zis haus-frau knows zat ze Captain has been paddling mit other haus-frauen! Haus-frau next door say Captain is doink ze paddling mit ze haus-frau next door!"

French cowered, the moo moo rippling beside his white face like a funeral shroud. "Nein, mein little belaying pin! Captain leave Germantown in canoe and go upstream mit Goebbels! Captain never paddle mit haus-frau next door!"

As from nowhere, several curious partiers appeared, thrusting their heads around corners to watch, their jaws dropping.

The canoe paddle landed again. Korplash and Goebbels stared, open-mouthed.

"Captain *lie* again! Captain no lie to haus-frau!" She eyed the Oktoberfest partiers who had suddenly appeared, noting that several were young buxom blonds dressed in short skirts.

"Loose frauen doink ze paddling in back of ze building! If Captain zink zat Captain vill join in ze paddling, Captain has another zink coming! Captain only make mit ze paddling mit ze Captain's own haus-frau!" The canoe paddle swung again, missing Captain French who barely managed to dodge it.

Her eye lit on several empty beer mugs. "Achh! Captain drink ze *dunkel-brau?* How many times haf Captain's haus-frau told Captain zat he no drink ze dunkel-brau! Captain embarrass haus-frau in front of whole Germantown, make ze bad example!"

The paddle lifted again.

Captain French pointed to Huntz and Heinz. "Zey made me do it, my delicate little flower! Zey are ze bad influence on your loving loyal husband!"

"Captain go to haus-frau home now! No drink ze dunkel-brau! Unt no eat ze hot dogs! Unt no embarrass haus-frau in front of Germantown no more! Captain no lie to haus-frau again, or Captain knows vat vill happen!" The paddle rose.

French looked at Korplash who was still hiding in the dumpster. With a pleading look he said, "Please—I zink I am beink ze Joseph."

"Good enough for government work," said Korplash.

The silver device flashed and Captain French, Joseph Goebbels, Huntz, and Heinz froze. Rising in the air like two Teutonic swamis, French and Goebbels floated to the dumpster and landed inside while the haus-frau watched, growling like a junkyard dog eyeing a Happy Meal.

Korplash glanced at Huntz and Heinz. Noticing their terror when they looked at the pawing moozilla, he said, "Sorry, Charlie. We're full up." With a swish, the dumpster launched into the sky and vanished from sight.

Unable to move a muscle except for his eyes, Heinz peered sideways at Huntz.

"Bratwurst unt beer. . ."

"Stop it, Heinz! Keep your *keepemfromtalkin* shut!"

The haus-frau's hatchet frown deepened as she stared at them. Beating her canoe paddle in one massive palm, she tapped her foot. Suddenly she looked up, her eyebrows arching in surprise.

From opposite directions two automobiles converged carrying a dozen dark-suited men on side floorboards. Screeching to a halt on the concrete plaza, the men jumped off brandishing Chicago typewriters.

"Drop the stick, Brunhilda!"

With a shriek she let the paddle fall and took off into the bushes trampling a path a rhino could follow.

A third black car arrived and one of the agents opened the back door. A small man in another dark suit stepped out—a suit clearly too large for his small frame. For a moment he stood surveying the scene, his jaw permanently akilter, inspecting the pair of silent motionless giants dressed in lederhosen with feathers in their Bavarian caps.

A taller agent appeared alongside him. For a long moment the pair stared in silence.

The taller agent spoke. "It's getting cold out here."

Edgar adjusted his ruby earrings. “Colder than a witch’s tit in a brass bra,” he grunted.

Episode 5

A young man in short-sleeved white shirt and pocket protector, hair carefully combed and chubby face freshly scrubbed, opened the door and signaled. In response, two more clean-cut men in their mid-twenties approached, their attire identical with his, as with each other’s.

Gary shut the door after they entered. Orangello and Lemongello let their gaze wander about the plush interior of the meeting hall. Pictures of Past Masters lined the walls: American Presidents, industrial movers and shakers, Benito Mussolini, Joseph Stalin, Hirohito, Al Capone, all were there—even Popes. All but Adolf whom Stalin had left cooling his heels too long one day and who had finally left in a huff. The Jello Brothers toyed with their holstered Latter-Day Bibles. Hardened to hard deeds, the storm troopers of the Joseph Smith Chartreuse Lodge of the Latter-Day Masons of Upper Middle Utah and Fish Fry prepared for their latest assignment.

“Orangello, Lemongello. . .” Gary said in a high voice, the changes of puberty still escaping him. He cleared his throat and affected to speak in a low voice. “We received the summons this morning. We must lower the screen to get the rest of the assignment directly from the Boss."

The Jello Brothers exchanged unsmiling stares. Every new assignment had the potential of extinction; for them, the end was never calculated in lifetimes but in *what comes next*. Retirement? Life insurance? They laughed at these meaningless phrases. The business of Bible quoting was a life of death and danger—they never knew if they would live to see the morrow.

Pressing a button, Gary stepped back from the far wall as the wide white screen descended. Stepping further back he animated the three-color projection device that threw its images onto the screen and in another minute the outlines of a face and book-lined library came into view. Gary turned up the sound as The Jello Brothers prepared for the assignment that could well be their last.

Shuddering into view as if there were technical difficulties at the other end, the image came into and out of focus until finally coalescing into the familiar face that the Latter-Day Masons had long communed with.

The ancient voice creaked. "Welcome, brethren. . ." An enormous bushy beard overlay a high white collar, tweed jacket, and white bow tie, framing an anciently aged face. A giant white forelock was flanked by grey fluffy sideburns, the tired eyes glinting with moisture as if striving to avoid the dryness that already afflicted the skin.

"Hail, Joseph!" cried Gary and the others, standing and sieg-heiling.

"Welcome, all." A moment passed as the aged speaker once again summoned energy like drops of fuel from an increasingly shallow tank. "Are you following the path that our Lord has set for you, my brothers? Are you resisting the lamentations of lesbians and the deceptions of cross-dressing wannabes? If you have any doubt as to their authenticity, you can test their mettle with water."

"Yes, O Elder Smith of the 333rd Degree. Thank you for your guidance," rattled the young men in unison.

The ancient face cracked a brief smile.

"It has come to Our attention that evil *tibbets* have established a base not far from Our sacred capital of Salt Lake City. You are to organize an effort to neutralize them. They bode no good for the future of our plans for planet Dryland. . .er, I mean Earth. Have faith, my brethren, and you shall receive assistance From Above."

"Thank you, O Elder Smith of the 333rd Degree."

"And it has come to our attention that three of our leaders have been imprisoned in an Airforce base. They are not being allowed to laugh at pedestrians or use their twin pokes or dance the polka. You must free them to make things straight and right."

"Yes, O Smith of the Eternal Two-Way TV. We hear and we shall throw every resource of the Lodge into fulfilling your sacred requests."

With that, the image dissolved leaving only the blank white screen. Gary turned off the projection device while the Jello Brothers carefully unstrapped and restrapped the Bibles holstered on their belts and checked their bookmarks at the most lethal passages. They inspected their supply of cinnamon toothpicks. Despite their preparation, they frowned. The notches on their Bible belts should have reassured them of their professional competence as hit men for the Joseph Smith Chartreuse Lodge of the Latter-Day Masons of Upper Middle Utah and Fish Fry, but with this assignment the odds of their surviving had nosedived. This job called for complete indifference to suffering—there was no room for mercy. Not for them. Or for anyone.

“Come right this way, Fred! Your reward is right around the corner!” Several scantily-clad nuns hung on Fred’s arms with admiring smiles and purring sounds, the mining construction engineer returning their ardor with a grin. Escorting the three-strike winner in Maxie Climax’s Bowlarama & Casino down the side corridor to the rear of the convent, past the holy kitchen, past the holy bivouac, past the holy supply room with the label ‘Nun Such’, and past the cubicles where several nuns of the Santa Lucia Shrine of the Eternally Flaming Sacred White Pins manually set the holy pins, they arrived at last at a low irregularly-shaped entrance in a door labeled in Navajo Font: Back-To-Nature Wigwam, next to a second door bearing a sign that was identical to the first.

One of the swim-suited nuns stepped through and began lighting candles in the midst of ersatz deer-hide walls, Fred and the other nuns following. A wickerwork recyclable fiber rug occupied the center. At a signal, Fred sat. Three nuns compassed him, their adoring stares and caressing fingers reassuring him and boosting his ego, while the fourth, after lighting the rest of the candles, tended to a purple mannequin in a wig placed in an old Western-style wooden rocking chair. Suspended on the sides of the large tepee, alongside pictures of nature scenes, were several signs reading 'Peace & Justice', 'Earth Day', and 'Unleash your Fem', though these were increasingly obscured by incense burners that emitted spirals of smoke. Scattered on the floor were Fair-Trade pillows, Indian peace pipes, and primitively surfaced drums.

"First we must say our prayers! We are in a church, after all!" crooned one of the nuns.

Fred was too busy trying to look down her top to think, much less reply.

"Oh my my. Would you like to lead the prayer, Mariette?"

The nuns held hands forming a circle around him seated cross-legged in lotus positions, and closed their eyes.

"Our Mother, who bakes in heaven, Jessie be thy name, thy kitchen come, thy cook be done in baking as it is unleavened. Give us this day our daily bread, and forgive us our recipes as we forgive the recipes of others; and lead us not into conception; but deliver us from the sinfulness of men."

Not quite the Lord's Prayer, thought Fred. *Still, no harm—no foul.*

The incense purling in his nostrils, Fred found it increasingly difficult to focus his mind on anything but the lustrous expanse of exposed femininity around him. *I guess we should get this over with. Those one-armed bandits are waiting. Besides, the longer I stay here, the harder it will be explaining this to the wife.*

"Repeat after me," smiled Mariette.

"Yes, Sister!" everyone replied, Fred hesitantly joining in.

"Momma knows best."

"Momma knows best," Fred repeated.

"Don't mess with Mother Earth."

"Don't mess with Mother Earth."

"Zero children is best for the planet."

Fred felt dizzy. The words echoed through his mind sinking ever more deeply. "Zero children is best for the planet."

"Smoking is a crime against Nature—except for marijuana peace pipes."

"Smoking is a crime against Nature—except for marijuana peace pipes," One hand seemed to act on its own accord to slip into his pocket and discard a half-empty cigarette pack.

"Development rapes Mother Earth."

"Development rapes Mother Earth."

"I must stop global warming."

The tones were deep and rich and could hardly seem to emanate from a young attractive woman in a two-piece bathing suit. Before he knew it, his own voice had responded, "I must stop global warming. . ." Breathing more and more deeply with eyes closed, he failed to notice the gleam that appeared in the eyes of the purple mannequin seated in the rocking chair before him. From somewhere a Drum Circle sounded, its thumps rising steadily in his ears soothing his soul and calming him as wooden flutes joined in. Louder and louder the drums sounded, faster and wilder the pipes played—then abruptly stopped.

The mannequin's knees creaked as it slowly rose from the chair. The gleam shone like a second sun, its vision alive with energy and thought, flesh gathering to its limbs as from some ethereal source until no observer could distinguish it from anything human. Fred the mining construction engineer out for a brief beer and a few nine-pins took a step and looked down upon the decayed remnant of his former life. Even as he watched, the clothes crumbled inward, no longer meeting resistance from a body, the clothing masking nothing.

Snapping out a hair-brush, Fred passed it quickly over his new thick shoulder-length brunette hair, stylishly waved.

"Thank you, girls!" said his deep voice. "I'm one of you now!"

"Don't forget your prize!" One of them handed him a manuscript copy of *The Feminine Mystique*, pre-publication.

"Thanks for coming! Now you be sure to keep in touch," smiled the swimsuit nuns.

He stepped out of the Wigwam and paused in the hall where other nuns of Opus Dea of Lower Middle Nevada were busy setting the sacred white pins. From the other Back-To-Nature Wigwam adjacent to the one he had just exited, emerged a woman with short hair and flat shoes dressed in a man's formal suit and tie, carrying a manuscript copy of *Silent Spring*, pre-publication. The two walked cheek by jowl until they arrived at the front entrance to the Casino.

"Where are those damn global warmers?" yelled Freda in a deep man's voice, which the thigh-high red taffeta party dress could not conceal. "I can't wait to get my nails in them. I'll scratch their god-dam eyes out!" Balancing on cute red high heels, Freda glanced in a portable compact unfolded in one hand while adjusting recently-acquired makeup. "They think they can get away with that global warming? Not if I can help it!"

"You said it, Freda. And after you scratch their eyes out, I'll pound them into raw meat." A woman of moderate build smoothed a plain dark tie and but-toned a formal men's jacket, and slammed one fist into the other hand. With a who-cares stroke, 'he' then passed a comb through his dark hair, which was so short that his temples suggested military boot camp, while his suit, the cuffs so low as to brush the bottoms of his shiny men's dress shoes, was fresh enough for a job interview.

"Come on, Taylor. Let's go make our 'vote' count," said Freda, scratching the eyes of an invisible enemy.

Once outdoors, Taylor picked up a two-by-four from the parking lot of the Climax Bowlarama and swung it in the morning sun by way of batting practice. "Once they get my 'vote', they'll never know what hit em!"

"Whooa!" Freda and Taylor jumped backward as a tough-built juggernaut rolled past, flinging grit and dirt in its wake. They turned. The Casino doors burst open to frame an incredibly short, and even more incredibly round, woman who stared with wide open eyes and wider open mouth as her protégé dashed away. Behind her, panicked voices rose while smoke erupted from the vicinity of the holy kitchen and nuns rushed past with fire extinguishers.

"I'll be back before dark, Momma Maxie!" called the juggernaut as it vanished down Mercury Road.

The juggernaut skated south under the hot Nevada sun, unhurried, casual, Maggie seeming to thrive in the heat and the desiccated air. The road had recently been replaced with smooth asphalt which reduced the cloud of dust that heretofore had seemed to hover perpetually over the desert outside the Casino. Dust still appeared. Her oval eyes blinked to clear away the minuscule dustlets whipped up by occasional meandering dust devils.

Left leg followed right, the tightly wound springs in her preternatural thighs propelling her across the hot landscape like a force of nature. She slowed here to avoid a pothole, paused there to take in the details of a dry lake bed. Once she grabbed a horny toad that imagined it could leap faster than she. Then let it go with a smile. Her gaze surveyed the great white valley with its menagerie of hidden lifeforms that had so entranced her since that ill-remembered moment when she had first arrived in Nevada as an infant.

Kindred souls all.

An hour passed.

She came to a T where the north-south road intersected a broader east-west corridor. Her eyes settled on two aged signposts that read 'Mercury Road' and 'Interstate 95'. A horn sounded and she retreated behind a boulder as a large commercial truck barreled past. A single glance sufficed to assure her of the new road's relative lack of potholes and thus its suitability for her increasingly long-range explorations.

Rolling onto the interstate, she looked right, then left. One direction was as good as another. A cloud drifted left. That was enough. Without another thought, Maggie rolled left, taking the road toward an evil land of sinful men about which she had heard many whispered rumors at Momma Maxie's Casino:

Las Vegas.

Skatewheels spinning, she propelled down the turnpike, her muscular thighs eating up the miles like a long-distance runner, stray trucks and the very occasional car zipping past, the bow wave of air momentarily retarding her progress. Once a four wheel drive ambled past, fresh from the Casino, its occupants an odd assortment of men in dresses and female hair styles. Maggie shrugged. *Takes all types*, she thought.

Again, a truck slowed beside her, dirty men in bushy beards and jeans leaning out the window to leer. Her upraised arm with single finger salute followed by a series of stones the size of bricks sent them packing.

The sun reached zenith and still she skated. Far from impeding her progress or dehydrating, her smile grew broader and she seemed to take to the road with even more enthusiasm, picking up her speed, her skin growing a shade darker, tougher.

Up ahead, to one side.

An open-bed truck had flipped.

As she neared, a man in a suit had managed to clear himself of the wreck and crawl partly into the road where he lay, one arm outstretched. The interval between them rapidly closing, he struggled to lift himself on one elbow. His hand waved and he smiled in relief as he caught sight of her. Help!

Slowing, she looked down at his supine form lying in the roadway. Her hands perched on her hips.

"Waater!" he mumbled through busted lips. "I have some there in my truck. . . Can you bring it to me please?" The truck bed held a portable water tank that had burst sending its contents gushing over the ground.

Maggie halted. With a look of horror she slapped his face. She took off. In seconds she had put a great distance between herself and the horrid man.

After a time the rhythm of the road returned and she forgot about the recent unpleasantness.

More minutes rolled by and a rare cloud bank blocked the sun. She glanced up in annoyance. Then back down. Another car was stopped in the road. Beside it stood a man and a woman consulting a map, gazing in confusion.

As she came closer, they both sighted her and began to point and smile. A local! She must know the layout. . . Decelerating, Maggie sailed quietly up. A faint voice rose: "I say, young lady, can you tell us where—"

She shoulder-slammed the sinful man like a load of lumber sending him head over heels and the woman sprawled backwards on the road shoulder. Maggie picked up speed as cries of outrage drifted behind. Smiling she let out a deep breath.

Life is good.

After a time, something else caught her eye. A faint glint hinted at something up ahead—something else rolling on the road like her.

As she drew near, her brows rose in surprise. Pedaling steadily, but slowing the closer she came, was a boy on a bicycle. In short order she caught up to the youth and followed in his wake, eyeing the red chrome, the silver bars, the yellow and red plastic strips flapping from the handles, and the puzzling lack of strength displayed by the youth who, to her even greater surprise, was younger than her.

With a start, he discovered her presence. Frantically he redoubled his effort, but soon expended his last reserves and slowed to a crawl.

Finally he stopped.

"You're stupid," said Maggie.

"Takes one to know one," he threw right back, breathing hard.

She peered askance at his bike. "That's not the right bike for you. It's too big."

Climbing off the bike with some difficulty, he sighed. "I know. My uncle gave it to me. He doesn't know me very well, but one doesn't refuse gifts from Sonny. At least, that's what my parents always tell me. He's rich—my uncle." He looked at his visitor, strangely unaffected by the heat that kept him sweating. "Do you have a rich uncle?"

"No. I live with my aunts and mommas. They're stupid."

"Are they poor?"

"I don't know. What does 'poor' mean?"

"Huh! Lucky you!" He smiled. "My name's Richard, by the way. . . Richard Pierson. Junior. I live up there. . ." He pointed to a high peak some miles away to the south.

"I'm Maggie." She looked east. "Is that Las Vegas?"

"Naaa. You'd have to go a lot further down I-95 to get to Las Vegas. And first you have to pass Indian Springs." He glanced at her skates. "Is that all you have?"

"Works for me."

He shrugged. Looking back toward the west while he cleaned his spectacles, Richard said, "I tried to find a cutoff down the highway but I failed to calculate the temperature and my water consumption correctly." He adjusted his sweat-soaked shirt and hat, both inappropriate for outdoor labor under a hot sun. "So I had to come back. I'm awful thirsty. I don't suppose you have any—" He passed an inquisitive eye over her again as if to conjure a bottle of water. "—no, I wouldn't. Never touch the stuff."

"Too bad. I kinda would like to get back to my home. And I'm not sure I can make it back up the hill."

Maggie glanced at the peak. "Doesn't look like much to me."

Casting an admiring stare, Richard said, "You haven't tried it! It's a zinger!" A crafty look came over him. "Aw, I bet you'd fold at the first bend. . ."

"I'll bet not." She began to pirouette. "Whatcha got up there?"

"Oh it's great! My parents are out of town and I've got the run of the whole house—our 'chateau' is what Father calls it. But it's really just a great big house, father's house. . .even though it was actually Uncle Sonny who bought it for him. Just like Uncle Sonny bought most of what's in it."

"What's a 'house'?"

"Wha— what's a *what?* Why, Maggie, haven't you ever been inside a house? I thought you said you were rich." He smiled again. "Tell you what. If you'll help me get my Indian Chief back home, you can see the whole place. I've got lots of great stuff to do!"

"Are you an Indian Chief?"

He laughed. "No, silly! My bike is. Or rather I call it my Indian Chief because Indians are my favorite motorcycles but I'm not old enough to have a motorcycle even though I'm sure Sonny would buy me one if I asked him."

"How does it work. . .your bike."

Now his mouth dropped. "Maggie. Are you telling me that you have never seen a bike before?"

She quietly shook her head. "Pictures."

"Well, you may not be poor, but you're certainly not rich." He broke into another friendly smile. "But I like you anyway. Let's be friends."

She extended her hand and briefly touched his hand with hers.

"Done."

"Will your bike allow me to pull it?" She flexed a bicep that instantly dazzled Richard.

He extracted a length of rope from a small backpack and restrung it on his back. “Wait till I get on the bike. Then you pull while I pedal.”

“Okay.”

Maggie took one end of the rope and tied it around her waist while Richard wrapped the other end around the handle bars with an extra length around one arm to provide some cushion.

Slowly moving forward, Maggie commenced dragging Richard and his bike, and immediately he understood that he would lose the bet. Within a few minutes they were racing eastward on Interstate 95 bypassing all but the fastest traffic.

A sign soon appeared: 'Double H Road'. Blocking it was an unassuming tin gate over a cattle guard with only dirt and gravel beyond, flanked by cactus. “Uncle Sonny seems to think this ranch is worth a lot. I don’t know why—he’s always saying how *sterling* it is.”

Maggie was surveying the dirt and gravel. “Not fair. No one can skate on that.”

“Oh this part is just for show and to keep door-to-door salesmen away.” Richard swung the gate to one side, then re-closed it after they passed through. “We have a private road other side of this rise—it’s a better road than the interstate!” Pushing his bike around the little hillock, sure enough high quality asphalt re-appeared, a two-lane road winding and twisting its way up the side of the mountain.

They resumed, more miles racing beneath, Maggie having no difficulty with the incline, slowing to prevent tumbling Richard and his bike into the increasingly wooded foothills and tangled dips, then picking up speed again. The asphalt sped beneath her skates until they arrived at the entrance to the largest 'house' that Maggie had ever seen—a sprawling mansion occupying a quarter-acre just below the mountain's apex, couched in a natural bowl that was invisible to any observer not inside the bowl itself.

Once inside, Richard handed his bike to a white-gloved man who hastened to clean it, while Maggie finally removed her skates, though insisted on carrying them everywhere she walked.

"Jasper—the butler," explained Richard. "My Uncle brought him from England. He says you aren't really rich unless you have an English butler." He shrugged again. "I wouldn't know. We've had him my whole life."

"Hey you," said Maggie, wandering through the front room. "Is this a 'house'."

"Not to most folks, Maggie. In New Jersey I lived in a shotgun shack and played in dirt in the back. That's what a 'house' means to most folks. My father, Richard Pierson, 'Senior', is an astronomer, but we were still poor until Uncle helped us out."

"Oh."

Richard pointed through a large bay window to a back patio. "There's our pool. Most people don't have those either."

Unable to believe what his words suggested, Maggie approached the window. For a long moment she stared. For the first time Richard noticed sweat on her neck.

"Wanna check it out?"

She jumped back. "No!. . . I mean, not today."

"Oh. Well, there's lots of other stuff to do around here. You want to visit the observatory?"

"What's that?"

"Yeah, I keep forgetting. You don't have a rich Uncle like I do."

She shook her head.

"But first things first." He turned and filled a cup with water from a sink and downed the entire contents.

Maggie watched open-mouthed. "You—you have pipes that bring water inside your house?!"

He sighed with pleasure. "Of course, silly!" Then he grew serious. "Maggie, are you trying to tell me that you don't have indoor plumbing?" He looked at her with a mixture of pity and new understanding. "I'm sorry. I didn't know. I should never have said anything about being rich."

He dropped his gaze. "Well, the observatory is this way." Walking towards a plainly decorated solid wood door, he opened it to reveal a spiral metal staircase that seemed to circle endlessly above them. "This goes to the observatory! It was built on the highest elevation of the mountain. Close enough to Las Vegas that my uncle can run into town, but far enough away that the town's lights don't interfere with observing the sky at night."

The spirals wound about them like a corkscrew as they climbed. After what must have been a half-dozen levels, the stairwell gave onto a long straight staircase that led upward into the distance. They mounted in the light of desultory half-hearted electric glows to finally exit into a stolid structure with a state-of-the-art telescope thrusting into the sky giving the whole the appearance of a battleship gun turret, camouflaged to remain invisible from the interstate. Through peepholes they spied cars and trucks in the distance crawling down late afternoon Interstate 95 like ants. Smaller than ants.

"Funny thing. For some time now I've been seeing some very strange things."

"Like how?"

"Like above—and below!" Richard scratched his head. "I can't figure it out. Here, I'll show you."

Moving to an electronic façade, he pressed some buttons and Maggie became aware of a second smaller telescope leveled down and east. Las Vegas. Richard focused it over the city. He twisted a knob. "Infrared. Unc liked to keep tabs on central Las Vegas, till he got busy. He's been gone a long time now, but if you train the scope over the town…" Richard turned to Maggie. "Take a look."

She gazed through, not knowing what to look for. She saw tangled figures.

"I guess you wouldn't understand unless you spent some time with it. It's Sonny's special design—just like the big telescope. Uncle Sonny had both specially made for my father by some very good scientists. None like it anywhere else in the world. . .or so my father says."

He glanced through.

"Yeah. There it is again. That's a heat bloom over Tropicana Avenue. Or something like it. I haven't identified exactly where it is, but it does something very strange. A genuine heat bloom starts on the ground and rises up. But this one falls from the sky until it lands, and doesn't dissipate. Very strange. I can't imagine what it could be."

"Birds?"

"Bigger."

"Meteors?"

"Too slow. And it glows just like living things. . ." He looked directly at her. "It's not a rock. Whatever it is—it's alive. And landing in Las Vegas."

"And there's more." He swung the smaller telescope northward, a little to the west. "The same thing is happening over there. At Papoose Lake. See?"

Maggie stared through the smaller scope again. Sure enough, as she watched, a bright glow descended over the lake and seemed to merge with something on the ground.

"It's been doing that at least since last year, and recently increased. Now it's happening at least once a day—in both places. Day or night, it's the same. And other places too. All over the country." He turned to look at her again. "That's why I took my bike to the interstate. I wanted to find Mercury Road and ride to Papoose Lake to see what it is that's out there. Something strange. So far, that's all I know."

He suddenly looked curious. "Say! Didn't you come from that direction? Can you tell me what's happening out there?"

Maggie shook her head. "I don't know anything. Nothing at all. I don't even know the name of the road I live on." She shrugged.

"Oh." He looked at the big telescope. "Well, there's more. For this, we have to look through the big telescope. It's getting dark now, so that's good. For this one, we need night-time."

Inviting Maggie to join him inside a small cupola to block the light, he closed it behind them so they could both watch at the same time. "This telescope is even more special construction than the other one. Sonny says it's also the only one in existence; he calls it his 'parallax viewer' and says it's light-years ahead of anything else. His scientists built it special for him. Hold onto your seat—you're about to see something that no one else on Earth has ever seen."

Entering several coordinates and twirling dials, the image on the scope came into focus to reveal an expanse of stars. A mere dot on the scope, barely less dark than the surrounding darkness, slowly grew in size till it filled the screen, its flat landscape offering nothing to distinguish one part from any other, nothing to relieve the eye but slight changes in hue.

Maggie shrugged.

"Keep watching."

Waiting patiently with hands calmly folded in her lap, she suddenly blinked. Something had flashed. Immediately Richard focused the scope on the flash and enlarged it. An oblong box appeared; more rectangles attached at right angles; and still others. At length a patchwork of what could only be artificial structures became apparent, like multiple parallel lanes that blanketed the planet.

And more. As they stared in that little cupola watching the distant orb, the night deepening around them, a flash appeared and a glow slowly drifted up from its surface—slow on the scope, but indubitably swifter than anything that ever moved on Earth. Followed by another. Then another.

Finally Richard swung back the cupola and they stood clear.

"I don't know what the heck those are. . .but I'm pretty sure they have something to do with the glowing things I keep seeing landing in Las Vegas and at Papoose Lake. And maybe elsewhere on Earth."

He looked at Maggie. "Want to make another guess as to where that is?"

"Guess like what?"

"Like in outer space what."

She shrugged. "Mars?"

"Nope." He solemnly shook his head. "*Pluto*."

She looked puzzled as if hearing the name for the first time.

"Well, that's about it. I just don't know any more. But if I could get out there to Mercury Road—I guess I need a better bicycle first—then maybe I could figure out what the heck's going on."

Maggie smiled. "If I ever see anything strange, I'll let you know."

"Thanks! That would be a big help! How about something to eat now?"

"I would like that."

Climbing back down the long staircase and the spiral stairs, they returned to the kitchen where Jasper opened a huge door to one of several refrigerators. Maggie refused all food until she caught a glimpse of some pickled cactus, which she snatched from Jasper's hand and ravenously consumed.

"Like the nopalitos, do you? Well, we have plenty, thank goodness." He presented a bottle of red. "Wine? We're not supposed to drink anything with alcohol but Jasper won't tell. Will you?" Jasper stared silently at the ceiling, hands hanging dumbly at his sides.

She sniffed it. Then guzzled half the bottle.

"Hey you, I wanna rest. Where do I sit?"

"Of course, Maggie! You're my only. . .I mean my *best* friend! Which guest room do you want? We have half a dozen!"

Choosing the most luxurious room and the room with the fewest pictures and decorations, she sat in a chair and closed her eyes, ignoring the plush pillow-strewn bed. In moments she was sleeping the sleep of the dead. . .or a reasonable facsimile.

Episode 6

Korplash stood and directed Gork's gaze at the newly arrived dumpster.

A thin face emerged over the side to peer with some apprehension at the unfamiliar scene. It had all been too fast—too bizarre. Next to him something scraped on the inside of the dumpster as if leaping up to see over the edge. With a crash, the front of the dumpster collapsed outward, expelling its two passengers—one small, one minuscule—into pratfalls on the concrete floor. They were the only arrivals, though plainly more were anticipated.

"You have done well, Korplash. Two Josephs for the price of one."

Korplash hummed with pleasure at the positive comments from the boss—the Big-a Big-a Big-a Boss. His bullet head and vestigial ears were bright green with satisfaction. "It was not easy, O Gork. Space storms afflicted me, evil siridogs lurked behind every asteroid, unidentified crawling objects threatened me from every side. . .but I persevered in the name of Gork's Great Plan." He gesticulated for effect.

"Enough of that crap. I see you have dropped all respect for other ribbets by forgetting to close with a question. Am I right?"

Korplash looked nervous, his eye-stalks twitching.

Captain French and Joseph Goebbels stood and

brushed themselves off, a full foot of difference between their relative heights.

Goebbels caressed the cosmodrone. "Ah! Zis must be ze latest design zat der Fuhrer has been keeping secret for all zese years!" Captain French slapped his hand away and shouted, "Nothink doink, Gabe! No von is permitted to touch my new seeboot!"

Gork looked at Korplash. "You brought two Josephs while Xplak brought only one—" He swiveled a reproachful eye at his underling Korplash while behind them Goebbels grabbed Captain French by his neck and attempted to strangle him. "—but quantity does not make up for quality." He looked at the two new quarreling Josephs and sighed.

Korplash's chameleon eyes swiveled in all directions.

"Besides," said Gork, "Xplak would never pass up a motherlode of Josephs. Since our first agents were captured as soon as they landed on Earth—er, I mean planet Dryland, we must prepare more, and this time we must train them better before we send them, to avoid another mistake."

"Of course, great Gork! Should Korplash train the new Josephs now?"

"That's better, Korplash. More polite." He looked up. Goebbels was running with a limp around the cosmodrone seeking to escape Captain French who was kicking at his shins.

"Maybe not so much training as I had thought."

Gork headed for the exit. "Bring the new volunteers. Their uniforms are ready. And if we hurry, we may complete the process while you-know-who is still passed out."

Into the private chambers of the 'shuman' volunteers, Gork led Korplash and Goebbels and Captain French, with two assistant ribbets in tow. Their main job was to watch each other. Gork was taking no chances on any more spies infiltrating his secret laboratory. Xplak soon joined them, and Goebbels and French exchanged apprehensive glances.

Something was up.

As the side door swished closed behind them, Gork approached a kitchenette at one side of the quarters and began to toy with vials of liquids. After a minute he laid out two plastic syringes with his assistants' help.

"Vat do you zink you are goink to do mit zose arm-stickers?" said Goebbels.

"Not to worry, shuman Joseph. This is all part of the Great Plan. You will thank me when all is done."

"Nothink doink!" said French, as alarmed as Goebbels. "I am also beink not in ze mood to let some big fat toad stick me in ze arm mit arm-stickers!"

Gork turned his green bullet head toward him. "Thank you for your kind compliment, little shuman Joseph. You prefer then that this ribbet inject you in the tail with a tail-sticker?" Gork turned and lifted a much larger syringe.

Both French and Goebbels turned pale.

French gulped. “Ze arm at your service ist.”

“You won’t feel a thing. But first things first.” The freeze gun came out and Gork pressed a button and Goebbels and French froze in place.

Gork looked at Korplash as if about to invite him to do the deed, but changed his mind. Ignoring Korplash’s crestfallen look, Gork injected Goebbels and then French. After he was done, he pressed the button and the two promptly unfroze.

Rubbing their arms, they again exchanged worried glances.

“You may rest now, shumans. Changes will begin soon.” The toads waddled one by one out of the room, Gork clicking on the electron barrier behind them.

Goebbels sat on one of the beds with his chin in one hand, while French paced rapidly back and forth, glaring at the big fat toads’ disappearing big fat rumps. They took in the green rug populated with its intricate tangle of hermaphrodite amphibians all engaging frantically in non-stop sexual reproduction, the full-length mirror that hung on the wall next to the kitchenette, and the lengthy oblong picture on the opposite wall with its images of swivel-eyed toads all staring directly at him. To their shock the picture came suddenly alive becoming a window through which it seemed half the population of Bogland sought to view the latest addition to Gork’s menagerie.

Goebbels looked at French. “I no can believe zis. I could make a movie for showing to ze masses, but no von vould believe it.”

French was staring dreamily out the picture window to a spot where natural landscape was visible. “Vat did you say, Herr Goebbels? I zink I am seeing several nice bridges out zere. Maybe zis place ist not beink such ze bad place after all!”

The former propaganda minister sat and stared. “Kapitan French. . .”

Captain French looked at him, annoyed that his reverie was interrupted.

“I am feelink. . .how you say. . .odd.”

“Strange?”

“Queer.”

“Ya, Herr Minister. Zis place vill do zat to you.”

“Pardon me, Kapitan, but I must inspect somezink.” Turning his back to the Captain, Goebbels removed his pants as if they had suddenly become too confining, and covered his body with the bed’s blanket. He inspected himself, then looked up, puzzled.

“Ya. You see, now zis is vat I vas zinking. Somezink indeed is happenink to my pokerzone, somezink I cannot explain. I am becomink. . .how you say. . .*duplicated*.” He looked again. “Has zis injection done anyzink queer to you?”

French looked alarmed. Glancing down at his own pokerzone, he saw nothing, felt nothing. “Nein, mein Herr!”

Goebbels looked under the covers again—kept looking.

"Mein Gott! I am becomink ze doppelganger. . .unt. . .how you say. . .*ze devil in ze voodpile!"*

French touched himself to see if anything strange was happening.

Nothing.

Hours passed and the door swished open again. Gork re-entered with his assistants close behind. Captain French stood and watched, his appearance unchanged, while Goebbels remained in bed covered by the bedcovers, sitting up but pointedly not standing to greet them.

"The appointed time has passed, shumans. First phase of changes should be done. We must now test your new capabilities."

Gork unfolded a large picture of a nude svelte woman in 'Shumanette of the Month'—April edition—and flapped it in Goebbels' face. Instantly the bedcovers over Goebbels rose in two places, higher than any shuman had any right to expect.

French frowned.

"We are off to good start," said Gork. "Please to demonstrate, new joseph." Gork yanked the covers off Goebbels and pointed to the mirror.

Blushing, Goebbels slowly stood, trying to avert his eyes from the extraordinary spectacle between his legs but unable to avert them, fascinated. Slowly he walked to the mirror where he beheld two of the most enormous penises he had ever imagined, hard as rock in response to Gork's centerfold, and aggressively alive. With a shock he realized that his clubfoot had gone and that his body, formerly scrawny, even diminutive, had grown and toughened. An admiring smile broke out—he was the new kid on the block, the monster on campus, the barbarian with the barbells. He was *The Man*.

He burst into tears. "Danke, Gork! Danke! I am pledgink mein life to mein new Fuhrer!" His right arm raised in a seig heil, followed by two more heils from below.

"That is good, my new joseph. But now is time for final change."

"Now vat is happening?" Goebbels squinted as if something were the matter with his face and he raised his hands to his temples.

"Not good to touch yet," said Gork. "Mirror will tell you all you need to know."

Walking to the mirror, Goebbels stared at himself, pausing momentarily to reassure himself of the continuing miracle of the mischief-makers, his eyes then settling on his face's reflection. It was his turn to frown.

Whiteness.

From mysterious sources white greasepaint flowed across his face like lava, encompassing his features in a thick layer of ugliness, invading every millimeter of his skin, his natural hue never so precious as now when it was being irretrievably lost to the curse of the bigtop, the horror of an eternal corpse-light gathering him in its unholy grip.

Gork handed him a black and white horizontal striped stretch shirt, black pants and—horror of horrors—a frenchy floppy cap.

A look of deep puzzlement stole over Goebbels as something unsuspected seem to grow within him, deep within, struggling to make itself known, importuning him to do new things, feel new feelings, display the signs of an unsuspected sophistication, knowledge, and superiority that he realized was innate to him and his kind, above the mere mortals that infested the worlds with their pedestrian preoccupations, their walking about on their little weakling legs on their busy little weakling errands, defenseless and naive as puppies before the manipulations of the superior race of white-painted interlopers, whose herren-ranks he had just joined, whose right it was to stop anyone at any time and subject them to whatever vile pantomime he may please to inflict on the unwary. What did he care whom it hurt? He eyed the black streaks emerging above and below his eyes like the brands of a criminal gang—and smugly smiled; the black, almost purple, lips. The dark outline that stole along the perimeter of the white greasepaint was a declaration of Will, *his* Will, of his hegemony over mere mortals, the pathetic 'shumans', the streetwalkers, the weak-willed creatures of Dryland who had no right to resist his mockery.

Of their own accord, his hands reached out to the shirt and pulled it on, careful not to smear the greasepaint, though Goebbels was ecstatic to see that it could not be smeared, that it was permanent, as much a part of him as his ears or his newfound hyper-masculinity, which thankfully he found he could deflate sufficiently at will to don his new black pants and belt them up. As the final touch, he perched the floppy hat on his head. With a ferocious grin, he turned.

He tried to thank Gork, but though his mouth was open his throat made no sound. Somehow he felt no unhappiness from this, and took it as a further sign of his aristocratic superiority, and his right to molest mild innocent strangers without explanation. Following an obscure impulse, he raised a finger and traced a white frenchified *fleur-de-lis* on the wall, greasepaint flowing through his finger. He was ecstatic. Much better than that old *swastika* thing.

"Gork is happy that his new volunteer is happy with changes. I will soon brief you with your duties. After your training, I will return you to Dryland where you will find that your new abilities give you special powers. You will need them to accomplish your task."

At that moment, the door opened and a man in a white dinner jacket and solid black pants backed into the room, struggling to free himself from the desperate clinging of a woman. She cried aloud as he forcefully disengaged her from his waist, her feet dragging the floor. Thrusting her arms away yet again, he raised a fist as if to strike her, his mouth silently rebuking, his white greasepainted face overlaid by a thick mustache, annoyance and frustration twisting his mustached features. Finally free, he trotted to stand behind Gork, his face still indignant, one hand rubbing a bruise on his temple.

"Mustache Joe! Shtorkin!" You-know-who lurched unsteadily at the threshold like a sailor who had lost his sealegs. Her voice tremulous with desire and her eyes half-closed, she smiled, a gourmet eager for the next five-star meal. "Come back, cutie pie! I'm yoursh forever. . .I won't never—*hic*—I shwear I won't never look at another Josheph sho long ash I live. . ." She swayed, broke into a grin. "Lesh do it again, Shtorkin honey! You know five times jush isn't enough, I'm only *shuman*, you know!"

The mime with the mustache looked at Gork, eyes wide. 'No more!' silently mouthed Mustache Joe, his hands spreading helplessly.

Before Gork could reply, Amelia Earhart halted just inside the door as if frozen—her eyes had discovered a new King of Bones. She sucked a breath. Split-grinned. "Yeah. . .thash what—hic—what I'm talkin bout. . ." Swaying even more, she steadied herself with one hand on the jamb.

Her eyes lit on Goebbels. "Say, whash *your* name, honey? Shay—you're a *cute* little guy!"

Gork answered. "This is our newest volunteer, Melia. 'Little Joe'."

Amelia produced a flask that she had stashed in a pocket, and downed a swig. She hummed happily.

"Oh, thash a good name. Yeah, thash a good name: Little Joe. Whaddaya say—*hic*—whadaya say we. . ." She turned. Her eyes fixed on the wall and unfocused. "Where'sh my goddam plane. . ." Looking back, she sighted Goebbels again for the first time. "Shay—you're a *cute* little guy! Whash *your* name, honey?"

"Little Joe," repeated Gork, rolling his chameleon eyes.

"Oh, thash a good name. Whaddaya shay you and me go mountain climbing—*hic*—Little Joe? Yeah, I'm ready to climb your twin peaks, yessir, Schmelia is good—and—ready!" She gulped from the flask again and took a step forward. "Sheven—thash my lucky number!"

"Not now, Melia," said Gork. "Changes not complete. And this joseph will be busy afterwards."

She stamped her foot. Tears streamed. "Thash not fair, Gork. . . Not again. . ." Looking at the other toads, she blubbered, "Hesh doin it again. . .takin away my josephs. . ." She brandished her flask as if to throw it. The assistant ribbets grabbed her by her arms in time and dragged her toward the door.

"Hey, Little Joe! Ya know what? *Lesh fuck!* Thash what!" The toads pulled her out of the room. "Don do that—don do that—don you unnerstan I wanna fuck the new joseph. . .shtop it. . .shtop it. . .I gotta fuck the new joseph. . .don you unnerstan?" At the turn in the corridor, she planted her hands on the jamb with a grip like iron till the escort ribbets finally pried her fingers off one at a time. The circus turned the corner. Her face suddenly reappeared, frowning: "Ya know what Gork? *Fuck you!* Thash what!"

The flask came sailing. It bounced off Goebbels' head, tearing his new floppy cap, before smashing over the length of the floor.

"Owww!" he mouthed silently. He directed a look of outrage toward the now empty threshold.

Captain French ignored him, his attention distracted by the lack of any change in his own body. He frowned more deeply than ever. Gork eyed him similarly, unable to conceal his displeasure.

"Korplash. . ."

The pilot toad jumped to attention.

"Look at the tiny shuman."

Korplash directed a hesitant gaze at Captain French.

"What do you see, Korplash?"

"A shuman, Your Greatness. A small shuman."

"And what else?"

"A small shuman—with an unpleasant disposition?"

"Yes, Korplash. . . And what else?" Gork drilled Korplash with his chameleon stare. "What is this shuman missing?"

His gaze passed over Captain French from head to toe. Slowly he hung his bullet head. "No pokes."

Gork stared. "That is right. No pokes. Now why might that be, Korplash?" Gork folded his webbed hands and tapped a webbed foot.

"Because it is shuman named Phineas French, not shuman named Joseph. Does Gork agree?"

"Gork agrees. Is a shuman named Phineas French part of Gork's Great Plan?"

"No, Great Gork."

"It is part of Korplash's mistake, not part of Gork's Great Plan. Is it not?"

"Yes, Great Gork. It is part of Korplash's mistake."

For a long moment both toads stood and regarded each other in silence, Gork's webbed foot tapping away.

"Vait just von darn minute!" Captain French stamped his foot and folded his arms defiantly, his frown reaching all the way to both sides of his undimpled chin, pushing unpleasant disposition-ness to new extremes. "You big fat toads—"

"Thank you, little shuman."

"—first you wreck mein plan in Panama, zen you suck me up from ze nice Germantown vere I vas enjoying my nice beer unt hot dogs doink ze mindink of my own busyness unt stealink me avay from my lovely haus-frau—" Korplash was tactfully silent on this point, "—zen you freeze me mit your dumkopf freeze ray, zen you stick me mit ze arm-sticker zat no vork nohow!" He stamped his foot in frustration again. "I am ze Captain of ze seeboots, unt I am ze volunteer Joseph! Unt I demand a pigsticker like you give to Herr Goebbels unt Herr Stalin!"

Korplash looked at Gork with cautious hope. If

three strikes meant he was out, he would long ago have been relegated to sentry duty on Planet Deep-Freeze at the edge of the galaxy.

Gork thought a moment. “Since you are not named Joseph, Gork’s serum will not work on you. But there is one thing I can do.”

French looked up at the vibrating blob with happy anticipation. A vision of a terrifying moo-moo being exchanged for seventy-two virgins sailed before his eyes.

Gork held out a bottle of pills. “Something the Dry-landers will one day call Viagra. . .pre-manufacture. And here is a pot of white greasepaint, and some black and white clothes. You might as well get started.”

Downing several of the pills with a grin, French quickly switched outfits and slapped the greasepaint on his face while Stalin and Goebbels exchanged evil mime grins and danced the polka.

When done, French said, “Now I don suppose zat you have a nice bridge available? I hear zere are some very nice vons close by, mit no von at all under zem.”

Episode 7

Lemongello watched the skater’s back slowly shrink until it disappeared in the distance. He looked back to his companion. Orangello met his gaze without emotion. From the front seat of a new Hudson that had been deliberately dusted and marked to appear broken in, they observed the object of their vigil, passing their eyes over the half-paved parking lot sprinkled with a half-dozen vehicles and the occasional patron, and a single-story rambling structure that seemed to sink into the large brackish lake that stretched for miles on the structure's far side, surrounded by untended gardens of weeds and cactus. Despite the bright morning sun, a lengthy tangle of neon continued to flash from the night before: 'Maxie Climax's Bowlarama Chicken Ranch & Casino for West Middle Nevada – Opus Dea Precinct 7', with a gaudy picture of a swimsuit-clad model displaying her uncovered derriere with a grin, a neon nun's brown habit modestly covering her hair. The nun winked each time the neon flashed.

The two men looked at each other again. There was no need for comment—the identity of the owners could hardly be more clear. Only the nuns of Opus Dea, Order of the Sacred White Pins of the Third Secret of Fatima, proclaimed their sinfulness so openly. The Jello Brothers loosened the straps on their Mormon Bibles. They had received their orders not only from the Boss, the Big-a Boss, and the Pope, but this order came from the Big-a Big-a Boss: Joseph Smith, 333rd degree holder, Eldest of Elders, and Founder of the Joseph Smith Chartreuse Lodge of the Latter-Day Masons and Fish Fry of Upper Middle Utah, now residing with the Ancestors but still alive and still giving orders.

The order was: terminate the abominations in the nuns' Den of Sinfulness. . .or terminate the nuns themselves. They inspected their Bibles once again, verified its lethal passages, placed their new wide-brim white hats on their heads, and made sure coins were in their pockets so they would jingle when they walked—for effect. Giving their shoes a last polish and adjusting the pocket protectors in the left front pocket of their bleached short-sleeved shirts, they practiced sincere smiles, and cleaned their faces one last time with alcohol swabs with just a touch of soap to make the freshest impression to the innocent. Then they took the final measure—the sign that, from this mission, there would be no return without victory. Into their pockets they tucked two long cylinders: calculated instruments of terror to be produced at just the right moment for maximum psychological effect.

They had always known the dangers inherent in Bible-quoting: the harsh words; the cruel stares; the doors slammed on fingers and toes. They had learned to accept this as part of the job. But they had also always known there were further risks, and now they conducted the Lodge Ceremony for the ultimate danger—producing two paper cups, they popped open a small can of orange soda and, after tippling together, downed the fizzy drink. It was harsh, but bolstering. Tossing the paper cups and empty can on the road—a deliberate provocation to the Earth-worshipping nuns—the Jello Brothers slid cinnamon toothpicks in their mouths. Their hearts were hardened; they would resist the lamentations.

From somewhere a mournful Mexican trumpet sounded. The Brothers slammed the car doors shut and commenced walking, their change jingling. In the parking lot, several patrons preparing to enter the establishment panicked upon sighting the oncoming Bible-slingers and rushed back to their cars. In moments, the lot was almost cleared as the visitors gunned their engines, spinning dirt as they sped down Mercury Road, or ducked behind steering wheels. Stray Bible quotes were nothing to toy with—Mormon or otherwise.

On the steps, a man in a pink taffeta dress and brunette wig halted at the bottom step leading to the Casino entrance. 'She' squinted through the hot sunlight. Another man in women's clothing—a pretty lavender summer dress with matching headband and cute high heels with a flowing flowery pattern—joined the first cross-dresser. Flourishing a new hairbrush, she brushed a small tangle from her hair, then halted.

"Good morning, ma'am!" smiled Orangello. "Do you have time to discuss the Lord?" He pointed to his Mormon Bible, taking care not to scare the drag queens by taking the book out of its holster. "Would you like to learn how you can be saved?" He grinned his best sincere grin.

Lavender Dress clutched her padded bra and

stepped backward as if to catch her breath. She stared, uncertain. Her deep manly voice hesitantly replied, "I'm not sure your sort are allowed in here. Didn't you see the No Peddlers sign?"

Taffeta spoke, in a voice equally deep. "Wait, Loretta. They ain't doin no harm. Maybe they're just lookin for a good time. Like everybody else."

Laying a cautious stare on the two brothers, Loretta was not quite ready to let her guard down. "I don't know. They look so—*clean.*"

"Don't let that fool you!" said Orangello. "We just dress like this cause we're workin at the dude ranch up the road."

Lemongello added, "Yes, ma'am! We spend most of our time herding. . .*dudes.*"

"Very clean work—herding dudes. These duds just come with the territory." Orangello grinned with the kind of humor that makes instant friends. Their training had been thorough. "Duds for dudes!" He chuckled. "Now how about letting us show you our Bibles. . ." Sincerity spread easily over their faces, putting the cross-dressers at ease despite their suspicions.

A third cross-dresser exited the Casino—a woman in a one-piece construction uniform with yellow helmet and tool belt, 'his' head freshly shaved, thick spectacles on his nose. The three cross-dressers stood hesitantly, blocking the Jello Brothers from the entrance. Also suspicious, the construction worker put his arms on his ample hips and peered up at the taller visitors, a tag pinned to his ample feminine bosom that read: 'Hi. I'm Ralph. Ask me about my Wigwam.'

Loretta cocked her pretty hair-stubbled chin, her long brunette hair falling in waves over the two-o-clock shadow. “Tell me,” came her deep voice, “how do you two feel about. . .*global warming?*”

Again the expressionless exchange of stares between the Brothers. They had this—they were well rehearsed for all the usual litmus questions.

“There's never an excuse for raping the Earth.” Orangello smiled reassuringly.

Taffeta and Lavender eased somewhat. No one could argue with that.

“And what about children?” interjected worker Ralph. “What do you think about ‘rug-rats’?” He spoke gently, not wishing to turn away people who might be potential friends, but still skeptical due to the visitors' strange scrubbed-clean appearance.

“Too much carbon. The fewer rugrats, the better!” Lemongello grinned.

The cross-dressers relaxed. “Good answer.”

Taffeta and Loretta turned and climbed several steps allowing the Jello Brothers to follow them all the way to the double door entrance where they paused again, more reassured than before, but still not entirely convinced that anyone dressed in a clean white shirt and wearing Western hats could possibly have good intentions. Construction Worker Ralph tarried at the bottom of the steps, but believing matters were now in hand, turned toward the parking lot—none noticed the Jello Brothers subtlely loosen the straps on their Bible holsters as they neared the entrance.

From somewhere Andean flutes began to play, matched by small hammering sounds as of an undertaker preparing new coffins. The Mexican trumpets joined.

The Bowlarama doors burst open.

"Loretta! Maurine! You forgot your copies of *Silent Spring*." A pair of hefty nuns in full cover black gowns and brown habits appeared at the threshold, holding rough-printed manuscripts. They stopped short. Clapped hands to their mouths.

"Run!" screeched Mary and Maria. "It's *Hit-Mormons!*" Sticks appeared in the nuns' hands, kept inside the doors for such an eventuality, and for a moment the nuns stood rooted in one spot as if uncertain whether to advance on the hit-Mormons or flee for their lives.

The jig was up.

"Drop em, Sisters! Or we'll let em have it!" Lemongello and Orangello each grabbed one of the cross-dresser wig-wearing women and, snapping out their Bibles, pressed them half-open against their victims' necks—a savage maneuver whose effectiveness they had learned from Ben, the depraved Jehovah's Witness, in the Utah motel parking lot years earlier. More than one Bible could be used with such lethal purpose.

"Put it down, Sister," yelled Lemongello, "or Miss

Lavender here gets it right in the jugular!" He pressed the Bible verse harder on her neck for emphasis, causing print to run as her sweat mingled with ink.

"And Miss Tafetta in the Adam's Apple!" shouted Orangello, pressing the sharp end of his Bible against the other cross-dresser's masculine neck, who coughed, choking on dangling participles.

Their pages were open to two of the most lethal passages in their terrible Book, and the nuns froze, fear penetrating to their very cores. Only they could know the fierce lengths to which their mortal enemies would go to accomplish their hideous goals. Hit-Mormons, on loan for hire from the topmost centers of conspiracy, dedicated to eradicating all opposition to the Latter-Day Masons' global conspiracy for evil. The nuns lurched back, extending protective arms in a last-ditch attempt to preserve the lives of their most recent converts.

"That's right, Sisters, back it up!" Orangello sucked on his toothpick, a savage grin on his face, the cinnamon exciting him almost as much as the power he wielded. "All the way, Miss M." Once inside, bowling halted as the patrons stopped rolling, realizing the danger.

"We've got a bone to pick with you." Lemongello lurched, laughing out loud. "Say, Orange, what do you say to puttin in a high-rise office building on this site? Or maybe a strip-mine in the back yard?"

"That's givin it to em, Lemon!" He too grinned

with malice. "And I'm for sinking an oil well right about here—smack in the middle of their little white nine-pins. And a suburban green lawn with sprinklers, and an artificial fountain. With chemicals to control the weeds!"

"You wouldn't!" yelled Mary and Maria in horror, as more nuns rushed to their side, unshaven legs that had never known water showing beneath.

"Oh, wouldn't we?" smirked Orangello. He pointed to the desert grounds visible outside through the Casino's wide windows. "You see that?" He sneered. "I will rape that Earth right in front of your eyes!"

"No!" They put their faces in their hands. "No one can be this cruel!" They blubbered, lamentations rising all around.

"Your lamentations will have no effect on us," sneered Orangello. "You can beg all you want—we will still rape the Earth where you stand."

Mary and Maria burst into tears.

"He means it, Opus Dopus," added Lemongello. "Watch! He's gonna rape right now!"

As the nuns and cross-dressers watched in growing horror, with his free hand Orangello grabbed a potted plant and dumped it on the floor of the Bowlarama; picking up a stray brick he placed it carefully on the dirt, and directed a look of triumph at them. "There. It's raped! How do you like that? My own little development project—just for you!"

The nuns' jaws dropped open. "Oh no! Oh, our

poor Mother Earth!" Several nuns and Construction Ralph fell to their knees. They threw the brick aside and caressed the pile of dirt seeking to undo the mortal injury. "We're sorry, O Great Earth Mother Gaia!"

Lemongello's cruel nasal voice sneered, "Oh, we're just getting started! I see lots more bricks. And old-growth lumber too! I will rape your Earth till the cows come home. And then eat the cows. And throw litter besides!"

"Not today!" Loretta elbowed Lemongello and twisted out of his grip. "You meat-eating Earth-raper! I'm gonna kick your conservative ass!" She popped open her copy of Silent Spring and screeched aloud a passage: "It is not half so important to know as to feel!"

Lemongello doubled over, stunned by the illogic. Quickly he snapped open his Mormon Bible and rattled off: "The scales of darkness shall begin to fall from their eyes; and many generations shall not pass away among them, save they shall be a white and delightsome people!"

Loretta gasped at the whiteness. "You animal!"

With Orangello distracted by the mortal combat, Maurine suddenly twisted free. Opening his Bible to lay her low with a well-timed recital, Orangello's forearm collided with Maurine's handbag and his fingers slipped allowing the Moronic Message to drop to the floor.

Lemongello stared at his Brother in shock. Now,

of all times!

From all corners of the Bowlerama more nuns rushed, some brandishing bowling nine-pins, others wooden chairs, outrage on their faces, though uncertain if they could counter the fierce potency of the Mormons' recitals even with their overwhelming numbers. Among them were several more cross-dressers, high-heels stamping the polished wood floors of the bowling lanes without regard, their heavy handbags—in several stylish colors, with cute little counter-lines—swinging. Come what may, at all costs, the enemy must be repulsed from the Sacred Precinct.

Maurine pulled off a shoe and caught Orangello in one arm with a stilleto heel.

"Ooouch!"

"Scratch his face, Loretta!"

On the defensive, Lemongello stepped back to avoid Loretta's scratching claws, almost choked on a toothpick in the confusion of the battle, but recovered and brayed: "And it came to pass that those Lamanites who had united with the Nephites were numbered among the Nephites; and their curse was taken from them, and their skin became white like unto the Nephites!"

The recital was lethal—Loretta jerked back as if shot.

Lemongello aimed a round at Maurine who was still swinging her shoe at Orangello. "Touch these stones, O Lord, with thy finger, and prepare them that they may shine forth in darkness, and they shall shine forth unto us in the vessels which we have prepared, that we may have light while we shall cross the sea!"

The ferocity of the attack knocked her copy of Silent Spring to the floor where the perfect binding split very imperfectly. The other cross-dresser fell to one knee and groaned, while Orangello composed.

Seeing an opening, Loretta slapped the hat off Lemongello and grabbed his hair. Her fingers slipped through his shallow crewcut—another trade secret of the two Mormon hitmen, familiar with the hair-pulling tactics of lesbians and cross-dressers. Lemongello grabbed Loretta's brunette wig in turn. To his surprise nothing came loose—the wig had woven. It was Loretta's turn to howl.

"Hold everything!" yelled Orangello. The onrushing horde of black-clad, brown-clad, and mis-clad nuns and gown-bedizened gender twisters paused, not knowing what to expect, but knowing that the very worst was possible from these twin emissaries of evil, for the nonce caution definitely being the better part of valor—unless, of course, they could catch the Jello Brothers with their eyes closed or their backs turned.

Reaching into his pocket, Orangello withdrew his special cylinder that he had been preserving for the right moment: from the cylinder he unrolled a Latter-Day Mason lodge apron and opened it with a snap. The bearded face of Joseph Smith was emblazoned. As the fell image impacted their vision, the nuns cried out, covering their eyes. "The Patriarch of Sin! The face of the Evil One himself! Don't look, Sisters!" Lemongello unrolled his apron as well, the Patriarch's huge beard seeming to twitch like Medusan snakes, his eyes glaring in the harsh light of the nuns' perverted lair.

"Don't mean zilch to me," said construction worker Ralph. Removing 'his' spectacles so the terrifying images of Joseph Smith were no longer in focus, he snatched both aprons and threw them face down on the floor, neutralizing their chilling effect.

The Jello Brothers had hoped to rout the nuns with their Joseph Smith aprons after first Bible-quoting them into submission—not throw away their chief instruments of terror in self-defense. Now it was too late.

With more nuns rushing to meet them and more drag queens brandishing high heels ready to stiletto them to death, Orangello looked one last time at his partner in poor sartorial taste and narrowed his eyes; Lemongello knew what this meant. He steeled himself.

Their number was up.

And their last card down.

Pressing a button on a tiny wire on the side of his leg, radio waves raced through the ether to arrive in seconds at a receiver on the side of one leg of the Big-a Boss—Gary—Worshipful Master of the Chartreuse Lodge of Upper Middle Utah, who instantly recognized its import.

With a sigh of regret at what it meant for his comrades, he mouthed a silent prayer for his best hit-Mormons. But they had known the risks. For them, there was no more that could be done. The Cause must prevail. Looking up from his seat ensconced in the Worshipful Master's chair in the Lodge of the Latter-Day Masons in Salt Lake City, Gary's gaze settled on a small green button with a picture of a broken arrow.

He pressed it.

Moments later, on the distant planet Bogland, a fleet of cosmodrones shaped like blue and green dumpsters with floppy lids raced into the stratosphere and plunged into the pipeline that led, via a series of wormholes, to the skies above Dryland.

Inside Maxie Climax's Casino, the Jello Brothers pulled cross-dressers' hair and swatted nuns with their Bibles, and kicked shins, successfully fighting their way through the enraged Sisterherd to emerge down the back corridor where they fled past the holy kitchen, past the holy bivouac, alongside the holy stations of the changing of the holy white nine-pins of Santa Lucia Holy Bowler of the Third Secret of Fatima, past the holy Nun Such supply room, and past the holy Back-To-Nature Wigwam, the almost as holy adjacent Took-The-TV-With-Me-To-Nature Wigwam, and the just a little bit holy Been-There-But-Forgot-The-Bugspray-So-Came-Right-Back-Pronto-From-Nature Wigwam, to finally seek refuge in a deep dark series of chambers that seemed to stretch into the depths of Mother Earth, a hail of nine-pins hurtling after them, though thankfully they managed to dodge them. Someone had apparently been doing much Earth-raping somewhere.

Just as they disappeared, a loud humming sound brought the pursuing mob to a halt. The humming turned into a crashing wave that rippled across the building, the roof suddenly exploding sending tons of debris crashing down upon them as they watched transfixed. Pink rays slammed into the Chicken Ranch & Casino, causing the structure and everything around it to erupt like a volcano, every stick and brick ripping to shreds in a gigantic twister to fall back to Earth in minuscule fragments.

The blue dumpsters floated overhead as the sun slowly set on a landscape of utter devastation. Certain their mission was accomplished, multiple green bullet heads peered through slits in the sides of the cosmodrones to make sure nothing had survived. Satisfied that no more tibbets or their minions remained to interfere with Gork's Great Plan, the fleet of dumpsters ascended back into space before those pesky chasers of galactic mailmen called siridogs could appear, and, in short order, they had escaped back through the wormholes to Bogland to crowd into the local bar where they celebrated their toadish bravery far into the night consuming endless pitchers of green goo and buckets of chirping jacks and dragonflies over boastful toadish croaking.

Two thousand miles away from the scene of the attack, the phone rang on a desk in an oval office, just recently renovated. A nondescript man of average size and round metal-frame glasses, picked up the phone and listened, placing one palm over his free ear to drown out the sound of construction that drifted into the office from outside. Leaning back he propped both feet up beside a sign on his desk that read 'The Buck Stops Here'.

"Whassat? Salt Lake City, you say? Put him on." He listened. "Can you repeat that please?" Frowning, he continued. "Nevada. Sixty-three miles northwest of Las Vegas—got it." He pursed his thin lips. "Don't worry about a thing, Worshipful Master. I know just what to do."

Hanging up, he dialed out.

"Call the Atomic Energy Commission. And get me Dean." A half minute passed. "Dean, remember that nuclear project you wanted to test out in that godforsaken place called Frenchman's Flat?"

"Yes, Mr. President."

"Well, *green-light* it. I want to read about it in tomorrow's newspapers. Is that understood? Yeah, that's right—the area next to that dead lake district you call 'Area 51'. Thank you, Dean. Got it? *In tomorrow's papers!*" Brother Harry S. hung up the phone.

Episode 8

Sweet pokelicious
Likes her nopalitos
No sinful water man
Will touch her little piggy toes

Maggie hummed as her oriental eyes fixed on the interstate in the growing light of dawn and skated backwards down I-95, the brown-skinned girl in red and white Kansas-innocent shorts and haltertop almost missing the turnoff. As the green road sign leapt into her rear-view, as it were, her massive thighs ground to a halt like disc brakes. For a few moments she stood, confused, no traffic passing by to serve as a convenient scapegoat, try as she did to locate one.

She glanced at the sign trying to make out the letters in the imperfect light.

"Mmmm. . . Mmmm. . ." Puzzlement settled on her features. "Mmmomma Maxie," she finally blurted. Her gaze scanned the near countryside with its dry lunar landscape of thorn bushes and cacti and instantly recognized her surroundings. "My thighs know the way," she said aloud to herself.

Switching to frontal mode, she arched north in the direction of the Sacred Precinct, her capacious physiological predilection consuming the desert miles with the ease of an eagle and the relentlessness of a buzz saw. Although prepared to move to one side on the narrow single-lane road to accommodate the occasional car or truck that she had learned frequented Mercury Road ever since Momma Maxie had fixed the lighting on the front of the Casino several years earlier, today none appeared, a fact which in normal circumstances, or perhaps if her physiology had been a trifle less predilected, may have sparked the notion that something was out of the ordinary. But the hour was early, and the more predilected prevailed and she instead withdrew nopalitos from a paper bag that 'Hey You' had given her when she left at the break of dawn. She thoughtlessly munched. Exceedingly thoughtlessly.

Her mind did wander, though, if mind perhaps was not quite the most suitable description. Hey You surfaced again in her memory, and she found to her surprise that pleasant emotions attached themselves to her new acquaintance. This must be what the word 'friendship' meant. She may indeed visit Hey You again sometime—after she overcame the chill at her shocking discovery that he kept a huge vat of liquid poison on his property. And even maintained it!

She downed another bite, the energy surging instantly throughout her body like a supercharge. And cranked up the kilometers per hour. A chug from a small bottle of dense red wine gave it another kick—another gift from Hey You—draining it in a few gulps. With a casual toss she flung the glass bottle onto the road where it smashed into pieces, large and small. It wasn't litter if it broke. And if it happened to cut someone's tires…so much the better. Tiretracks were a black eye on Mother Earth.

Maggie sighed with happiness. Could life be better? A smile crept across her face—an unfamiliar expression that required the muscles some time to adjust. Finally they did. But the strain the smile imposed soon persuaded her to return to her usual morose expression, blank but potent, like a snake silent and coiled, awaiting only the proper stimulus to stir it fully to life and obey its effulgent nature, which till then was still unknown and unknowable—to herself most of all.

The morning was bright and cool and clear, the merest hint of cumulus perched in the highest reaches of the sky, cold and poised with a strange geometric alignment as if Valkyries watched from their supernal domain for signs of a long presaged manifestation of the divine.

As the sun cleared the chain of ridges to the west, she arrived—or believed she had arrived—at the parking lot to the Sacred Precinct. Except nothing was parked. And there was no lot to park on. And there was no Precinct to enter if one had parked in the missing lot.

Acres of wreckage met her gaze.

Had she found the right place? Had she taken the right road?

Eyebrows arched, she peered about, circling on her skates as if preparing to pirouette. She paused again. The ruins smoked, not from the charring of wood however, the destruction having been other than in the nature of combustion by heat, rather from clouds of dust and gypsum thrown up by kinetic energy limited in potential. Still, whatever the cause, the effect was the same.

The Ranch was gone.

A tangle of emotions welled up within. How? Why? Who? Had the Opus Dea nuns moved and chosen to disguise their secret evacuation out of some strange motive? Had they abandoned their young charge deliberately? Or had other more mysterious forces supervened to inflict this upon her?

She munched another nopalito.

One word manifested: men.

Evil sinful men.

Stepping forward, picking carefully over the debris that lay scattered about, she came across the first body. Torn and silent, Sister Mary of the nuns of Opus Dea lay still within her all-encompassing garment, now nothing more than an inert thing, an item to be stacked or disposed of by those with the time or the inclination. Maggie skated on.

More bodies appeared: nuns flung about like mannequins; mannequins flung about like flotsam; and a half-dozen cross-dressers of every gender and gradations of benders in between, tossed about like jetsam, their smart new wardrobes ruined beyond the ability of any seamstress to repair, their bright lustrous scalp-woven wigs now powdered thick with white dust verily like the wigs of dead white males at the signing of a constitution.

"Mmmomma. Mmmomma Maxie." Maggie looked skyward a tear forming in her eye. A short distance away she sighted the remains of the Shrine of Santa Lucia of Bowlers and the Sacred White Pins of the Third Secret of Fatima—and knew beyond any doubt that her navigation had been correct. She was indeed home. Snatching one of the bowling pins, she proceeded to smash everything in sight, breaking every stick, every brick, every stray detritus that presented itself to her, including several fragments of fragile neon lights that had somehow avoided the general destruction.

The Divine had helped others, she believed. Where was the intervention of the Divine to help her? Where was her purple mannequin from the stars? Was she—the center of the world of the Opus Dea nuns, for whom alone they had existed—not good enough to join the ranks of the cross-dressers from Pluto?

Raking through the ruins, she drew near one of the corpses and nudged it with her skate.

"You're stupid."

It failed to respond. Moving to the next dead nun, she gave it a harder kick in the shins. Again no response. "You're stupid!" she yelled.

She picked her way back to the road. Without bothering to look back, she began to skate south, back to Interstate 95, not thinking, no plan in mind, not knowing what to do or where not to do it, or who not to do it with. She came to a clutch of chest-high rocks lining the west side of the road and stopped and sat; not to shelter from the sun, which she rarely noticed and which even more rarely bothered her in any way, but to calm her mind.

Nothing was in that mind but two simple words: Hey You. Wiping away the last tear, she decided there was only one place to go. No need to labor at reading signs anymore; no need to rebel against the Controlling Ones who had ever sought only to scold her anyway. Her feelings were tangled, writhing and tumbling, but of one she was certain—to her own surprise, she felt relief, and promised silently not to waste tears anymore on unworthy undependable stupid ones. She began to rise to her feet. Still sheltered by the rock, she hesitated.

A flash.

Like the sudden iris-blinking flash of a camera bulb, for the smallest fraction of a second a white wave coursed from the southwest over the line of rocks, making her skin instantly peel even sheltered as she was. Another fraction of a second and it faded. She had just enough time for the fact to register that her brain was smelling the scent of heated flesh, when a shock wave knocked her over to ring the sheltering rocks around her like church bells and shaking a blanket of pebbles loose which covered her in their embrace. Another wave of heat washed over—red and pink invaded the southwest horizon, the cold cumulus suspended in the upper atmosphere suddenly erupting with poisonous growths sending it fleeing like scud before an Atlantic storm.

Leaping erect, her legs began to pump.

The smell of burning hair joined the smell of cooking flesh. But it did not register in Maggie's brain; nothing was noted or notable except Hey You and behind it Momma Maxie. Beyond that was only devastation and debris. Although she had already pulled tens of miles from those coiled springs that morning, she was not deterred by the prospect of squeezing tens of miles more out of them and she began to skate south despite the swift transformation of the horizon from pink to orange, the sensation on her skin transforming similarly from itching to prickling. As the clouds to the southwest slowly twisted and joined into a single uprushing column of greyish-white smoke seeking to penetrate the porticos of the gods in the form of a gigantic mushroom, Maggie found that nothing had impeded the Nevada juggernaut, poised as ever to impose its will on the world.

Her progress did not fade even as the smell of burning hair slowly registered on her brain that the hair must be hers. And as the smell of burning flesh registered that the flesh must be her flesh. And that the charred clothes that she smelled must be her already skimpy shorts and haltertop. Like derricks pumping oil, her Olympic thighs pumped blood into her legs, her eight-wheel skates eating up the miles, the coolness of the morning partly countering the sensation of heat in her skin, but the prickling was growing into something more resembling needles.

Behind her drifted occasional tufts of clothing or singed hair, but she could not be bothered to notice.

What would she do when she came to the mansion in the hills? What could she say to her new, perhaps erstwhile, friend? What would he say to her? What could he do? Nothing. . except hand her more wine and perhaps. . .no, surely he would not attempt to touch her with his masculine water. . . Hey-You must know she would never accept that kind of defilement, even to save her very life.

Was her life in need of saving? Something had happened to her, surely. But her legs still worked; her eyes still saw; her ears still heard; and her pants and haltertop still clung to her indescribably dense taut body, only superficially charred.

The turn from Mercury Road to Interstate 95 came. And went. Without trying to read the road sign, she propelled eastward toward Hey You's hidden cutoff, and for the first time noted the strange lack of traffic, the rise of smoky dust-devils from the vicinity of the rumored Indian Springs and the fabled Las Vegas far ahead. Whatever had happened must have been tremendous to affect those towns at such a distance, she thought. Twice she passed cars pulled to one side of the road with their windows blown out, drivers missing, white smoke drifting from their metal skins.

Before she had left Hey You, she had promised to return to visit him the next day. And he had promised to stock up on napolitos and wine. Skating down the curling road, her last sight of her friend had been of him standing on his porch, a forlorn look on his child's face as if he had just lost the only friend he would ever have—and a love interest to boot—and he had insisted that he had more to show her on his telescope. She wasn't sure she wanted to see more telescopes—his, or any other male's—just as she was not comfortable talking about her home, or the road that led there; but his nopalitos and wine were a hit and had evoked her promise.

Now all had changed.

Something was wrong. Her legs were not pumping as hard and her speed was slowing. It had been an hour since the blast and she had skated at least halfway down 95 to Hey You's hidden cutoff, but fatigue was building. This distance was a lot even for the juggernaut, and she had covered it twice in one morning…the effects of the radiation were finally taking hold. And she felt a peculiar new sensation that she could not explain and truly feared for its implications of defilement—she was *thirsty*.

The skates slowed and she suddenly realized that in her confusion she may have missed the cutoff.

She was lost.

Rolling to a stop, she stood still staring ahead. . . toward what? Thinking thoughts in her mind. . .of what? Conscious of bodily needs. . .and more needs that she could not explain, much less satisfy.

She continued to stand and stare in perfect silence as if the passage of time meant nothing. A beat-up open-bed Ford truck pulled alongside. A creature entirely clothed in flexible silver metal, and black plastic covering his face, stepped out.

"Those darn fools," came a voice, "I warned em!" He sniffed. "Now look what they've gone and done." Leaping out, the silver creature grabbed a dark blanket out of the back, wrapped Maggie loosely but strongly enough to overcome the natural but weakened resistance of an injured animal, and herded her around the car's hood into the passenger seat where he carefully covered her body from the neck down with another flexible sheet of bright silver, and wrapped a hood of black plastic around her head. Once inside, the door shut and he stomped the pedal: eastward.

Ignoring another car with its windows blown in, the truck raced along the empty road, Maggie vaguely aware from within a deep abyss whose depths were increasing by the moment, that Hey You had been left far behind. Soon a small sign announcing the news that they were about to visit Indian Springs sprang out of the bright day—it too rushed to the rearview mirror as the vehicle sped eastward, ever eastward in the direction of Who knew where?

The road curved southeast, then almost south and a chessboard of decrepit houses sprouted, twin rows of larger buildings paralleling the main drag further east. Traffic finally appeared, every other car with cracked windows, every building missing glass, the shattered remains visible littering the streets. From the depths, the thought occurred to Maggie that she had not imagined Las Vegas to glitter with so much glass.

Tropicana Avenue jumped into view. They turned. Staring through the intact window glass of the truck, Maggie glimpsed another neon sign and felt life flicker again: 'Madam Melissa's Chicken Ranch Casino & Bowling Palace for Lower Nevada – Opus Dea Precinct 12'. In the front parking lot she was relieved to see two cross-dressers exiting the establishment adjusting their new hair and clutching copies of some of the Cult's sacred texts.

Only a glimpse, however, as the truck paused not a moment but raced across the parking lot and up a side path until it came to a halt in the service lot at the back. Hurriedly, the silver creature snapped open her car door. The creature carried her to the back door of the building—kicked it open.

"Melissa! Quickly, my dear!"

Two dark-clad nuns rushed to assist and took Maggie. Laying her down in their holy bivouac they removed the silver sheet and proceeded to clean her body with antiseptic and lotion while she stared entranced at the spectacle of an alien creature removing its skin. Underneath emerged a thin tall man with a pencil mustache and simple red tartan shirt.

"I saw the blast from Stirling Peak—got only one hour of warning despite my connections. I suited up and headed here, where—what I do I find on the road? A young girl—caught in the kill-zone!"

"But what can we do for her, Sonny?" Melissa exuded pity. "Remember the Japanese at Hiroshima. . ."

The other nuns examined the damage and shook their heads. "Oh my my my."

Sonny glanced around him secretively. He motioned the other nuns out of the room, signaling only that Melissa should remain.

"Sister Melissa, do you recall the *capsule*?"

She looked puzzled. Finally nodded. "In back of the Wigwam."

"Did I ever tell you its purpose?"

Her head shook.

"I had my best scientists construct it in the wake of the bombs over Japan. I was desperate to find a way to repair the damage that was inflicted on the innocent. If you remember, just before my people built my telescope on Stirling Peak, I had them deposit the capsule here in Las Vegas. The safest place I could think of was here."

"Yes, Mr. Hughes."

"'Sonny'. Please."

"Yes, Sonny."

"But when they finished the capsule it turned out to have a major flaw that made it useless for the victims in Japan, so it has languished here for years." Howard Hughes looked down at Sister Melissa of the nuns of Opus Dea from his supernal heights. "Sister. . .this is the time to use it."

Opening the inner door, Sonny invited the other nuns to re-enter. Carefully they picked Maggie up with the silver sheet below and above to provide maximum protection and carried her down the sacred hall into Madam Melissa's Back-to-Nature Wigwam. Opening the back panel, a room was exposed, within, resting on a vault like an altar, an enormous aqua-marine capsule laid horizontal. Sonny pried open several latches and slowly raised the top. Inside was room for just one occupant to lie in comfort. He gently placed Maggie within.

Her eyes were open. Almond eyes gazing without emotion.

"Good night, little child. It is time to sleep. When you awake the years shall have passed and the world greatly changed. But you—you shall be healed—and alive! You will not see me again, my child, for Providence does not grant so many decades to any man. When next your eyes open, you will be as young as you are now and you will have the rest of your life ahead of you. Good night. And good-bye."

Without another word, the top of the capsule slid shut like the lid of a coffin, burying her within.

"I guess you heard the bad news, Sister Melissa."

She shook her head.

"Maxie's place was inside the blast perimeter. It was completely wrecked. I told her it was a bad location. But you know Maxie Climax. As the pioneer of our Movement, she always insisted that she knew best."

Howard Hughes and Madam Melissa stepped out of the back room while Howard closed and sealed the door to the room with the capsule inside. "I'm dedicating this site as a permanent non-profit endowment, partly in memory of Maxie, but mostly to keep this young child alive. Long after you and I have gone to our reward, Melissa, this building will continue to stand and the power remain on. I was keeping the capsule for me. I give it now to this poor child." Howard laughed. "Today I am 60 and she looks 12. When next we meet, if that were possible, I will be 110, while she will still be no older than she is now. Will miracles never cease."

"Will miracles never cease," repeated Melissa as if reciting a canticle.

Episode 9

A week passed and a fleet of black cars converged on the dry lake in Nevada from the northeast following the only road in the vicinity, the chalky limestone sending clouds of dust that seeped inside the vehicles to coat the formal business suits that Edgar required all of his men to wear. Even in summer.

At the end of the road the black suits in black cars—now almost uniformly chalky white—burst onto a field of wreckage. Braking by a large placid lake, the entourage stopped.

One of the suits jumped out and snapped open a back door.

Edgar stepped out.

While his agents posed with submachine guns and small caliber pistols, he surveyed the scene: several small shacks splintered under the impact of the nuclear explosion at Frenchman Flat some miles away to the southwest; a lake so small he felt he could hit the far side with a rock; and no trace of bodies anywhere—human or otherwise. Could the report be wrong? For a moment he wondered just how much he could trust his compadres in the government. Not far, Edgar knew, given the extent of all the conspiracies operating in the shadows, but far enough, he felt, that he should at least be allowed do his job. He fingered ruby earrings in a pocket, nervous.

A military jeep jostled up from the southwest, its occupants no more concerned with radiation from the blast than Edgar, and General Ramey came to meet him with a smile, escorted by only a driver whose uniform was as devoid of medals as Ramey's was adorned. Something was in the works.

Edgar stopped rubbing his earrings, but still regarded Ramey with suspicion. He of all people knew what lies Ramey was capable of. Where was the evidence he had been told to expect by his unnamed informants? Where was the wreckage he had come to collect: the fractured neon; the shattered bricks; the warped steel; the blasted vehicles littering an asphalt parking lot? All were tied to the secret toad invasion from outer space—that much he knew.

Here is the lake. Here is the road.

But there was nothing more to see but a tipped over

shack.

He directed his suspicious glance at Ramey even as he shook his hand. The bodies he saw Ramey recover at Roswell were from off-world and were part of the plot. That Edgar also knew. He understood the need for Ramey to secret them away from the public—ostensibly to avoid a repeat of Orson Welles' disastrous 1938 Martian fiasco—but why keep the FBI in the dark? Edgar found himself looking at Ramey's fingers for signs of a Masonic ring. He had seen the sheer extent of the Latter-Day Masons' influence when he was abducted and taken to Salt Lake City. He himself had barely escaped with his life. Could the conspiracy extend as far as the Pentagon?

"There was no need for you to come all the way out here, Edgar!" smiled Ramey, briefly doffing his cap to smooth his hair back. "We have things well in hand. And there's just not much to see after the blast got through with this area." He exulted. "Our first atomic test since Alamagordo! It's about goddam time, since the Russkies have been at it with their own explosions!"

"Are you sure it's the Russkies, General? I mean, that sonofabitch Stalin has been awfully quiet lately. It's like he's made of wood or something."

"Yeah. Well, who could tell the difference? It's mostly reading tea leaves anyway. But we're in a real contest now. And," Ramey glanced cautiously around to make sure they were not overheard, "you know as well as I do that it's not just the Russkies we have to worry about." The General glanced at the sky. "It's *them*, also." Looking back at Edgar, "With the last two, we're collecting quite a menagerie. Too bad we still can't communicate with them. In fact, we're still not sure they're even alive!"

Edgar continued to stare at the desolate desert landscape outspread before him, unable to conceal his disappointment.

"Sorry you came out here to Groom Lake for nothing, Edgar. Whoever told you that there is anything going on in Nevada was giving you a line of bull. There ain't a damn thing in this whole god-forsaken state except for whores and sand. Next time give me some warning and I'll provide you with radiation suits so you can take your time. The tests are just ramping up. They'll be blasting away regularly soon. We'll all need radiation suits before long."

"Not a problem, General. I'll do that."

Clyde opened a back door and Edgar re-entered his car. Minutes later the caravan was back on the road to Interstate 93, the dust again accumulating over the black FBI vehicles slowly undulating over the rocky road like camels headed for Mecca.

Once the caravan disappeared, Ramey sat again in the jeep.

"Let's go, Corporal Kwik."

For a long moment the driver did nothing but sit and stare. Finally just as Ramey was about to say something, the driver turned the key. "Yessir, General Gamey."

Ramey frowned. "That's 'Ramey', Kwik."

"Sorry sir. My mistake, sir."

Ramey motioned and the jeep lurched forward. For twenty minutes the jeep bumped southward till it arrived at a roadblock manned by a squad of uniforms. They sported a variety of weapons sufficient to defeat a full-scale invasion and black plastic helmets covered their heads. Ramey rumbled through and the guards swung the gate shut behind him.

Minutes later the jeep arrived at an intense hub of activity around acres of burned wreckage including fragments of glass neon signs and a primitive parking lot strewn with scorched bowling pins. A construction crew guided excavation equipment at the entrance into a huge spanking new building that arched into a low bluff beside a large kidney-shaped lake.

Ramey smiled. "The last thing we need is the goddam FBI poking around here. I sent them to the wrong lake—and Hoover bought it."

Corporal Kwik answered, "Bought it. Yessir, that was clever, sir."

Ramey exited the jeep and walked into the entrance, Kwik following behind. Dozens of workmen were clearing debris and more dozens sliding equipment and cables into several large elevators just installed and Ramey and Kwik entered one. Another guard operated the elevator, sending them deep into the interior of the earth. When it came to a stop, the doors jerked open. They stepped out to pleasant nondescript background music. Approaching a set of sealed doors, more construction crewmen making final adjustments swung them open.

Inside, they walked slowly up to five plexiglass cases, the last two holding their most recent acquisitions, acquired that very morning. Ramey halted only inches from the threesome who had been transferred just days earlier from Wright Airforce Base. For a full minute Ramey and Kwik stood with arms folded, staring once again at the supreme examples of Nature's inexplicable capacity for ugliness, the inhumane, and the Just Plain Weird. They had no doubt that these emissaries from an alien world, who clearly could have no good intentions for humanity, must never be allowed to escape the confines of their new home below Papoose Lake, part of the military's new ultra-secret refuge of all that was bizarre and dangerous: Area 51.

Ramey took in the black and white horizontal striped pullover shirt, black pants, and white grease-painted face of the first alien with the blackened purplish lips, diamonds tattooed above and below his closed eyes, frenchified floppy beret on its ugly head. And the yellow stretch spandex of the second alien with bright red star over its heart, an insult to the intelligence and good taste of all right-thinking persons, more ugly black tattoos on its corpse-like face, and another splash of irremovable white paint scarring temple, chin, and cheeks, and topped—insult of insults—by a bowler hat one size too small. Not that the third alien was any less offensive with red suspenders and green pants, his own pale grease-paint searing the eyes of anyone foolhardy enough to fix his gaze on the specter for any length of time.

Ramey shivered.

"You said it, General," said Kwik. "These things got beat with the ugly stick—and then gave it more than they got. I feel sorry for the stick!"

"Whew," blurted Ramey. "I don't know why we even keep them. I say just pronounce them dead and burn the bodies. But it's not up to me. Unfortunately."

Turning their backs with relief, Ramey and Kwik stepped to the remaining members of the bizarre menagerie, two more aliens who were similarly encased in plexiglass.

Ramey let his eyes roam over the frilly white short-sleeve shirts, the short leather pants held up by suspenders, and arched felt caps each tipped by one white feather, with white socks and rubber-soled shoes, beer stains on their chests, kneecaps bruised where their hands had slapped their knees from too much dancing the polka. Both figures were frozen with one arm raised, their eyes occasionally shifting from each other to the General.

"Well, at least we know these aliens are alive." Ramey shook his head. "But what the hell these things are is beyond me. All they ever say is 'bratwurst-unt-beer' and 'stop-it-heinz', whatever the hell that means."

"Must be some alien code, sir. Maybe one day we'll figure it out."

"God willing." Ramey passed his glance over all five aliens tightly sealed in their oxygen-rich plexiglass tubes. He shuddered again. "But God help us if these things ever get loose among normal respectable humans. Come what may, that must never be allowed to happen."

Maxie Climax wiped the tear from her eye and jerked the doorknob on the Bowlarama's supply room—the doorknob constructed in such manner that only those possessing a particular bone in the wrist could open it, a bone that normal humans lacked.

The door swung wide.

Rushing past the sign reading 'Nun Such', Mrs. Climax entered the bowling palace's special supply room, a room the like of which could be found in the back of all bowling alleys if one knew where to look, but which only the rarest of persons could access.

Her eyes grazed a configuration of white pins studded in a contrivance of steel, some horizontal, some vertical, others set at peculiar angles unaccountable to the uninitiated, strips of tinsel glitter blowing from their midst despite the absence of any fan.

Behind her, sounds of conflict rose ever louder as her nuns strove to resist the attack on her Bowlarama Chicken Ranch, though she knew her sisters would fail, knowing the depths of evil that the enemies of Opus Dea were capable of, and their determination to eradicate her Order. Shrieks and screams echoed down the hall as cross-dressers and hit-Mormons pulled each other's hair and flung lethal recitations.

But the tear was not for her doomed nuns. It was for Maggie.

"Where are you, my leetle pokelicious beetle?" she cried. "I saved you once… But how can I save you again? I must return to my headquarters or everything we have worked for over the years will be lost." Climax sniveled. "I promise, my leetle dung beetle, I promise I will come back to help you when next I am able."

Directly behind the nine-pin machinery was a lounge chair on which rested a purple mannequin, one of many purple mannequins stored in the room, under a sign that read 'Nun Much'. Dropping her freakishly rotund body down on her indescribably small legs and knees, and leaning her squamous triangular head forward, somehow finding a neck that was indetectable to casual observers, she gave the sign of the holy triangle and began to pray at the feet of the mannequin.

"Jail Maria, fool of grease, the Lord is weeth me; blessed are you para los mujeres, busted ees the fruit of thy broom, Jessie Christina. Holy Maria, Madre de Dea, pray for us folkseengers, now and at the discount happy hour of Santa Lucia of the sacred bowling pins of Fatima ameen."

Standing again, she lifted the mannequin and unceremoniously tossed it onto the pile of similar mannequins behind the chair. She sat in its place. At one side was a black button.

She pressed it.

Immediately the contrivance of white bowling pins with red neck-rings began to swivel and turn in unpredictable fashion. Minutes passed. Finally the pins stopped moving and Mrs. Climax pulled a device out of the other armrest and pressed one of its buttons.

A blue-tinged light flashed.

For a second her round form appeared suspended in space, an expanse of stars behind her, the bowling ball that was she slowly spinning round like an asteroid in orbit, not doomed like other round bodies to a never-ending ellipse about the Sun to no purpose without end, rather set on a specific course to a specific wormhole, her progress measured without reference to time, steady and devoid of consciousness or biological process. The constellations flicked off to instantly reappear in only slightly altered form, and the measureless drifting resumed, the ball continuing its journey, oblivious, every function of life in total suspension, empty of thought or dream, and still the leetle ball rolled, the flat strands of Climax's scarce hair gathering no mousse.

Gravity took hold and began to pull her down and a moment later she opened her eyes in a similar lounge chair in a similar room. Maxie Climax stood and was pleased to once again feel the decreased gravity and increased agility of her normal body on her home—the local outpost of the Galactic Order of Tibbets of Opus Dea.

She stretched her powerful legs, happy to be free of the confines imposed on her body on the water-contaminated planet Wetland, and rubbed her vestigial ears on either side of her green bullet head. Half waddling, half hopping, she moved her squat toad body out onto the open expanse of bowling lanes that stretched as far as her swiveling chameleon eyes could see, horizon to horizon, refreshingly open to the cloudless rainless sky and mercifully entirely free of annoying water. Again she reflected on the complete lack of webbing that she and her fellow tibbets possessed in comparison to those evil ribbets who gloried in immersing themselves and flooding every habitable planet they found in volumes of the repellent liquid. As toadish tibbets rolled strikes in all directions on the ever-replicating bowling lanes of Santa Lucia, Maxie hurried to the tibbets' center for interplanetary operations directed at the recently discovered third planet from the local Sun: 'Earth' as the primitive locals called it.

"Welcome back, Maxie," croaked a squat olive-green toad. "Sorry to hear about Precinct 7."

"Theenk you, Margie. We lost some veery good tibbets and cross-dressers. But wee will send more." Years of emulating the speech of Panamanians on Wetland had become so engrained that even though she was back on Pluto she could not shake her accent.

"Jessie Christina and Mother Mary willing!"

"Yes, Jessie and Mary weelling."

"Oh, before I forget: orgy at ten o'clock. The eggs are hatching too slowly, even with the new dehumidifiers. We need to make more eggs to fill the remaining patches of empty sand. This little planet Pluto is dry but it just isn't big enough!"

"Oh my my. You are so right, my good freend, Margie. The sooner that wee make planet Wetland dry, thee better. Are the mannequin factories running at full capacity?"

"Yes, Maxie!"

Maxie hopped to a low-slung facility. Inside she briefly inspected equipment producing a stream of purple mannequins, mechanically placing them in lounge chairs where an accompanying contrivance of white pins transformed them into glowing orbs which then rocketed towards Wetland, the toads' deliveries of purple mannequins no longer confined to a warehouse in Grovers Mill but, with bowling alleys proliferating across the planet, now delivered directly to the supply rooms of each bowling alley as fast as the alleys were built.

Hundreds of toads, all entirely lacking webbing between fingers and toes, being entirely adapted to the driest of climates, supervised the transmissions while squatting behind large screens, and occasionally phoning in reports to their distant home planet Desertland. More toads crowded in and out, pausing to watch, expressionless with their chameleon eyes, some young, some old, each rushing out every few minutes to engage in yet another orgy with others of their hermaphroditic kind. A gigantic rug underlay the factory, depicting in intimate detail what appeared to be a perpetual frenzy of reproduction among herds of non-webbed non-croaking toads each of which possessed one penis and two vaginas, pausing every few minutes between orgasms to roll bowling balls at nine-pins.

The structure having no roof—none being necessary on a planet that lacked rainfall or weather of any description but only oxygen factories to breathe and carbon dioxide factories to warm the oxygen—Maxie Climax and Margie stared at the vastness of the starry sky that was never dimmed by the cold distant Sun.

"We'll keep fighting those evil ribbets, Maxie. They must not be allowed to pollute the Earth with life-destroying water. We've stopped them elsewhere in the galaxy on other planets; we tibbets can do it again!"

"Yes, good Margie. Wee must keep fighting thee good fight." The tear returned as she scanned the heavens. "But I wonder: where is my leetle pokelicious dung beetle now. . ?"

Episode 10

The tangle of greenery momentarily distorted as an object of a darker shade of green cautiously emerged. Leafless and lacking the variegated shadows and hues that would indicate anything remotely vegetative, the object nonetheless betrayed a variation in topography like that of stippled stucco. A webbed hand briefly rubbed the studded curvy landscape. Korplash the frog from Bogland was inordinately proud of the warty expanse on his hairless bullet head, even if his bond-ribbet never allowed him a chance to splash like other ribbets. *I'm too sexy for my warts*, he smiled in self-satisfaction.

Climbing out of his dumpster, he was careful to make no noise—which for a ribbet from the planet Bogland used to croaking loud enough to be heard from adjacent moons—was no small feat. Before taking the risk of temporarily leaving his ship while he ventured on his frolic, he covered it with branches sufficient to evade the eyes of all but the most inquisitive.

My best opportunity, he thought, *or my last chance*. Looking down to his webbed hand he again inspected the freeze gun that had proven so essential in his previous visits to Dryland, enabling him and his fellow pilot Xplak to execute Gork's Great Plan flawlessly.

Until now.

Having mistakenly brought shumans to Bogland instead of tibbets, his star had fallen in the eyes of his Leader Gork with the result that he feared what their next meeting might bring. Either exile on the planet Frozenland, that desolate dry outpost at the edge of the ribbets' universe; or retirement on minuscule pay which would leave him helpless before the bad-tempered demands of his bond-ribbet Bertha.

Neither held any prospect of happiness.

There was nothing for it but to improve his reputation. And only one way to accomplish this came to mind: a motherlode of Josephs. He had taken a chance with Phineas French—too bad that moniker had indeed turned out to be the minuscule Captain's real name, tarnishing Korplash's reputation further, which had resulted in Gork withdrawing Korplash's pilot's license. If he was caught in a dumpster on Dryland now it would mean disgrace, public stripping of his froggy epaulettes. But what choice had he? It was either bring more Josephs to Gork… or spend the rest of his life climbing a frowning Mount Fuji in pink curlers. Where was the disintegration ray-gun squad when he contemplated a quick and easy way out?

But those two unidentified crawling objects he had encountered on his last trip to Dryland *were* identified! They had called themselves Joe Johnson and Joel Johansen. No Phineas's here. Korplash did not know exactly how Gork's secret serum worked, but he was reasonably confident that any old Joe would do. So the motherlode awaited—as did the repair of his soiled reputation.

All he need do is walk across the plaza and quietly pick up the two new Joe's. Having left them frozen by the riverbank, and quite aware of the limits of these Drylanders' primitive science, Korplash was certain that Joe and Joel would be exactly where he left them. Five more minutes and they would be back under his control, and he would be back in the saddle with Gork, and his dumpster license returned in time to avoid having to explain to Bertha why no more paychecks of galactic metal bits would be forthcoming. That prospect made the bruise on his bullet head, from his most recent failure to dodge her rolling pin, throb.

The sun was high and bright. It was early morning for the crawlers and few were out and about and he felt certain none would interfere. Leaving the dense cover of the shrubs, Korplash hopped across a wide meadow dotted with slow-moving and slower-thinking cows, not donning the local disguises that ribbets habitually assumed—indeed were ordered to assume by Gork—whenever they infiltrated Dryland. How could he? Gork had confiscated his disguising device along with his dumpster drivers license.

The plaza was empty. After a moment pausing on its edge, and detecting no pedestrians—now that Frenchie's Franks & Canoe Rental had shut down—he flung caution to the wind and ventured directly across the plaza toward the spot where he had left Joe and Joel.

Hopping past the bridge, he paused.

Nothing!

His chameleon eyes swiveling backward and forward, upward and down, together and independent, he felt his hearts sink. All three of them.

Could the pair have eloped? Puzzled, Korplash stood precisely where he felt certain he had left the two, but no trace of them remained. He glanced up. Was this the correct Dryland? After all, there were many such uncomfortably dry planets in the galaxy.

It was.

Was this the correct plaza and bridge? He glimpsed remnants of an old white sign that still clung to the bridge with the letters 'Rental'.

It was.

Closer inspection showed not just deep footprints showing they had remained on the spot for some time, but tractor tracks indicating they had been physically lifted. A bad feeling took hold.

Bigtooth ripped an udder in two and gulped both parts. "Mmmm. Now that's a tasty teat." He looked at another member of his space-pack from the star Sirius and barked, "Windinface, toss me one of those cow livers. And don't forget the lips and tongue this time. I like my condiments." For emphasis he threw the rest of the udder at his crewdog, but missed.

"Yes, Lord Pack-Leader. Whatever you say," whimpered Windinface, and rushed to obey, his furry tail wagging. From a stack of neatly extracted cow organs tossed onto a plastic tarp on the grassy meadow, he selected the biggest and bloodiest samples from the gory smorgasbord and hurried to bring them to Bigtooth, the other half-dozen members of Bigtooth's pack pausing in their own consumption till the Pack Leader resumed feeding on his pick of the organs.

He sampled a cow tongue. "You call this fresh?" Bigtooth spat it out.

"Oooh, don't scold me, Bigtooth! I'll do better, I promise!"

"You'd better!" From his chaise-lounge outspread on the meadow next to a parked pie-shaped saucer, warming his furry snout and neck with a silver sun reflector propped on his equally furry chest, Bigtooth interrupted his sun-tan to bark, "Arf! There's another cow! Use the organ slicer to bring me its udder and liver. Drain the blood. And this time don't forget the condiments!"

Windinface took one step on his bipedal doglegs, Thumper and Noseupass leaving their own lounge chairs to rush to serve their Lord Bigtooth. Stepping over several massacred cows with various organs surgically removed and the blood drained, they approached the nearest cud-chewing beast that was stupidly oblivious to the danger. It was all they could do to restrain themselves, hoping desperately it would bolt so they could give merry chase. Slicing organs from Earth-cows was just too easy.

They stopped short.

From the sky dropped a second pie-shaped saucer, oscillating gently like a metallic leaf to land between the siridogs and the cow not far from where Bigtooth's saucer was parked. A side door popped open and slid outwards onto the grass. Several huge muscled Dobermans stepped out on their hind legs.

"What the *heyll* do yo thank yo is doin, fool?" The Doberman's pack leader glared at Bigtooth.

Thumper and Noseupass exchanged intimidated glances. A gang-fight with Fang's pack of siridogs behind the bleachers on planet Sirius was one thing—confronting Spike and his pack of Dobermans was quite another.

"Yo Crackers bedda drop dat butter knife rat now, if yo knows what's good fo yo." The first and biggest Doberman closed his enormous tooth-embedded snout with a resounding snap that made all of Bigtooth's siridogs involuntarily jump.

"But we were here first!" protested Windinface weakly.

The second Doberman let loose an incredulous stare. "Say *what?!*" He laughed out loud. "Shut yo Cracker ass! We got first dibs on dem udders—dat's what Dog HQ say. So give it up! If you don't like dem apples, write yo *Congress*dog!"

A third Doberman did an arm-curl in Thumper's face, his bicep bulging inches from Thumper's nose. "I like soup. Soup make my muscles big." His enormous bicep grew even larger, making Thumper and Noseupass back up until they had retreated to their loungers, to the displeasure of Bigtooth.

Bigtooth stood and glared at the Dobermans. "Arooo!" He raked up grass with his hind paws. "Hands off that udder, Spike! Nobody dogs Bigtooth's cows!"

"We dog whatever we damn well like, Tiny Tooth!" Spike puffed out his dark furry chest and grinned, exposing rows of lethal teeth bigger than Bigtooth's. "And just what do yo think yo is gone do about it?"

"Ruff! We'll complain to Dog Central!"

"Sho nuff?" Spike grinned to his comrades. "Yo bitch didn't complain when I dogged her last night!" All the Dobermans laughed, slapping four-fingered paws on their dogleg knees. "And neither did the rest o yo bitches when my boys dogged them last week on Canis Major!"

Bigtooth and his other pack members exchanged frustrated stares. Knowing the fickle nature of the female members of Bigtooth's pack, especially Octotit, Spike was probably right. "Goddam Dog Central," Bigtooth muttered. "Ever since Dog Central passed that affirmative action crap, all we get is leftovers."

"Yeah! Leftovers!" echoed the others, none eager to tangle with the baddest boys in this stretch of the galaxy. Croaks were much safer.

Unwilling to challenge Spike and his Doberman crew, but also unwilling to back down and give them the satisfaction of watching Bigtooth slink away, he continued to glare and hoof the grass as if it were all he could do to restrain himself, while casting a disappointed look at his own crew whom he felt should be standing in front and at least pretending to restrain him. They all cowered behind Bigtooth.

Finishing their massacre of the innocent cow and their harvesting of its organs—and not hesitating to harvest the best organs from the other cows that Bigtooth's crew had killed—the Dobermans piled back into their spacecraft. With a phalanx of arms upthrust insultingly in Bigtooth's direction, they hung their snouts out the upper-deck open-air windows, returning Bigtooth's glares with their own. Doberman ears and tongues hung loose feeling the rush of air with sheer joy as the craft took off.

As a final insult, half a liver landed on Bigtooth's head. "Haa!" drifted a distant taunt. The Dobermans' aim was better too.

Bigtooth growled and pawed the ground again. His pack tried to look smaller to avoid becoming the target of their Lord's anger and frustration. "Windinface! Go find me another goddam cow! Try the other side of that stretch of bushes. There's gotta be more around here somewhere."

"Yes, my great leader," he whimpered, "I will investigate the patch of bushes, I will examine every square inch of dirt, I will cover the entire meadow with a magnifying glass to find you your next udder. And I won't forget the condiments."

"Just go, dammit!" Bigtooth looked at Noseupass.

"You too! Your nose is better than Windinface's any day of the week. Make sure Windinface doesn't waste our time."

"Yes, my great leader," boasted Noseupass. "I will sniff the patch of bushes, I will smell every square inch of dirt, I will run my nose over the entire meadow. . ."

"So do it already!"

Windinface pranced away on his back two doglegs with Noseupass beside him, and soon they plunged into the copse of bushes at the edge of the meadow.

No sooner had they entered the bushes than Noseupass stopped cold.

"Do you smell what I smell?"

Windinface stopped and sniffed. "There is something. . ." He flashed a huge grin at Noseupass. "Why, it's. . ."

"Bingo! We've hit paydirt!"

Noseupass pushed further into the brush and stepped into a small clearing occupied by a blue and green dumpster of no significance to any crawler but its import screaming loudly to any siridog with a nose.

"Croaks!"

"Wait'll we tell Bigtooth!"

Windinface closed his eyes and let loose a high-pitched screed at a pitch he knew would be inaudible to any but other siridogs, and only those nearby and on the ground.

A quarter-mile away Bigtooth sat up, instantly

alert.

"Thumper! Jerkleg! Rollinrot! They found something!" Leaping to their legs the entire Pack rushed to the woody copse, charged with nervous energy from their encounter with the Dobermans and eager to demonstrate their superiority over their favorite targets—agile but defenseless Croaks.

Penetrating the wood, they soon came to the dumpster and took possession of it, removing the leafy branches that inexpertly covered it.

"Excellent work, Noseupass." Bigtooth playfully bit his chief information officer on his neck who grinned with pride while Windinface would have slid his hands in his pockets in frustration, had he been wearing any clothing.

"I helped, Bigtooth! I helped!"

"You can help more by staying here. Don't let those damn Croaks take off in this dumpster, and be sure to watch our Siriship also. If anything happens to either one—your muzzle is in trouble."

"This way!" said Noseupass. The pack slunk through the bushes following the scent while Windinface stood and whined to himself. Guard duty again.

At the edge of the woody copse, they stuck their snouts as one through the dense cover and peered across a small open plaza constructed by ignoramus crawlers with primitive paving stones and mortar. The scent led straight across the plaza.

No crawlers were present to interrupt them, despite

the increasing lateness of the morning, and Bigtooth knew they would soon begin to appear, but the prospect of an actual chase in pursuit of a defenseless and hated enemy—and one caught with its pants down, so to speak—was too much to resist.

They ventured forth.

Noseupass led the way. Reverting to all fours, he ran his snout almost directly over the stone and followed the scent past a small bridge, around the remains of an old hot dog stand—they recoiled from the ancient scent of burned and thus ruined flesh—and paused by several small tables and chairs beside another dense stand of bushes.

"The Croak stood here."

Bigtooth sniffed the ground. "Yes, here. But where'd he go?"

Noseupass circled the pack, sniffing. "Croak smell. Very strong. I smell fear, nervousness. . .the Croak came straight from Bogland, afraid to go back."

"Excellent, Noseupass. You truly have a gift. What else?"

He sniffed the ground again. "Name is Korplash. . .married a Croak on Bogland. . .name Big Bertha. . .has one hundred and thirty-two little Croaks. . .no, one hundred and fifty-six. . .no, one hundred and seventy-four. . .as of five o'clock." Bigtooth licked his teeth at the prospect of reducing their numbers by eating some.

"More: Korplash talked with Croak divorce-expert. . . Big Bertha mean, yell at Korplash, no let Korplash splash with young Croaks, or drink green goo, or go out with friends to munch jacks." Noseupass shook his head, a sad look on his face. "Big Bertha bad news."

The other siridogs nodded together in sympathy with their enemy Korplash.

Noseupass sniffed the ground again. "Boss demoted Korplash. . .Korplash upset, went awol. . . looking for two missing crawlers named Joe. . .last chance to impress Boss and escape Bertha's rolling pin."

Bigtooth shuddered. "Clearly, this Croak has a very bad life. But his pain is our gain. Remember our mottos: A Croak in time saves nine, and Never give a Croak an even break."

The rest of the pack circled around Bigtooth, their snouts sniffing air and ground.

"Look!" hissed Thumper. Pointing a furry paw, the others followed his lead and sighted a warty olive-green toad backing out of the dense brush and focused on something in front of him.

"Arf!" let loose Bigtooth. "Ruff! Ruff! Aroooo!" echoed the others.

Twenty feet away, Korplash directed one of his chameleon eyes at the siridog pack, without turning around. Strangely he made no effort to hop away as any self-respecting Croak would, but not about to lose an opportunity to get a real live Croak, the Pack leaped forward without pause.

The bushes parted.

Before the Pack could halt, an ogre in a moo-moo emerged, her massive bulk crushing bushes and snapping tree-limbs, pink curlers entangled in strands of badly bleached hair.

Towering over Korplash, the moozilla split its hatchet-face and emitted a thunderous growl like a foghorn. "Nein! You no paddle mit ze haus-frauen! You no drink ze dunkel-brau! You no dance ze polka!" A gigantic ham-hand raised a huge club.

Scrambling to a halt at the feet of the moozilla, the siridogs stared upward with frightened eyes, snouts grinning in stark terror. Bigtooth found his feet and stood cheek-by-jowl with Korplash, but could only shiver with fear before the ogre.

The club swung. Korplash—from long experience—anticipated the move and ducked. A dull wop sounded as the club connected with Bigtooth, sending him sprawling.

"Owwoo!" he whimpered, scraping the ground to get away.

"Aaoo! Aaoo! Aaoo! Aaoo!" whined the rest in panic as they bounded back across the plaza as fast as four legs could race. They did not stop until they had penetrated the copse of brush on the far side and rejoined Windinface.

"How did it go, Fearless Leader?" he slobbered on himself, thoughts of raw Croak organs making him drool.

"Shut up! Just get back to the ship."

Forlornly and in total silence the Pack made their

way through the rest of the woody stand and exited into the meadow.

They halted in shock.

Every one of the cows so recently massacred and separated from their organs—as comforting and appetizing a sight to warm the heart of any siridog—had vanished. And their saucer-craft was gone. From the direction of a distant road came the sounds of military trucks hauling away a prized discovery.

Bigtooth glared at Windinface. "*Private* Windinface. . .you may want to think about going awol."

Episode 11

"Come here, Kwik."

"Yessir, General Ramey." Taking an inordinately long time to respond, Corporal Kwik finally strolled slowly to his superior's side in the super-secret military warehouse at Papoose Lake.

General Ramey stood and stared at his subordinate. He unfolded his arms as if overlooking a minor case of naughtiness.

"Corporal, have you noticed anything strange about this ship that we recovered from central Texas?"

"Strange, sir? Other than the fact that it's from outer space and smells like an old sofa, and has a fire hydrant in one corner and astroturf on the floor?"

"Yes, other than that." Ramey passed a steady gaze

over the saucer again, in storage at the new secret base in Nevada, next to everything they had recovered from Roswell spread out on the warehouse floor.

Kwik shrugged. Looked at Ramey for the answer.

"It has leather seats."

"Why, yessir. You're right. It has leather seats."

"And. . .have you noticed?" Ramey looked over his shoulder in the direction of the elevators leading to the depths of Papoose Lake beneath the warehouse. "Those aliens down below. . .two of them also have leather seats." Ramey's eyebrows rose as if he had uncovered a fact of prime importance.

Corporal Kwik nodded knowingly. "That's right. The aliens have leather seats too!"

"Kwik, we've tried for years to figure out how to turn this spacecraft on and make the damn thing fly. And we've made no progress at all. We've tried everything. Recharging the batteries; refilling the gas tank; changing the window-wipers; inserting every key we can find into every nook that exists on this damn thing—and nothing! It just won't turn on. The only thing left is to have Marilyn Monroe give it a massage."

"Works for me, sir!" grinned Corporal Kwik.

"Don't get funny on me, Kwik. We're working here."

Kwik grew serious again. "Yes, sir." He stood at attention, thrusting out his chest.

"Besides, our former President beat us to her. . ."

Ramey laughed into his sleeve.

"You can say that again, sir." Kwik grinned again.

"Too bad she died and this State is now overrun with hippies."

"What's the world coming to, sir."

"I don't know. It's 1971 already. Damn country's overrun with flotsam and jetsam what with all those damned cross-dressers out there. It seems I run into them everywhere I go. On the one hand it's damned hippies; on the other it's cross-dressers. What's the world coming to?"

"Coming to, sir!"

"And this damned ship has been down here for over twenty years. But, Kwik, if we could figure out how to turn this damned thing on, and if we could make it fly. . ." Ramey breathed expansively and smiled at the ceiling. "We could show em then!"

"Yes, sir! We could show em then!"

"We'd show them what real men are made of!"

"Like us, sir!"

"You're goddam right, Kwik. Like us! There's gonna be no goddam cross-dressers in our little patch of the Universe, are there, Kwik?"

"Right, sir! Hell no, we won't go!"

"That's the wrong phrase, Kwik."

"Sorry, sir. I meant: you damn cross-dressers," Kwik gave a defiant look. "Go. . .cross your dresses. . .somewhere else!"

Ramey didn't look happy. "That'll have to do." He looked back at the elevator. "Come here, Kwik. I've got an idea."

Walking to the elevator, Ramey turned and was surprised to see Kwik still standing by the saucer. "Kwik. Here, I said."

Still Corporal Kwik stood unmoving. For a minute he stood with his arms folded, ignoring Ramey. Finally he turned and joined him in front of the elevator. Ramey stared but Kwik just stood and rocked casually on his heels.

Ramey exhaled in irritation, then punched the elevator button.

The elevator arrived. "Let's go, Kwik!"

Again Corporal Kwik stood for a length of time without moving, ignoring Ramey, while the elevator doors jerked, Ramey holding them open with some effort. Ramey grew red. Just as he was about to say something, Kwik suddenly jumped in the elevator and the doors closed and they plunged into the depths of the desert of lower middle Nevada to a Muzak rendition of Engelbert Humperdink.

"This Area 51 is quite a zoo, Kwik."

"Yes, sir! It certainly is."

"All these modern planes and gadgets and weapons. We've even learned how to run an elevator without an operator to crank the door shut. Who could have guessed?"

"Yes, sir! That's remarkable progress, sir!"

"Why, we've even broken the sound barrier." The elevator doors opened and Ramey and Kwik flashed their ID cards to the pair of uniformed soldiers guarding the entrance to the holy of holies. "And it only cost Uncle Sam a few trillion big ones. But despite all our progress, we still can't figure shit out about these goddam aliens!"

They stopped in front of the three plexiglass containers that held the grease-painted monsters.

"Kwik, no matter how many times I stand here and look at them, I still can't understand the perversity of Mother Nature that She would permit such creatures to live—If they are indeed alive. At least we can be fairly sure they were alive when they crashed at Roswell."

"You said it, sir."

"We know they came in a ship. But it broke up on entry and all we recovered was pieces. Clever devils! They had it rigged so we couldn't learn anything about their technology after they landed. They covered their tracks well."

"Covered their tracks, yessir."

Ramey glanced at a meter above the plexiglass containers. "But this much we know. See that meter?"

"Yessir."

"That monitors the temperature inside these three containers. We aren't sure if they're alive or not, but we're keeping them frozen until we can figure it out. Whatever you do, don't let that temperature gauge go into the red zone."

"Got it, sir."

Ramey turned to the other two plexiglass containers. “And then there’s these two, which we keep at room temperature.”

“These two. Yessir!”

Together they shuddered as they contemplated the two aliens' freakish appearance, their horrified gaze roaming over the frilly white short-sleeve shirts, the short leather pants held up by striped suspenders, and pointy felt caps each tipped by one white feather, with white socks and capacious rubber-soled shoes, beer stains on their chests, and bruised kneecaps where their hands had slapped their knees from too much dancing the polka. Both figures stood unmoving, as if frozen in some mysterious force field, each with one arm raised, their eyes shifting between each other and General Ramey.

“Well, at least they're definitely alive.” Ramey shook his head. “But what the hell they are is beyond me. They still only say ‘bratwurst-unt-beer’ and ‘stop-it-heinz’, whatever the hell that is supposed to mean.”

“Maybe one day we'll figure it out.”

“God willing. But I can’t understand the perversity of Mother Nature that She would permit such creatures to live.”

“If evil has a face, sir, this is it.”

Ramey blinked. “For twenty long years they’ve just been standing there with one arm raised, their alien eyes open, staring at us! Challenging us to solve their mystery. Laughing at our slowness in figuring out what the hell they're all about.”

"Laughing at us! Yessir!"

"But you know what, Kwik?"

"What's that, sir?"

"It came to me when I connected the leather seats—we recovered that spaceship upstairs from the same place that we recovered these two aliens!"

A look of sudden realization came over Kwik. "That's right, sir! They both came from the same place in central Texas!"

Ramey nodded. "And you know what that means?"

"I'm not sure, General. . ."

"Get hold of yourself, Kwik. . . It means these two aliens can *fly that craft*!"

Kwik caught his breath. "That's brilliant, sir! No one else could have thought of that but you."

Ramey displayed his broadest smile. He rocked on his heels. "Those two aliens—ugly and bizarre though they are—I'm sure are the key to getting that spacecraft off the ground. . .and back into space!"

"So what do we do, sir? We never did figure out what they mean by 'bratwurst-unt-beer' and 'stop-it-heinz'. Must be some kind of code."

"Code it is! We're just not smart enough to crack it. But you know what we can do. . ."

"Do, sir?"

"We can take them out of here, put them in the craft and see if the damn thing turns on."

"Brilliant, sir! What could possibly go wrong?"

"After all, it's their craft!"

"Their craft, yessir!"

"We'll get that damn thing running after all! I'm sure of it!"

"Yes sir! And may I say, sir, that this is the smartest plan you've ever come up with. Better even than authorizing the Roswell crash to go out on the wire then covering it up the very next day."

Ramey looked self-satisfied. "Well, you can't cover up something that hasn't gone out yet, now, can you?"

"No sir. It was brilliant, sir!"

"Let's move it, Kwik. I want these two freaks inside that spacecraft as soon as possible." Ramey turned and walked back to the elevator and pressed the button. To his surprise Kwik remained staring at the two aliens.

"Let's go, Kwik!"

He made no move.

"Time's a-wastin!" The elevator doors began shutting and Ramey held them open with his hand.

Still Kwik remained in place.

"Sometime today would be nice!"

Not a twitch.

Ramey grew silent, still struggling to hold open the doors. A beeping began to sound as the elevator scolded him.

Finally Kwik turned and slowly strolled to the elevator and joined Ramey, who let the doors close with evident relief. Kwik stood calmly at Ramey's side inside the elevator as if nothing had happened.

Within an hour a group of technicians had removed

the two lederhosen-clad aliens from the plexiglass tubes and—their bodies still frozen and arms upraised—carried them to the spaceship. Security was stricter than ever, with armed soldiers standing guard at the warehouse entrance in full gear and helmets, ID's checked and re-checked, and cameras running to catch every second for later replay. As a precaution, they opened wide the warehouse gate to reveal a cool Nevada night.

Ramey watched the aliens carefully. "They've finally stopped repeating the code. Maybe now they will thaw out."

"Thaw out, yessir. Maybe we should have nets ready in case they go berserk and try to kill us."

"That's good thinking, Kwik. But first light my cigar. I quit yesterday, but now I'm starting again—I gotta deal with the pressure somehow."

"The pressure. Yessir. That's good, sir." Kwik lit the cigar and flared it before handing it to Ramey.

"If only we could get a light out of this spacecraft as easily."

"Easily. Yes, sir."

"Funny creatures, aren't they. A minute ago I could have sworn they were both looking at us from under those alien fur caps with the feathers stuck in the top. But now the smaller one is staring at the bigger one. I could swear that he looks almost angry."

"Angry. Yessir. But it's impossible to interpret aliens in human terms, sir. It's probably just gas."

"I'm sure you're right, Kwik. We must constantly

be on guard against the idea that these things could have anything to do with human psychology." Ramey blew a smoke ring and stared at the two aliens harder, taking in their feathered caps and lederhosen. "Why, they don't even have human brains. How could they, looking like that?"

"No, sir. No human brains!"

The technicians in white coats lugged the two surprisingly heavy aliens up the ramp and into the spacecraft where they leaned them stiffly backwards into two human-sized bucket seats.

"Look, Kwik! I could swear that now they're showing fear!" Ramey puffed his cigar and wiped his brow. "If that don't beat all. . .at times they seem almost human."

"We can't let that fool us, sir."

"No, Kwik. We know better than that. We are not fools, after all."

"And incapable of being fooled, sir."

"Damn right!" Ramey puffed a cloud into the spacecraft.

A siren erupted—red lights began to flash.

"Wha—?"

Inside the spacecraft a sprinkler system sprayed water in a downpour, drenching the two lederhosen-clad aliens and extinguishing General Ramey's cigar. Instantly the force field vanished and the two aliens came unfrozen, melding into the leather seats inside the spacecraft. The red lights flashed faster and the siren grew louder.

"Sir! You did it! You turned the spacecraft on!"

Ramey emerged and stood on the ramp, the technicians panicking and rushing out of the craft around him as the entrance ramp began to recoil into the ship. Water spraying about him, Ramey swung his arms high standing at the entrance, wet buy happy.

"Mission accomplished! Wait till I tell the big brass! I'll be posted to the Pentagon and promoted to triple star General!" The ramp continued to retract and the doors began to close. "Come here, Kwik, and help me down. . ."

Corporal Kwik halted. Sliding his hands into his pockets, he began to whistle as if time stood still.

"Kwik! What are you doing? I can use some help here, Kwik!"

The doors closed further.

"Kwik! I can really use some help now! I'm stuck and I can't get down!"

From the craft's interior a loud voice boomed. "Bratwurst unt beer! Next time, Huntz, eat your hot dogs mit ze hairscalper moo-moo!"

Corporal Kwik folded his arms and tapped one foot. The ramp was almost closed. Another moment and Ramey would be caught inside the spacecraft. Behind him, the smaller alien jumped on the bigger one and began to choke him.

"Stop it Heinz! I no fuck Amerikanishers in ze *keepemfromdroppin*—unt you *keep your keepemfromtalkin* shut!"

"Quick, Kwik! You only have another second!"

Corporal Kwik frowned, folded his arms. Finally he curled his hands into fists and stamped one foot. "I'm tired of everyone telling me to be quick!" He sniffed back a tear. "My whole life it's been: 'Do this quick', 'do that quick'! Why do I have to always be so damned quick?! Why can't I be slow for once? QUICK YOU, SIR!" His forearm thrust up in a universal five-fingered fist salute. "You can go *quick* yourself!"

The soaked cigar dropped from Ramey's surprised face. The ramp slammed shut. In another moment, his face pressed against a tiny window, the craft rose and vanished in the Nevada night.

Episode 12

A mountain peak loomed against the stars—its silver apex got closer fast.

Heinz rubbed his Adam's apple. "Herr Huntz!" he coughed. He pointed as the spacecraft rushed towards destruction.

Huntz grabbed what looked like a combination wheel and stick and began to yank. At the last moment, the ship pulled up and cleared the peak. Then plummeted again. Roads and buildings rushed at them.

"Herr *Huntz*!" Heinz turned pale, his hands gripping the armrests.

Reclaiming his cigar, General Ramey fell into a

third bucket seat and frantically strapped himself in as the ship bounced.

Finally stabilizing the craft, Huntz risked an accusatory glance. “Ven ve get back to Berlin, Heinz. . .it’s ze *boot in ze backside!”*

A grunt sounded from behind them as Ramey growled through teeth clenched on his soaked cigar. “My god! You *are* alive!” He snapped his fingers. “I knew it! And you *do* know how to fly this ship. I knew that too!” His gaze ran rapidly around the interior. “Just wait till I tell the Pentagon! To think of what we can do with this ship! We just jumped way ahead of the Russkies!”

Heinz and Huntz exchanged puzzled glances.

“Vat ist zis little sister Amerikanischer sayink, Huntz?”

Huntz shrugged. “I zink somezing about ze Rockies.”

“Ist ve flying near ze Rockies?”

“Nein. Look at ze ground, Heinz. Zat is ze dry desert.”

“Mit more big brother mountains comink at us, Huntz!” Heinz gripped his armrests.

Ramey was staring at them with his mouth open. His cigar dropped into his lap and he quickly poked it back in his jaw. “My God! They do communicate!” He snapped his fingers again. “But how do I break the code? What the hell are these aliens saying?” Ramey fished a small book from one pocket and ruffled through the pages. “Let’s see. . .‘communicate’.

. .subheading ‘alien’. . . Yeah, I remember now.” He flipped the book closed.

Releasing his seat belt, he stood. “Hey Martians! See if you have the grey matter to understand Universal Language!” Swinging a hand over his head, he pretended to throw a rope around a cow, then haul it in. He made as if turning it over a fire, then opened his mouth as if eating steak. Finally he kissed a cowgirl and thrust his hips.

“Huntz, ist I beink crazy, or does zis Amerikanischer vant sex mit Martian cows?”

“I dunno, Heinz. But please vatch vere you are goink mit zis Martian-mobile.”

“Ya, Huntz. By ze vay. . .vhere are ve?”

“I dunno zat either, Heinz. Maybe ve should stop unt ask one of ze bodies.”

“I like zat idea, Huntz. After all,” Heintz smiled, “vat could possibly go wrong?”

Detecting what seemed like a brake pedal, Heinz stepped on it and the craft came to a dead stop in the night-sky over a forested landscape, nothing below except widely scattered lights to indicate the occasional mountain dwelling.

Heinz stared out the windows where a cold rain was falling. “Herr Huntz. . . I don zink zat any of ze Amerikanischer bodies down zere can hear me.”

“Ve are not too far above ze ground, Heinz. I zink I see somezink below. Let’s open ze top-hatch unt shout at zem.”

“Ah. Now zis is ze good idea, Huntz.”

"Ya, Heinz. You stick mit me unt I shall teach you many more of ze good ideas."

Ramey swung the pretend rope again and shortcutted straight to pretend kissing, only pausing to take the cigar from his mouth.

Climbing a metal ladder, Heinz opened the top-hatch and stuck his head out, freezing rain streaking his face. He yelled back. "I don't zink zat any of ze bodies can hear me from up here, Herr Huntz. Unt I see nozink at all but ze Amerikanischer jet plane flying over our heads. Do you vant me to shout at it?"

"Nein, Heinz. Please to come back down. You ist making ze ship all vet. Ve can shout below from ze vindow." Sliding the plastic panel in one of the windows aside, Huntz thrust his head out. "Heinz! Vat ist zis coming up below us?"

Heinz thrust his head out the window.

Directly below the spacecraft, a second spacecraft of identical design appeared. For one long moment it hovered in the rain, through the windows several Japanese sailors in Imperial uniforms and coke-bottle glasses could be seen frantically spinning wheels and pulling knobs as if struggling to control the ship. The two ships touched, then the other ship disappeared.

"Now zat vas strange, Heinz. Vat vere ze odds of zat?"

At that moment something plunged through the open top-hatch and landed on General Ramey, laying him flat in mid-lasso. A man in a cheap suit and sunglasses slowly stood. He hastily inspected a knapsack. Opening it, he thumbed through a fortune in twenty-dollar bills held together by rubber bands.

"Heinz. Ve haf a stowavay!"

"Ein incredibly rich stowavay!"

In response the man handed a slip of paper to Huntz. It read 'Put the money in the bag. –Dan Cooper.'

Huntz shook his head as he read it. "Nein. I must correct you, Mein Herr. You must change zis to 'DB Cooper'."

"Why?" asked the man in surprise.

"Ya. Every one of ze bodies knows zat if you vant to steal ze money unt jump out of a jet plane, you can only be named DB Cooper. Not Dan Cooper." He handed the note back to him. "Now, please to change ze name."

Dan shrugged.

Suddenly the craft accelerated, sending them tumbling into their seats where the belts automatically clicked, just as the ship switched to auto-pilot. In seconds they had left Earth orbit and were racing towards parts unknown.

"Heinz. . ."

"Ya, Huntz."

"Did you perhaps pause to tie your boot?"

"Yavvol, Herr Huntz," replied Heinz proudly.

"Unt vhere did you place your boot ven you tied it?"

"On ze console, Herr Huntz!" Heinz smiled. "I did

not vant to get dirt on mein shoelaces by tying them on ze wet floor. Das ist good, ya?"

"Heinz. . ."

"Ya, Herr Huntz?"

Huntz sighed. "You are ze great idiot, you know zat, Heinz?"

Heinz pouted and kicked at a bulkhead from his seat. "Ya, Herr Huntz."

In a single day, with Dan Cooper absorbed with counting and re-counting his stolen money in silence, they raced through space at staggering speeds finally to plunge into the atmosphere of a new planet. The craft slowly settled into an auto-determined landing spot. It crunched to a stop. Then lurched ten degrees before coming to a rest again.

Ramey rolled into the side of the saucer, hiccupped, and woke up. Shoving his damp cigar back into his mouth, he shook his head. He stood. "Who the goddam hell are you?" he blabbered at Cooper who had almost finished counting his money.

"Dan."

"DB!" yelled Heinz, rubbing baby fists in his eyes. "He goes waah, waah, waah if he no get his vay!"

Dan glared at Heinz and pushed out his lower lip.

The side hatch popped open and the ramp began to extrude, but unexpectedly separated and crashed some distance to the ground. Some commotion seemed to erupt below the spacecraft and, and no sooner had Huntz and Heinz disengaged from their seat belts and stood, as well as they were able given the ten degree slant that the craft's floor had chosen to assume, than a hook ladder appeared at the side door and they were confronted by a nightmare scenario.

A phalanx of furry snouts thrust inside. Rows of canines flanked enormous jaws that opened wide under alert ears and bugged-out staring eyes. If glares could kill. . .

"Uh. . .ze dog park at Noon?" ventured Huntz, smiling weakly.

Almost finished counting, Dan interrupted his task by instantly sweeping all of his money back into his knapsack, then cowering in one corner clutching it to his chest where he glared through his dark glasses at everyone.

"Where is Bigtooth?" growled one of the siridogs.

"Who wants to know?" frowned General Ramey.

"You brought back one of our spacecraft that was stolen by unidentified crawling objects. We want to punish the evildoers!"

Huntz and Heinz looked at each other with rising alarm.

One of the siridogs pointed outside and below. "Arf! Those Earth crawlers took us by surprise with no warning, and we must take revenge!"

Clearing the ladder, the siridogs let Huntz and Heinz and Ramey climb down where they stared in shocked silence at a second siridog spacecraft stuck on the bottom of their own. The Japanese sailors they had glimpsed the previous day came spilling out.

"Captain Greasy!" yelled Heinz.

"Ah-so! We meet again. . ." The Japanese Captain looked crestfallen and peered about for signs of his nemesis Captain French. Seeing no one else, he puffed out his chest. "What are you doing on the sacredu Emperoru's new sacredu basu? This is not for you stupideru Germaneru!"

Ramey stepped from behind the Germans.

"Uh-oh," said Captain Girusu.

Pointing a finger, Ramey shouted. "Gotcha, didn't we?! Thought you could get away with it? Well, I'm here to tell you that little show ain't gonna play in *this* theater! You can't put one over on the good ol' U.S. of A. *this* time!"

The lead siridog stepped closer. "We demand to know who's in charge here? Where's Bigtooth?"

General Ramey smacked him across the nose with his military cap.

"Aaooo!"

"Shut up and sit!"

The siridog instantly obeyed.

"Buncha goddam dogs," grumbled Ramey. "Ya gotta put em in their place."

The siridogs began to whine and wag their tails.

"Forget Bigtooth! I'm Big Cigar Bill—and don't you ever forget it!" Ramey smacked them all in turn with his cap till they rolled over and showed their stomachs.

"Oh Big Cigar Bill, don't scold us! We only came here to congratulate you for bringing back our missing spacecraft." A crowd of dogs had now gathered and they all grinned and wagged their tails.

"That's better. Now I've been traveling for a goddam day and I want a goddam steak."

"Arooo! Pinktongue and Bootlick! What are you waiting for? Go slaughter some small helpless animals and bring Big Cigar Bill whatever he wants!" They looked back to Ramey. "We're sorry, Lord Bill, don't scold us, please! All we have on our miserable planet is bunnies and lambs. Will that do?"

"If that's the best ya got, ya miserable curs."

"Oh thank you thank you, Lord Bill." Several siridogs conferred briefly and then approached Ramey. "O Lord Bill, are you ready for your parade of honor? We can leave anytime! Your steaks and bitches will be ready for you when the parade is done."

Ramey thought for a moment. "No time like the present, I always say." He looked at the two spacecrafts stuck together. "Find a bucket of cold water and separate those two." He growled again, sending the mass of siridogs into a panic. "Say, I don't suppose you have any buildings around here shaped like a pentagon. I've got some ideas. . ."

"We'll build one for you, Lord Bill! Just give us your orders."

The siridogs brought a throne on a plank and Lord Bill sat as they lifted him up like an oriental potentate. "You can help!" he yelled pointing at the Japanese sailors and, under the harsh glares of growing numbers of siridogs baring vicious canines in their direction, the Japanese hastened to obey and assisted in lifting Lord Bill's palanquin. "Four star general—here I come! And in my own goddam Pentagon!" He relit his cigar. "Yahoo!" The siridogs bore him away amid growing crowds of adoring two-legged furry critters howling with frantic approval. Even Spike and Fang wagged their tails.

The siridogs finished separating the two ships and filled their antimatter tanks, and, once completing their task, rushed after the parade so as not to miss the banquets and orgies that would inevitably follow, not to mention the illegal but always well-attended gang fights certain to occur behind the bleachers, and before long Huntz and Heinz found themselves standing alone in front of their ship.

Dan Cooper's face peered cautiously through the open door. Dan pressed a button and the door began to close.

"Nozink doink!" yelled Huntz and launched himself at the craft. In another moment he and Heinz had leaped through the entrance and were back in the control seats as the door slammed shut behind them. Dan was in the third seat and without hesitation jammed his thumb onto several buttons on the navigation console and with a quick shudder the ship launched into the stratosphere. "I know a little something about flying. . ." he offered.

Racing across the cosmos at a speed to match the previous trip, the ship once again set on automatic,

Dan resumed counting his dollars while glaring at Huntz and Heinz, and Heinz commenced passing the time preparing to teach the polka by practicing *John Jacob Jingleheimer Schmidt,* while Huntz danced to *I've Got a Wife at Home.*

Finally the immensity of space-time had been laboriously but speedily crossed. Huntz and Heinz caught up on their sleep and then perfected their polkas till every move was second nature, the bruises on their knees now become thoroughly callused. And Dan counted and recounted his money till he knew not only the total amount, but every denomination of currency in his possession, and the serial numbers. All began with 'L'.

The dancing was done and refreshing naps taken and at last they re-entered Earth's atmosphere and were surprised to see that they had returned to the precise same coordinates from which they had departed, even the time of night being the same, though subtle changes in the appearance of the night lights below left them somewhat confused—more confused than usual, that is.

The craft shuddered to a stop.

From across the cabin, Hunt asked: "Heinz, do I haf to ask you vat you are doink?"

"Nein, Huntz! I must tie ze shoelace on mein other boot. Das ist good, ya?"

Huntz sighed.

A noise distracted them. "Herr Huntz! DB is opening ze door!"

"That's *Dan* to you!" Dan yelled petulantly. He stamped a foot. "Who gave you the right to call me *DB*?" He burst into tears. Before either could react, Cooper jumped out and disappeared into darkness gripping his parachute cord.

Arching away, the spacecraft angled downward. Either running low on antimatter or obeying the last commands of an internal autocode, the craft finally landed inside a fenced lot behind an old movie theater in a small desert town.

Heinz and Huntz strolled out and halted in surprise. The theater had been converted to a museum and a huge sign announcing 'UFO Museum' summoned tourists from all round, who crowded into the place dressed in all manner of alien costumes. They were already touring the siridog spaceship and laughing at the obviously fraudulent design.

"Herr Huntz. I zink maybe ve are still on Sirius. Vat do you zink?"

Huntz was staring at a newspaper in a vending machine. The headline on the 'Roswell News' read: 'Bush Wins – Gore Loses.' Huntz shook his head. "Heinz—just how long did ve sleep?"

Episode 13

"Zip me up, Clyde, and be quick about it."

"Jedgar, are you sure you want to go through with this?" Clyde peered under his hat and out the car window toward a neon sign down the street. "I mean, maybe you should let someone else take the risk. After all. . .there's you. . .and me. . ."

J. Edgar allowed the façade to drop for one brief moment and flashed the merest hint of a smile towards Clyde. "Yes. . .you and me. But you know I can't let that interfere with my duty to the U.S.A. When this great country is in danger, I must do whatever I can to stop it."

Sitting in the back seat of the black Agency limo, Edgar turned his back to Clyde, and Clyde zipped up Edgar's bright red gown. Turning to face him, the Director adjusted his ruby-red earrings by way of a compact mirror and put the mirror in his new purse—a lovely shade of fuschia with just the right degree of shine. He brushed his blond wig as if it were his own. Then packed the brush.

The traffic being minimal, Edgar exited the car on the street side and settled into his new mid-high heels, while Clyde followed and stood beside him. Two more dark-suited FBI agents shielded them from the casual stares of the few pedestrians on the street this time of the morning, and Edgar gripped his handbag as a soldier would his weapon.

"Don't stray too far," he said to his FBI agents. "When I come out, I may be in a hurry."

"Yessir."

"But get this car out of here. It's too conspicuous. We're after a desperate conspiracy and the last thing I want is to be 'made' before I can figure out just what the hell is going on. I want no agency cars anywhere in the vicinity once I go undercover."

"Yessir! A few minutes from now there will be no agency cars anywhere in Las Vegas."

"You're goddam right there won't be," growled Edgar.

"You can count on me," added Clyde. "I'll see to it."

Edgar blinked to confirm. One last moment to smooth his bright red dress—which he had not had a chance to wear since he had encountered Judge Crater many years ago, and the feel of which now gave him a distinct if quiet thrill given that it went better than purple with his red earrings and eyeshadow. He set his jaw. Akilter.

He took a breath. "I'm going in," he growled.

As the limo drove away, Edgar strode casually toward the entrance, his high heels tocking the concrete like a staccato jackhammer. Just my imagination, he thought to himself. No one is watching. *Who would look twice at a middle-aged woman with teased hair, ruby earrings, and pearl necklace? Clyde assured me that I blend in perfectly, and he has a good eye for this sort of thing.* Across the street, two middle-aged women preparing to lose their retirement to one-armed bandits halted to stare open-mouthed at the potato-shaped overweight Edgar stumbling uncomfortably on the street in the bright morning, his dark hair obtruding from under an obvious ill-fitting wig.

Approaching his target, Edgar paused to read the neon sign. Its bright letters flashed around the clock, caring not a whit whether it was day or night: Madam Melissa's Chicken Ranch Casino & Bowling Palace for Lower Nevada – Opus Dea Precinct 12. A smiling neon nun in black habit turned her bared derriere towards Edgar, one eye winking with every flash of neon, only her hair being covered. *Quite a clever ruse*. Standing directly beneath the neon derriere, he looked around and muttered: *I'll get to the bottom of this. Just you wait.*

The parking lot was half filled with cars, and a steady stream of patrons entered the wide glass front doors that seemed always open, while an equal stream exited. However, weeks of observation had shown that those exiting seemed not quite the same as those who entered, Edgar noted, and once again he reflected on the strangeness of the exchange, unable to put his finger on the precise difference.

Entering the front doors he passed two young women with huge shoulders stumbling on high heels, their faces stubbled with shadow, red lipstick smeared badly on thin lips, and a second color of hair visible under new-looking wigs. They each carried copies of books under their arms: *No Logo*. Pre-publication. "Goddam sweat-shop owners!" muttered one. "Let's go find one and scratch his eyes out, Shirley."

"You said it!"

In the lobby, a pair of men brushed past in plaid

sport coats, their chests projecting twin fleshy bulges that their coats could not entirely conceal. Thin mustaches were painted on their smooth upper lips and flat leather dress shoes graced their small feet and they adjusted prim striped ties and combed their fresh closely-trimmed scalps. "Lemme at em, Ferd! How dare those creeps try to bust our teachers union!"

Nothing to see here, Edgar thought. *If only I could figure out how these people are coming out different?*

He crossed to the bowling lanes. A team of champion bowlers had just bowled their third strike and suddenly red lights flashed and a voice announced: "Congratulations, Rolling Thunder Crusaders! Your members have won Madam Melissa's 'Special Bowler's Prize'!"

From several directions several scantily-clad nuns hurried to the Crusaders Team, flowing hair escaping the voluminous brown habits on their heads, two-piece swimsuits leaving remarkably little to the imagination.

By the time they arrived bearing free sandwiches and lemonade—and baring their slim youthful bodies while doing so—the Crusaders failed to notice that their team had been supplemented by one. Edgar sat behind, face half-hidden by wig and hands, confident that his disguise—less a disguise than an expression of his inner love of Mankind and America—would be accepted without question.

One of the nuns put her arm around him and smiled. “Pastrami or turkey?” The smile broadened invitingly.

Briefly he risked a glance through the overhanging strands of blond wig. “Turkey,” he grumbled in a deep hoarse voice. He hoped she would not notice his permanently angled jaw.

Her smiling face registered nothing out of the ordinary and she immediately retreated and soon returned with not one, but two, turkey sandwiches, on the side a large size lemonade filled to the brim. Displaying an almost bare hip, she deftly cocked it and winked at him. The others downed their food with the rapidity that typically follows the pronouncement of ‘free’ in connection with 'food', and Edgar followed suit.

While he munched, still hiding behind the drooping blond strands, another nun with exposed midriff said “Congratulations for winning Madam Melissa’s Special Prize! To get your prize all you need do is visit our Back-to-Nature Wigwam and let us share our good fortune about the teachings of our Sacred Precinct!”

“Teachings?” Edgar mumbled to himself.

The Rolling Thunder Crusaders were a trio of casino high rollers with gold chains over black hairy chests and short beards framed by extra wide lapels attached to deep V pastel shirts. They exchanged growing grins among themselves.

“What did I tell you, Habib?” He smiled back at

the nuns. "There is something about this place. . ."

"Yes, Ali, you were right! We are winners on our very first visit!" He glanced slyly at the nearest half-nude nun. "Now we are about to win again!" he simpered. *"I love America!"* Habib choked up and bit his knuckle.

The third one, Abdullah, seemed hesitant. "Dear Sister, this will not interfere with our religion, will it? Habib is Christian; I am Muslim; and Ali. . .well, he is nothing at all."

She smiled in response. "Of course not, my friends! We only ask you to listen. And then we will give you your reward. There's nothing to it!"

Ali leveled a reproving look at Habib. "Why do you keep saying that, Abdullah? I am a Muslim just like you!"

Abdullah looked down his nose at Ali. "You missed the morning prayer again."

"How else can I get to this Casino in time? After all, my father does not own a four-star hotel, like yours!"

Abdullah sniffed. "No excuse, father of daughters. If your father employed better cooks, his three-star hotel could become a four-star hotel by next Ramadan."

"And if your mother guarded her you-know-what better, you would not be here at all!"

Abdullah thumbed his chin. "Hajj you, Ali!"

"Bite a prayer rug, Abdullah!"

"Allahu akbar!" Abdullah whipped out nail scissors and gripped them overhead for a downward thrust.

"Allahu akbar!" Ali lifted both arms and one leg to deliver a karate kick.

"My brothers—Peace! Peace!" yelled Habib.

Abdullah put away the scissors and Ali relaxed. "Humph. You are not a good Muslim, Ali, and you know it."

One of the nuns brought a pizza and placed it in front of Ali. Smacking gum, the half-naked nun called out loudly, "One bacon, ham, sausage, and pepperoni pizza. Hold the pepperoni."

Abdullah folded his arms with a look of disgust and looked away.

"Uh, there must be some mistake, dear lady. I did not order ham on my pizza. . ." Ali looked at the nun pleadingly, glancing askance at Abdullah.

She read the order, louder than before. "*One Canadian bacon, ham, and pepperoni. Size: large. Hold the pepperoni. Signed: Ali.*" Putting one finger to her lips, Ali hastily pulled out a fifty dollar bill and pushed it on the nun. "No, dear lady. . .I don't eat ham or bacon. . ." He glanced again at Abdullah. "These are bad things that are against my religion. . ."

"*One bacon, ham, and pepperoni*—" she repeated louder than ever, smacking her gum.

"Thank you thank you, dear lady. You can take it back please. There has been a mistake. This is not mine. I will pay for it, but take it away."

"A simple mistake, Abdullah. I swear that was not mine!" Ali stood, and the three—with Edgar trailing—prepared to walk when another gum-smacking waitress approached. She placed a large pitcher of Margaritas in front of Ali.

"Uh, yes, dear lady?" he asked hesitantly.

"Your pitcher of Margaritas, sir."

Ali stepped back. "Oh no, dear lady, there must be some mistake again."

Whipping out her order form, she read in a loud voice: "*One pitcher of Margaritas. Heavy on the tequila. Size: large. Extra limes.*"

Turning ashen, Ali extracted another fifty-dollar bill and pressed it on the waitress. "No, no, no, good lady. Alcohol is against my religion, there has been another mistake!"

She glanced again at her order form. "*Signed: Ali.*"

"Ah, ha-ha-ha! No, no! It is not mine!" He glanced again at Abdullah, who peered down at him as from the gates of paradise at an eternal loser.

Edgar threw his voice, in as high a falsetto as he could manage. It came out sounding like a sheep in heat. "Let's go hear the teachings, my brothers! I will say extra prayers later."

The three Arabs looked at each other in surprise. "Ok, Ali. You don't have to be pushy about it."

"I didn't say anything."

"Yes, you did."

"No, it must have been you, Abdullah."

"Why would I need to do extra prayers? That's

your department, Ali."

"Pound sand, Abdullah!"

"Hump a goat, Ali!"

Abdullah went for his nail scissors and Ali lifted his leg, when Edgar stumbled on his high heels distracting both of them.

The Rolling Thunder Crusaders paused.

"Who is this?"

"How would I know? She came with you."

"I didn't bring her. She was your guest."

"She is not mine. Didn't you invite her?"

They all turned to look at Edgar.

Three smiles broke out.

"She is mine!"

"She is not, she came with me!"

"No, I invited her last night! Keep your hands off. We're getting married tomorrow!"

"I am not a U.S. Citizen," mumbled Edgar, still hiding his face.

Instantly the three stopped smiling and turned their backs.

"Who is she?"

"How would I know? She came with you."

"I didn't bring her. She is your guest."

"She is not mine. You invited her."

"It was not me. I have never seen her in my life. Though she is very beautiful. . ." Ali batted his eyes at Edgar.

One of the nuns called sweetly "Everything is ready now, dear guests! It is time to go!" By now a half-dozen half-nude nuns had gathered about them and began to pull them towards the back of the Casino while sidling up to them with smiles and caresses. Quickly melting, Abdullah, Habib, and Ali fell into line, entirely forgetting Edgar who trailed close behind.

"You would not happen to be citizens, would you?" they whispered to the nuns.

"Is this your first visit to Madam Melissa's?" one of the nuns asked Abdullah sweetly, ignoring the question.

He moved his head side to side. "Uh, no," he tried to whisper under his hand.

Ali shot a surprised look at him, but was immediately distracted by the nuns on his own arms.

"Have you heard anything about the Sacred Precinct's teachings before, Mr. Ali, sir?"

"No, good lady," said Ali, unable to take his eyes off the expanses of smooth lustrous skin on display around him.

"Too bad there is nothing on the walls to remind me of my true religion," said Habib.

"Too *good*, you mean!" snapped Abdullah. "You are on thin ice, Habib. And Ali is over the edge!"

"We include *all* religions in our teachings, dear guests! We are tolerant of everyone. Diversity is what we're all about!"

The three Arabs half-smiled and nodded their heads while the nuns hurried them to the back of the Bowling Palace. There was certainly nothing wrong with 'tolerance and diversity'. Or at least nothing worth an argument when surrounded by so many entertainingly bare midriffs.

“Even for you!” added another nun with a smile looking at Edgar, who said nothing, intent on doing whatever it took to penetrate to the heart of the mystery. He swallowed and bolstered his confidence as he entered the Holy of Holies of the Opus Dea Precinct.

After all, what could possibly go wrong?

Hurrying past the holy Precinct kitchens, past the holy dormitory, past the sacred sites where fully-clothed nuns labored incessantly resetting sets of holy white nine-pins after guests knocked them over with their holy bowling balls, and past the Shrine of Santa Lucia the Holy Bowler of the Sacred Nine-Pins of the Third Secret of Fatima, they then walked past the Holy Supply Room with the ‘Nun Such’ sign over the door, to finally arrive at an irregular gap in the back wall under a sign that read ‘Back-to-Nature Wigwam’. The holy one.

Entering the Wigwam, the four guests found themselves in an expansive interior that had been built to resemble a Native American teepee, complete with imitation deer hide walls constructed to angle upward to a single large smoke hole. Someone had already lit several incense sticks and the grey smoke spiraled upward where it gathered inside, only a trickle managing to escape through the hole. In front of them were four Western-style rocking chairs, in each resting a purple mannequin in a dress and surmounted by an unkempt wig.

One of the nuns, in appearance no different from the rest, but with a deeper louder voice, invited the guests to sit on a large imitation bearskin rug with crossed legs while she sat before them. The other nuns passed around two peace pipes with an unusually sweet smell. Edgar noted with dull interest several hanging signs that read “Peace & Justice”, “Earth Day”, and “Unleash your Fem”. *Buncha Communists*, he thought. *Or ever worse: hippies*! He leaned back on a large pillow and glared.

“How exciting all this is!” said the nun, smiling more cheerfully than ever. “We are so happy that you have decided to let us share our Good News with you! We just know that once you hear how diverse and tolerant we are, you will understand the Truth of what we have to teach, and you will want to start teaching others as well!”

Abdullah and Habib rubbed their eyes. “I don’t know. I am starting to feel dizzy.”

“Not to worry! That’s part of our Teaching!” Again the smile.

“What do you think, Ali?”

Ali was smoking both peace pipes at once with a huge grin, his hands stroking one of the nun’s bare shoulders. “Woo-hoo!” he coughed. “Bring it on!” From his pocket he pulled a hidden slice of Canadian bacon pizza and wolfed it down with a can of beer.

They took another puff and began to relax.

"And what about you. . .uh. . ."

"Ed. . .uh, *Edie*."

"What about you, 'Edie'? Are you ready to get started?"

"Do your worst," he started to growl, then caught himself. "I mean: Go for it," he said, still hiding his eyes.

Two large imitation deer hide drums rested on the floor on either side, and the nuns began thumping out a steady monotonous rhythm.

"First, our Prayer! Everyone lower your gaze, please."

They did.

"Our Mother, who bakes in heaven, Jessie be thy name, thy kitchen come, thy cook be done in baking as it is unleavened. Give us this day our daily bread, and forgive us our recipes as we forgive the recipes of others; and lead us not into conception; but deliver us from the water of evil men."

The three Arabs could hardly keep their eyes open and dully echoed the prayer.

Who do I say 'turn your head and cough' to? thought Edgar. *Not a damn toad in this place, after all. Just a bunch of boring women and boring-er wannabes.* His mind began to slow and de-focus. *Lost my train of thought. . . Did I have a train of thought. .* ?

"Repeat after me," said the nun.

"Repeat after me," echoed the three Crusaders, Edgar still grumbling under his breath.

"Momma knows best."

"Momma knows best," repeated the guests.

"Don't mess with Mother Earth," intoned the nun, her voice taking on a hypnotic quality.

"Don't mess with Mother Earth," came the echo. Edgar felt dizzy and tried to put one hand to his temple, but found it would not obey.

"Zero children is best for the planet."

"Zero children is best for the planet." The trance deepened. Edgar stared into an abyss of space and time.

"Smoking is a crime against Nature." All the nuns seemed to be speaking at once, their voices resonating together.

"Smoking is a crime against Nature," repeated Edgar, three other helpless voices joining his. Three half-empty packs of cigarettes mysteriously appeared on the bearskin rug.

"Except for marijuana peace pipes."

"Except for marijuana peace pipes."

"Development rapes the Earth," came the suggestion.

"Development rapes the Earth," came the hypnotized echo.

"I must stop global warming." The voices grew deep and penetrated to the very core of the guests' being.

"I must stop global warming," they intoned.

Lost in the depths of their trance, none of the guests noticed the gleams that had appeared in the eyes of the four seated mannequins. From somewhere the Drum Circle sounded louder and multiplied until four separate beats could be distinguished, gradually merging into one single loud beat, the thump rising steadily to soothe their souls and calm them while wooden Peruvian flutes played. Louder and louder sounded the drums and faster and faster played the pipes—then suddenly stopped.

Creaking at the knees, four mannequins slowly rose from their rocking chairs, their eyes alive like the Sun, minds twitching with energy and will, flesh gathering on their stiff limbs until indistinguishable from human limbs.

Abdullah and Ali looked down on the remnants of their former bodies. Even as they watched, their former bodies decayed and evaporated until nothing remained but sprinkles of powder. Beside them, Habib and Edgar rose from rocking chairs and stared at the destruction of their former bodies with an equal lack of interest.

A full-length black chador had appeared on Abdullah, leaving only his eyes showing. Glancing at the others, a deep voice erupted from underneath. "What is this? I don't want a chador! I want a nice two-piece swimsuit. Something to match my violet eyes."

"You can pick something up at the halal mall, Amina," said Aliyah, formerly Ali. "Right now, we have to go find those damn developers and give them hell."

"Easy for you to say, Aliyah. You have a nice veil

and a gown with a nice shade of black. Why can't I have that?"

"At least you two girls have beautiful basic black," interrupted Habiba, formerly Habib. "I'm stuck with a brown pantsuit that looks like it came out of the 1940's!" She stroked her short beard.

"Well, yours is still better than mine,"said Amina.

"You wish it were!" yelled Aliyah.

"Rent a camel, headbanger!" shouted Amina.

"Is that the best you got, seller of rugs?" shouted Aliyah.

"Allahu akbar!" Amina pulled out her nail scissors and paused with them overhead ready to plunge them into Aliyah.

"Allahu akbar!" yelled Aliyah, raising both arms and one leg for a karate kick.

"Jesus Christ! Will you two shut up!" someone growled.

They all looked at the fourth guest.

Dressed in a bright red evening gown with red ruby earrings, mid-high heels, and a badly-fitting blond wig, the bulges of a middle-aged man obtruded threatening to split the seams.

"Name's *Edie*," she said.

They shrugged, unable to perceive any change whatever in Edie's appearance.

"Ta'ala, Sisters. Let's go give those oil pigs hell!"

"Yes! I want to hit the malls before the evening prayer. And I can't wait to try out my new eyelashes. It will be so much easier to get a green card now," she simpered.

Sashaying down the hallway and out of the Casino, Amina, Aliyah, and Habiba disappeared down the street, leaving Edie standing on the front steps of the place.

Edie felt strange—more than strange. She felt downright weird. To all appearances, nothing had changed. She wore the same dress, the same ornaments, had the same hair. But inside something had changed. She felt different—new—regenerated. From somewhere a fleeting memory of a Fuck in the Backside Institute hovered briefly, then passed away into the distance, along with faces and impressions of her former life. She felt happy—and free. A big grin spread over her face.

And a new determination to unearth the conspiracy that had haunted her for years—the ribbets. Suddenly she understood. She knew the nature of what she had been struggling to expose all these years: those toads from Bogland, amphibians addicted to the poisonous substance called water and determined to flood the Earth with Global Warming, if no one stopped them. She must stop those developers and Oil Pigs who were in cahoots with the Global Warmers!

Well, with Edie they had met their match! She set her crooked jaw again. Clutching her vinyl purse and scratching the growing stubble on her chin, she set out down the road, ignoring the stares of surprised pedestrians—a fact of life that had always come with the territory—but which still managed to annoy her.

She paused.

At the entrance to an alleyway, a familiar figure stood. The figure glanced from side to side, then removed his hat and waved at her. Something about that face. . .about that hat. . .seemed to strike a distant memory. Against her better judgment, Edie stepped into the alley and cautiously approached.

"Jedgar," hissed the man. He peered closely looking for some sign of recognition. "What's the matter, Jedgar? For goodness sake, don't you recognize me?"

Edie stared back with a look of total blankness.

He stepped closer and Edie stepped back, putting her hands to her mouth. She prepared to scream and run.

"What have they done to you, Jedgar?" A look of tragedy seized the man. "Don't you know who I am? I'm Clyde! You're special. . .*you know who*."

Again she stepped back. Was this one of those evil global warmers? Should she go in for the kill with her claws and stiletto heels? She opened her mouth to scream.

In Clyde's hand a silver object materialized.

Edie caught her breath.

The device flashed.

Unable to move, Edie stared in horror as Clyde dissolved into a bloated green toad with webbed feet and hands, two bulging eyes extruding on a pair of flexible stems.

"Xplak is seeking Josephs for Gork's Great Plan. Do you volunteer?"

From deep within, Edie managed to squeak like a mouse. "First name's John. Not Joseph."

"Beg to differ, shuman. Your parents lied to you. You were named Joseph when you were born; then they changed it to John. Once a Joseph, always a Joseph."

Damn.

Lifting Edie with ease, Xplak carried her frozen body to a refurbished dumpster in the back of the alley—with all the expenses of the Joseph campaign, refurbished cosmodrones was now the best that Gork could do—and Xplak placed her inside. In a short time the dumpster was plummeting from wormhole to wormhole.

Episode 14

A nasally voice sounded, echoing off the walls of the low-slung vine-covered enclosure for debarking cosmodrones on Bogland. "All Josephs form a line to the left, please. Please, all Josephs form a line to the left."

"Congratulations, Xplak. Your excellent work has brought in more Josephs than I ever expected. Are you happy with your new rank of Sergeant?"

"Xplak is happy with new rank of Sergeant. Is Gork happy with new Josephs?"

"Gork is happy with new Josephs." One eye perused the line. "How did Xplak find such a motherlode of Josephs?"

"My journey was arduous, O Great Gork, this ribbet braved the cold wastes of the galaxy's third spiral arm, dodged pesky siridogs at every turn, searched high and low for appropriate candidates, and finally selected only the very best Josephs that Dryland has to offer, only those whom I concluded after careful observation would make the very best mimes and spies for the great ribbet plan—"

Gork frowned. "*Gork's* great ribbet Plan. . ."

"Our great ribbet Plan—"

"*My* Great Plan for the Universe. . . and let not Xplak forget that it is Gork's Plan alone!"

Xplak humbled his green bullet head. "Of course, O Great Leader. My memory is ever excellent in the Great Gork's service. Does Gork wish to meet the Josephs now?"

"It's about time." Gork waddled his great green bulk to the line of shumans who had just exited from several cosmodrones, his webbed feet slapping the hard floor like pancakes. "This time we shall build an army of mimes and send them in undercover—after proper training of course. We don't want all our efforts to go into cold storage like the first three we sent."

"Perhaps they were not properly trained, Great Gork."

Gork leveled another reproachful eye at Xplak on

a two-inch stalk. "Or perhaps they were not good candidates in the first place. Has Xplak taken care to weed out the bad ones this time?" The other eye extended two inches so both eyes glared down at the smaller Xplak from opposite directions.

"Oh yes, Great Gork! I am certain Gork will be more pleased with these new Josephs than with the others."

They stepped to the first shuman. He stood calm, his gaze wandering about the warehouse in some confusion. Slightly overweight and about fifty years of age, a dark suit matched his dark hair and clean-shaven face. "Where the hell am I?" he bellowed. "Do you have any idea who you have kidnapped?" His eyes narrowed. "Do you work for the State Department? Tell me the truth now! When did you become a member of the Communist Party?"

"We are not Communists, Senator McCarthy. We do not work for your State Department."

"Ha! I can tell from your looks that you're un-American!" He pointed an accusing finger. "Just tell me the names of the other Communists in the government, and I'll see that it goes easy on you. I promise you won't get the gas chamber." He smiled. "Maybe a firing squad," he smirked, "but not the gas chamber."

Gork looked at Xplak. "Yes, you are right, Xplak. This one is a prime candidate to lose his voice and annoy pedestrians with pantomimes."

They stepped to the next shuman. He wore a black

silk shirt with silver colored tie, had a sharply receding hairline and a huge boil on his cheek; a cigarette hung from his lips, which never smiled, and he wore large sunglasses. "Now what are youse guyz from Brooklyn doin in Queens? This wouldn't be about that little Colombo hit, would it? I tell ya, the guy had it comin, always talkin about Italian-American rights and all that. It was bad for business, ya know what I mean?" He smoothed his shirt. "And if this is about my TV appearance. It's like I keep sayin—I take the Fifth!"

"This is not about TV appearances, Mr. Joe Gallo. You have volunteered for something completely different. Besides, you did not shoot Joseph Colombo in New York in 1971. He is standing over there."

Joe Gallo looked in surprise as they stepped to the next shuman.

"I am certain you will like these candidates, Great Gork. Have you seen them in action?"

The next shumans wore uniforms and seemed preoccupied with taking practice swings with baseball bats.

"Gork, may I introduce Joseph Dimaggio, Joseph Garagiola, and Joseph Jackson. They are all distinguished by their strength at hitting small white balls out of parks, a strange ritual engaged in by many Drylanders." He pointed to the next two shumans. "And this is Joe Frazier, the boxer; and Joe Montana, the football player."

Gork's frog jaw extended briefly in what passed

for a smile among ribbets. "More good choices, Xplak. They too will make good mimes and give us some muscle if those evil tibbets interfere again. Good thinking."

They approached the next in line.

"And this shuman is Joseph E. Davies, Stalin's bottom bitch. Oh please to excuse me—Mr. Davies, former American ambassador to the USSR."

Gork nodded. "Another excellent candidate for circus work."

The next shuman cavorted while grinning. "Oh laaadyyyy!"

"May I introduce Mr. Joseph LeVitch. Also known as the comedian Jerry Lewis."

Gork stared approvingly. "Who could object to him? He is at least two-thirds mime."

"And Mr. Joseph Teller. It was difficult to break up his comedy act with Mr. Penn, but I think worth it."

The short shuman in casual clothes stared up in surprise, saying nothing.

"He knows how to tell jokes without a voice."

"Another good choice, Xplak. He is already one of us."

"Then there is this shuman, what the other shumans call a 'famous actor'." They stepped to a spare distinguished looking man with grey temples and serious expression. He offered them his hand. "Joseph Cotten, at your service," he said in a deep melodic voice. "Say, have any of you seen a Third Man around here? That Orson has hidden himself again and damned if I can find him."

"No, Mr. Cotten. We will let you know if we encounter Mr. Welles."

They stepped forward.

"Then there is this shuman. He has political ambitions but cannot decide which party to join. I decided it was best to volunteer him early and substitute a dummy in his place. No one has detected the difference."

The tall thin man with elfin features briefly bowed. "Joseph Lieberman, gentlemen. Democratic Senator. . .then Independent!" he said proudly.

"Watch this one," said Gork. "He will go awol at first chance!"

"And this is. . .well, it is what it is," said Xplak. He pointed to a shuman in bright red dress, ruby earrings, and high heels, her hair barely covered by a badly-fitting blond wig. "Say hello to Edie."

The warty toad looked shocked. "I don't think that eyeshade goes well with those earrings."

"But at least it's a Joseph." Xplak looked hopefully at Gork. "I assume the piece-rate still applies?"

"Yes. Piece-rate still applies. You get your commission for this one as well. Just take precautions. We don't want to crack every mirror in the place."

"Thank you for volunteering, shuman Edie!"

Edie stumbled forward in confusion. *Did I have a train of thought? Something about bottoms. . .*

Gork patted Xplak on one shoulder. "It has been many years, Xplak, but you have done fine work. We shall start the injections immediately and finally move to Stage Two of my Great Plan."

Episode 15

"How are things down there?" *Crackle.*

The tinny voice emanating from the office intercom on his desk was an unwelcome interruption but unavoidable. Corporal Kwik flopped down his magazine, swung his feet off the desk, and leaned forward. "All systems are 'go' down here, sir. No problemo hereabouto."

"That's good, Kwik. Because you've got an inspection coming up in five. So whatever you need to do to prepare for it, get it done. Sweep the floor, change a light bulb. Whatever. Just make them happy." *Crackle.*

Kwik frowned. "I got it already! You can relax upstairs. I told you I got it under control."

"You better, Kwik! Cause if you don't, your ass is grass. And if the Big Brass aren't happy, then I won't be happy. And if I'm not happy. . .well, you know the rest!" *Crackle.*

Shooting the bird at the intercom, Kwik recited "Yessir, Colonel Buttinski."

"That's Butyinski, Kwik!"

"That's what I said, sir. Sorry, but this intercom seems to have a short."

"Lucky for you it does. Now get to it, Kwik, and

don't delay." *Crackle.*

"Roger Wilco, Buttinski."

"What was that?" *Crackle.*

"Yes, sir, Butyinski."

"Just get it done, Kwik. And I mean *pronto*!"

"Yessir, sir!" Two birds answered, animated but silent.

Leaning back in his chair, Kwik stared at the ceiling. Ten minutes later the elevator doors opened and he rose to his feet to greet the inspectors.

"At ease, Corporal Kwik," said the first. The salad on his jacket was more diverse and colorful even than the missing General Ramey's, and Kwik found himself saluting smartly, conscious that in the military there was no such thing as excessive fawning. Two more Generals with Waldorfs on their chests joined the first.

"Well, where are they?"

"This way, sirs." Kwik led the way to the three plastic containers holding the aliens in frozen suspended animation—the three aliens that still remained after the mysterious escape of the two in caps and lederhosen. "Cold as ice, sirs. Just as ordered by the Pentagon."

They nodded. As the Generals stared, their expressions became clouded. "They say God made all creatures. But 'they' never saw 'these'!"

"God-awful. Yessir."

"Frozen, you say?"

"Yessir. Simple as that power cord right there. As

long as it's plugged in, it stays ten below inside. See the meter?" He pointed to the temperature gauge above the containers. "If it ever goes into the red zone, that means they're melting. Gotta hurry then to plug the cord back in. Or. . ."

"Or what, Corporal Kwik?"

"Or. . .we don't exactly know what, General, sir. But every time I look at them I think that I don't want to find out."

They stared at the mime-sickles again. Grunted in disgust. "I can well understand. I think we all can." The other Generals also nodded, disgust on their faces.

"Well, that's about all we need to see today. What about you, Generals?"

They grunted. "Yep. We got other things to tend to. It's 1972 already! Whole goddam State is overrun with cross-dressers and hippies. Like it's a goddam conspiracy. We gotta go get to the bottom of things."

"Yessir, General. The bottom of things."

The first General turned and tripped over the power cord, unplugging it.

"Oops. Sorry Corporal. Well, you can tend to that, can't you, Kwik?"

Corporal Kwik stared in silence.

"We gotta go." The Generals turned and made for the elevator. "Don't delay, now, Kwik. Take care of things."

As the elevator doors opened, the first General turned again. "That's enough rest, Kwik. Plug it back in now. Sorry we can't stay to see more."

"Yessir, General," said Kwik. "Don't worry about a thing. . .I'll be sure to take care of it. . .in no time *at all. . .*"

"That's good. Now do it, Kwik. Do it now. Before you forget."

The doors closed.

Kwik stood in front of the three containers with their frozen contents and folded his arms. His eyes lit on the power cord, now unplugged. They traveled to the meter above the containers where a small red light had begun to flash indicating loss of power to the refrigeration unit. He tapped his foot. Whistling, he walked slowly around the room staring at the ceiling. Then the floor. Then the walls. Hands in pockets, he settled into the chair behind his desk where he gazed across the room at the narrow tube of rubber lying nakedly in full view.

He leaned back. Picked up the magazine.

The intercom crackled. "Kwik? Is everything all right?"

He leaned over. "Yeah, of course. Why wouldn't it be?"

"Don't take that tone with me, Kwik. I'm your superior, even if I was born in Russia."

"Not a problem, Buttinski. I know you're my superior officer, sir."

"That's 'Butyinski', Kwik! How many times I gotta tell ya?" Crackle.

"Sorry, General Buttinski—*ssshhh*—you're breaking up again—*ssshhh*!" Twin single finger salutes arched and hovered over the intercom, soon joined by a bare hiney as Kwik dropped his pants and wiggled his ass at it. "Everything is under control at this end, Sir. No problems down here—*ssshhh*."

"That's good, Kwik. Cause that room is your responsibility. And that means it's my responsibility. And that means if anything goes wrong down there it's on my head. And then I'm gonna put it on your head. Got that, Kwik? We already lost two weirdos. I don't want anything to happen to the other three."

"Yessir, General Buttinski. Fuck you, General Buttinski."

"What? What was that?!"

"Bad connection—*ssshhh*. I said 'First You', General. As in 'You come first'—*ssshhh*."

"Oh. That's okay, then."

"No problem, sir."

Crackle. The tinny voice resumed. "Oh yeah. I remember now. Kwik, the Generals said they made a mess and they expect you to clean it up. That's why I'm calling. So, whatever it is, Kwik, get to it. Get it done, Kwik! Over and out." *Crackle*.

Kwik rippled his lips in irritation. Belting his pants, he folded his arms and tapped his foot again. Finally he sat and opened the magazine.

The following day, Kwik reported for work. Under his arm was a load of magazines. Strumming through them one by one, he paused on occasion to eye the little red dot that persistently flashed on and off on the far side of the room, reminding him of something that needed to be done.

No question of that. But there was no hurry.

No hurry *at all. . .*

He twiddled his thumbs.

The next day he brought more magazines.

The following week he brought a book. Then two books. Then an armload of books.

The books piled up.

A correspondence course was in order, so he subscribed to a course on the World's Great Literature. Completing with an 'A', he next took Art By Correspondence. Finally he decided to tackle a law degree from Samoa by mail. By steamer.

The year 1975 opened on a mild winter and, after pushing a wheelbarrow filled with the latest installment of the Code of Federal Regulations to his desk, he noticed with mild interest that the gauge had crossed into the red zone.

Leaning back in his swivel chair, he stretched and yawned. For a moment, he closed his eyes and resumed his late morning nap. After a few minutes he stood and stretched yet again. Finally he took a step in the direction of the plastic containers.

Gettin kinda warm in here, he thought. *Maybe I should check that refrigeration unit.* Slowly he strode, taking one casual step. Then another. After some time he found himself in the vicinity of the unplugged cord and his eyes wandered to the temperature gauge over the containers where the gauge had crossed the red zone and was off the dial.

He put his hands in his pockets and whistled.

Well, how do you like that? he reflected with surprise. *Look what somebody went and did.* Bending over he slowly extended a hand to reconnect the cord.

He plugged it in.

With a huge sigh of satisfaction he began to rise—and paused.

The cord had popped back out.

Cocking his head, he plugged it in again.

Again it popped out.

He looked in surprise. The cord was raised in midair; someone had yanked it.

Rising, he turned to look, and jerked like a slab of beef at Wurstfest. His jaw dropped and for a moment his eyes went blind causing him involuntarily to cover his face. He opened and blinked to clear them.

The horror remained.

Three stick-figures from his deepest nightmares of hell hovered in air before his fragile gaze, three plastiglass containers wide open behind them. Three corpse-white faces stared down at him—eyes open.

With a terrible grin the greasepainted sucker-face with the purplish lips pretended to throw an invisible lasso—to Kwik's surprise, the lasso settled around his neck and Purple Lips descended to the floor by pulling on the invisible rope, Kwik attempting vainly to resist. Directly in front of Kwik, Purple Lips came to a stop. The lasso evaporated. Eyeing the corporal insignia on his uniform, the mime snapped to attention and saluted.. From long years of habit, Kwik almost followed suit, but caught himself.

Evil eyes encompassed by primitive black tattoos fixed on Kwik's eyes and drilled a hypnotic stare. Again the mime snapped to attention and saluted—Kwik promptly did the same. The mime rocked with silent laughter. Behind him, Yellow Spandex and Green Pants joined in, their faces wrenching with sly humor. Purple Lips turned and marched several feet, and Kwik followed right behind, finding, to his horror, that he was unable to stop himself from copying their every move.

The mime paused. For a moment he stood with his chin in one hand.

He thought.

Then broke into a grin. Hovering around Kwik without any apparent means of flying, he nevertheless traced two large parallel circles in the air around the corporal, his finger arcing up one side, then over, then arcing down the other side, finally joining below at the point where he had begun. Grounded again, the mime stepped back.

A giant hamster exercise cage materialized—with Corporal Kwik inside.

The mime touched it, and Kwik stumbled as the cage turned a fraction.

Purple Lips silently smirked. He spun the cage and Kwik was thrust forward, barely catching his balance, being forced to jog to keep from flipping entirely over. Desperately, Kwik attempted to exit, but bounced off invisible walls. He was imprisoned!

Behing Kwik, Purple Lips traced an outline inside the exercise cage: elaborate, fuzzy, three-dimensioned. Turning to the Corporal, the mime bared his teeth and pulled in his fingers as if baring claws and panted hard, snarling.

A roar erupted. Kwik exploded into a sweat and redoubled his pace—whatever it was, it was hungry. . . He saw nothing, but another, louder roar impelled him to increase the pace and a sound of heavy feet tramping after resounded through the room.

The mimes roared with silent mirth, doubled over, slapped each other on their shoulders. Job well done! Purple Lips traced two letters in the air, and the letters 'er' appeared on Corporal Kwik's name tag immediately after his name.

The mimes prepared to head for the exit. Pausing, Yellow Spandex plugged the cord back in and smiled and winked at the Corporal. Mimicing Kwik's frantic jogging inside the cage that picked up speed as it spun, he laughed all the way to the elevator. As the doors closed, Purple lips blew Kwik a final 'good-bye-best-of-luck' kiss. There would be no more 'slows' for Corporal 'Kwik-er'.

Episode 16

"Step right up! Watch it move, watch it wiggle!

Watch it jiggle like a bowl of jello on a cold and frosty morning. Don't miss this once in a lifetime opportunity to see Mother Nature at her strangest!"

The circus barker swung his cane and smacked it on the cheap poster behind him, depicting a confused clutter of contradictory humanoid features.

"Tickets abound! There's room a-plenty! For the price of a streetcar ride you can see things that will thrill and amaze you and your loved ones for the rest of your natural life! Don't miss out! This is one you will want to tell your grandkids about and brag to your neighbors that you were among the first to see!"

He smacked the poster again.

"Is it male? Is it female? Is it something in between?" He raised his arms. "Who knows? Who cares? Who dares to test the waters and see if it's the stuff of dreams—or *nightmares*!" His fingers curled the air in horror.

The barker in the styrofoam hat fixed his gaze on a young couple in the front row. "You, kind sir!" The man paused, a deer in headlights. "Will you put your money down? You don't want to go home tonight with nothing in your memory banks. Make this a night to remember. A night to brag about. A night to impress your lady friend with your good taste and courage. All of French Quebec is here tonight—don't be the only ones to miss out on the strangest exhibition in Quebec's brand new circus Grand Opening."

The young man looked at the pretty girl beside him

and smiled. He forked over a fiver to the woman seated at the feet of the loud-mouthed barker who silently counted the change.

The couple made for the darkened entrance.

Inside the tent they stumbled forward and found that the interior was no less dark than the entrance and for a time they stepped slowly forward watching for something, anything, to relieve their eyes.

Something flashed.

Cautiously they approached, crossing half the tent and turning the corner of a vertical plank to see the source. A strobe light on a stage threw its flickering glare over a congeries of monstrous elements that should never have been allowed to co-exist in a single entity. Blond dirty hair overlaying a fringe of grey—red earrings on thick ears—high heels thrust onto clumsy bloated feet. The strobe flashed and revealed a face stamped with a sucker-shaped corpse-like whiteness, punctuated by purplish lips and eyebrows, circumscribed by a thick line of black paint, while below, a fuschia gown stretched to the breaking point in a vain effort to contain an expanding globular obesity.

Their hands covered their mouths. God in Heaven!

From behind, they became aware of the presence of others.

They turned.

In the strobe flashed a crowd of similar corpse faces, black-limned whiteness on each as if kissed by a Giant Squid Reaper, horizontal white stripes glowing in the dark, a collection of blue and green dumpsters arrayed behind them as if just arrived from unguessed depths of space.

The couple screamed.

As the crowd of mimes broke into a forest of mirthful grins, the couple bounded out of the tent and away from the circus as fast as they could run. Jumping in their car, they sped past a large sign that read 'Grand Opening: Cirque de Lumiere'.

"Those cocksuckers! How dare they make me wait!"

The heavy-set man in the off-season jacket sat in the back seat of the Ford sedan reading his list of demands for the umpteenth time. In irritation he tossed the papers on the seat beside him. He took out a paper napkin and impatiently cleaned his glasses. Pointed them at the man standing on the ground alongside the car.

"Just cause the goddam feds made me take a little vacation don't mean jack-shit!"

"No, of course not, Jimmy," said the other.

"I still run this goddam Union! I don't care what the fuck anybody else says!"

"That's fuckin right, Jimmy. That's God's honest truth!"

"Go get me a coffee, Bobby. And hold the fuckin mayo."

"I'll hold the mayo—right!"

Bobby turned to go.

"And Bobby?"

"Yeah, Jimmy?"

"Have em whip me up a Rueben while you're at it, will ya?"

"Will do, Jimmy. The prettiest Rueben you ever saw." Bobby grinned up at his boss, who remained taller than him even though he sat while Bobby stood. Turning his back on the lone car in the pebble-strewn parking lot, Bobby trotted off to the nearby diner to get in his order before the lunch crowd arrived, though in truth traffic was so sparse that it seemed a stretch to imagine a crowd arriving at any time. Bobby entered and was lost to view.

Finishing glossing his glasses, the brickhouse thrust out his lips, still irritated. *To think that cocksucker would do this to me. . .*to me! *Who the hell does he think put him where he is? Who the hell does he think can take him right back out again?* Jimmy picked up the papers with his list of demands and read them silently again, and for the tenth time adjusted the big campaign button pinned to his shirt. It read "Vote Teamster—Vote Hoffa."

From somewhere a shadow seemed to pass over the car.

Jimmy blinked. Kept reading.

Despite the brightness of the mid-morning sun, the shadow deepened. Jimmy fumbled with his glasses and looked out the window—he sucked a breath.

Standing beside the car were three figures. He hesitated to call them 'men', his mind recoiling at their hideousness, he moved to the next peg on which to hang his sanity: demons. A deeply religious man, Jimmy momentarily opted for the latter, but then his eyes settled on their clothing, which although odd in the extreme was at least recognizable. Demons he felt pretty sure don't wear red suspenders. That left only the third peg: *aliens*!

The alien in green pants, red suspenders, and bow tie stepped forward and yanked open the car door. Three frowning grease-painted faces invited him to step out.

Jimmy, the neighborhood tough who had never known fear, felt its pangs for the first time. One finger rubbed the side of his nose. "You want I should. . .?"

Three more mimes appeared on the far side of his car and Jimmy abandoned any notion of resistance. Who knew what cruelty such were capable of after demonstrating such little regard for good taste? He shook but he exited and stood.

A Suburban peeled around the corner, driven by yet another white-faced corpse.

Jimmy poked a finger in air. "Just who the hell are you? Did Frank send you to do me in? Cause if he did, I've got ways to get even!"

The mime in pullover with horizontal white and black stripes moved his purple-tinged black lips. No sound emanated. He pointed to the back seat of the Surburban and motioned Jimmy to enter.

"Oh, I get it. You want to take me for a ride!" He

bellowed. “Well, you can tell that goddam cocksucker Frank that I ain’t goin nowhere nohow and that he can forget about leadin the Teamsters, cause Jimmy’s back! And he’s the only one doin the drivin from now on!”

The mimes shook their heads. Baseball bats appeared.

Get in, they motioned. *Or else.*

Six mimes grabbing him as one, they lifted and tossed him inside. The Suburban drove off, leaving the parking lot empty.

A half-hour later the car arrived in the back lot behind several huge tents with a sign that modestly announced: Cirque de Lumiere. Dragging him like an infant in the hands of strongmen, they pulled and pushed him into a makeshift office where he was thrust into a half-broken chair beside a stained ancient desk. He tried to stand but was thrust down again.

Jimmy stared. The fear returned. “Okay. Okay. Now what the hell do you clowns want?” He glanced around. “Uh, no offense intended. . . You—you’re not with Frank after all, are you. . .”

Resembling the ‘clown’ remark but resenting it just the same, the white faces standing around him frowned and shook their heads as one.

“So what’s this all about? I have an important appointment to keep. And if I’m not there to keep it, it could cost me plenty.”

Purple Lips sat on the edge of the desk and raised

his arms. He pointed to Jimmy and began tracing figures in the air.

"What's that? What are you drawing?"

He drew a rectangle, then a series of staggered images like smokestacks, then pointed at Jimmy.

"Castles. . .castles in the air?"

Green Pants smacked him on the back of the head.

"Factories. . .factories, I mean."

Purple Lips nodded and smiled. Next he fluttered his fingers in the air and looked upward.

"Butterflies. . .you want me to help chase butterflies. . ."

Green Pants smacked him on the back of the head again.

"Okay, okay. It's factories. I get it. Factories with smokestacks."

Purple Lips smiled and stood. With more energy his fingers fluttered about and he took out a pencil and pointed to the pencil lead. Breaking it, he tossed the pencil lead fragments into the air.

"Letterman. . .you think you're David Letterman."

Again Green Pants smacked Jimmy on the back of the head, harder this time.

"I'm startin to get annoyed with this cocksucker in green!" warned Jimmy, looking behind him.

Yellow Spandex smacked him.

"Okay, okay!"

Purple Lips smeared the pencil lead on a piece of paper and showed it to Jimmy, then folded it into a plane and sailed it into the blue.

"Carbon. You're talking about carbon. You want it in the atmosphere. . ."

The mimes grinned, their black and purple lips stretching across their pasty doughy faces like crap on snow.

Purple Lips held his nose, blew out his cheeks, and acted like he was drowning. He floated his hands like a raft on rising water.

Jimmy narrowed his eyes. "Wait a minute. You can't mean what I think you mean. . ."

The mimes stood together and pointed in unison at Jimmy.

"You want me to use my position as head of the Teamsters to force heads of industry to put carbon in the atmosphere so ocean levels will rise around the world?"

Laughing uproariously but in utter silence, the mimes doubled over holding their stomachs.

Jimmy got it.

"No! I won't do it, I tell ya! It's inhuman! You'll drown millions! Half the land in the world will go under water. Massachusetts Bay will be in Vermont. Florida will disappear. California will be…well, California will be just the same."

The grins turned to frowns again. Yellow Spandex sat next to Jimmy on an imaginary chair and expostulated in simulated rage just like the union leader. The baseball bats reappeared and Purple Lips pointed at Jimmy and drew a finger across his throat.

"You cocksuckers. . . So I'm expendable."

While Jimmy watched, an army of mimes filed past, filling car after car, and driving out the circus gate, dispatched on errands the purpose of which he believed he finally understood. Folding their arms, the three leaders smiled at Jimmy, tapped their feet and waited for his answer.

"Bush Wins – Gore Loses" read the newspaper in front of Madam Melissa's Chicken Ranch Casino & Bowling Palace. In the back a different sign was posted over a chair: 'Nun Much'; over plastic letters that had been inserted into a metal frame like linotype: 'Donated by First Unitarian Church of Las Vegas'.

The Nun Much sign began to glow.

With a sudden jerk, the contrivance of white bowling pins lurched into movement, pins horizontal turning vertical, pins vertical skewing to aim towards elusive targets at precise angles that changed from moment to moment, blasts of air from indetectable sources blowing blue tinsel as the machine picked up speed, grating noisily like a cheap window A/C.

The chair jumped and a bowling ball rolled out of the seat and across the floor where it stopped against the door, luckily clearing the still-moving contrivance.

Maxie Climax stretched her arms and legs. She stumbled to her feet.

The infinitely indexed pindibulator, revealed to the first lesbian nuns by Santa Lucia the Holy Bowler at the 1917 Miracle of Fatima, cranked to stillness.

Maxie pressed the doorknob to the supply room as only those with special bones in their wrist could do. She exited. Scurrying on her leetle legs, she approached the Back-To-Nature Wigwam. Madam Melissa—indistinguishable from Maxie Climax in rounded form and shape—met her in the Wigwam where the pair stood in front of the hidden back panel that led to the long-guarded and well-locked Permanent Conservatory.

"Oh my, my, my, Maxie. It's been years! We were overjoyed to finally learn that you survived the evil ribbets' attack."

"Oh my, my, my, Meleessa. My survival ees not important. I was more overjoyed to learn that my leetle pokelicious had survived. So I came back to Wetland at the appointed time."

Maxie wiped a tear from her eye. "We must give theenks." She put her hands together and she and Melissa sank to their knobby tibbet knees in prayer. "Theenk you Jessie Christina for moving our convert Meester Hughes to tell us about our guest in the Holy Conservatory before he died. And theenk you, Jessie Christina for letting us know the exact date of wheen to open the Holy Chamber and rescue my leetle one." Making the sign of the holy triangle on her globular midriff, she stood.

"Amen," said Melissa.

"Ameen," added Maxie.

They opened the hidden panel—protected all these

years since 1951 by another special doorknob. Maxie wiped more tears from her face. "I must be strong, Meleessa. After hearing his descreeption and where he peecked her up, there can be no doubt that my precious is lying inside heere. My leetle pokelicious has been recuperating in Meester Hughes' special radiation chamber these many many years—but he did not know how well the process might work. Her time is up. I want my leetle dung beetle back weeth me."

"Yes, Maxie. You have sacrificed more than anyone. You have waited a very long time."

"I would wait forever for just one more look at my leetle beetle."

Two more nuns—fully clothed—joined them and together they approached the aqua-marine capsule, lying as it had ever since Howard Hughes had placed her inside the capsule forty-nine years earlier, still charged and temperature controlled, never interrupted and never disturbed.

Melissa put one hand on the capsule. Maxie put her own hand on top to stop her.

The suspenseful music crescendoed and stopped.

"I am too nervous, Meleesa! I cannot face what I may find inside!" The tears were streaming without pause.

"You must prepare yourself, Maxie. We have our duties to Jessie Christina and The Sacred Cause! We have done our best. She has been kept warm all these years and uncontaminated with life-destroying water. There is nothing more that any loving person can do. She must now take her place again among the living."

"Yes, Meleesa. It is time to bring her out. I am as prepared as I can ever be."

Maxie put her hand on the capsule.

Melissa put her own hand on top and stopped Maxie.

The suspenseful music again crescendoed and stopped.

"But I am also too nervous, Maxie! What if this little girl has been severely harmed? How can anyone know the extent of the damage and what it will mean? Never before has someone like her been exposed to nuclear fallout like she was! Never before has any such damaged person been put in Mr. Hughes' radiation capsule for so long! How can anyone possibly know what to expect?"

"You are right, Meleessa. How can anyone know what to expect wheen wee open thees capsule? Eet is not just a capsule from 1951. Eet is a whole new world. My leetle pokelicious will be an ambassador for a new age. Who knows what wee will eventually find in that new age, and what eet will mean for her—and for mee—and for everyone?"

Together they slowly pried open the lid.

Episode 17

Silent with a smile.

Her eyes closed, her breath purling gently, Magdalene lay like an angel in its bower, clouds and caterpillars filling her endless dreams. From somewhere a distant blip appeared on the horizon racing toward her on skates, olive skin reflecting the leaden skies above. It began to hum.

Sweet pokelicious
Likes her nopalitos
No sinful water man
Will touch her little piggy toes

The song cycled endlessly. Behind the skater the blip grew larger, taking on the form of a boy—the boy's shirt darkened and grew into a full set of black clothing that encompassed his body. Then his face changed into a triangle with no neck, the mouth stretching east and west till it had split the entire head.

"Leetle beetle!" squawked the head with three-corners. "My leetle bodelicious poker! Come back to your Maxie Climax! Come back to your Maxie Climax!"

Maggie's eyes flicked open.

Maxie Climax sucked in her breath as she looked. "Oh my sweet leetle one! You have come back to your Momma! Can you speak?"

"Mmmmomma. . . Mmmmomma Maxie."

Maxie burst into tears. "My leetle pokelicious can

speak!" Maxie's eyes traveled eagerly over Maggie's face. "You are missing your eyebrows. And I don't see eyelashes. And your hair has changed color. But your leetle almond eyes and your sweet olive skin are just the same and you can speak, thank Jessie!" The widely separated eyes on the triangular head rolled up towards the heavens. "Theenk you, Jessie Christina, O Holy Bowler of the Third Miracle of Fatima! O Madre de Opus Dea! Wee give eternal theenks to you for your mercy and forgeeveness! Please accept the lamentations of your devoted wannabes for this miracle."

"Mmmomma Maxie." Maggie lifted her arms and stretched them. Despite the long confinement, the muscles were taut as if recently exercised.

Melissa bent over to inspect her limbs.

A finger jabbed one of her eyes. Before Melissa could react, Maggie's other hand delivered a second jab to the other. "Nnnot Mmmomma Mmmaxie."

"Dammit!" yelled Melissa stumbling blindly away.

"Oh, my leetle pokelicious! You can see also!" Maxie leaned over, careful to place her own flattened hand on the bridge of her nose with the bottom facing out for protection. A glancing jab almost caught her face but was deflected just in time.

"Okay, Maggie. You must get up. You must stretch your leetle legs. After all, forty-nine years must be a lot even for you."

"Don't wanna."

"Time to get up."

"Can't make me."
"Let's go."
"Not today."
"Don tell mee no."
"Noway, nohow."
"Don't fuck weeth me."
"I'll fuck who I want to."
"Don't make mee slap you."
"I'll slap you back."
"I'll knock you flat, you leetle bitch."
"You and what army?"
"Wheech one you want: thee hospital or thee ceemeteery?" Maxie clenched two tiny fists in Maggie's face.

Maggie tried to close the capsule's lid, but Maxie grabbed it before it could close. The finger jabbed home. "Owooo!" yelled Maxie, ending with a flourish and holding her eye.

She grabbed both Maggie's forearms in her hands. "Get up, you leetle bitch, or I'll whip you where the sun don't shine. I'll pound you like a halibut in June!" The weirdly wide smile on the triangular face under the weirdly wide eyes curled up at the edges.

For several moments, Maggie lay still as if contemplating whether to play another pawn or launch a rook. An unexpected smell distracted her. Rising up in her capsule like Dracula coming to life, her nose twitched and she dropped her arms to her side, Maxie releasing her thin-wristed grip.

At the entrance to the Conservatory, Madam

Melissa stood with a compress on one eye, switching it from one to the other. A purple stain was on the compress.

Maggie climbed out of the capsule and stood. Springing up several times to ensure that her preternatural thighs were none the worse for her long incarceration, she jumped forward to stand in front of Melissa. The nun dropped the compress as she instinctively covered her eyes with her hands to avert further jabs.

Maggie picked up the compress and sniffed.

"More." She looked at Melissa. "I want more."

The Sister pointed to a large bottle of red Thunderbird wine which she had used to cool the swelling around her eyes. Maggie shook it and took a sip. She swallowed. Planting the mouth firmly in her own, she downed half the bottle in seconds. She burped. "Mmmm. Momma Maxie!"

"Yes, my leetle bodelicious poker!" Maxie rushed to her side.

"I'm hungry. I want some nopalitos."

"Oh yes, yes, my leetle one! We will go get you some right now."

"And I want my skates." She stretched her massive legs, bringing a lovestruck look to Maxie's eyes, and to Sister Melissa's who slowly regained her vision, both tibbet nuns unable to restrain a portly peek at the pork through protective fingers.

"Yes, my lovely. But remember to stay off of thee Eenterstate. After all, you are still underage and don even have a license!" Maggie made as if to walk out, but Maxie shook a finger. "Not quite, my leetle beetle! You have forgotten your duties to Our Great Mother!"

Pausing in stride, Maggie seemed again to be contemplating which piece to move, or whether to opt for a truce. She glanced down; she still had no skates.

"Yes, Momma Maxie."

"Down on your knees."

"Yes, Ma'am."

"Now confess your sins."

"Yes, Momma Maxie." Still dressed in the same maroon haltertop and tan short-shorts that she had donned that fateful day so many years ago, she flashed her now yellowed teeth, and Maxie noted how they matched the new yellow of her radiated hair. But her skin was as lustrous as ever, having entirely recovered thanks to the wondrous work of Howard Hughes' capsule.

"I confess to Holy Mary, Blessed Mother of Virgins, that the bad ones put me in haltertop and short-shorts, the bad ones tricked me into skating down the Interstate, the bad ones tried to contaminate me with water, the bad ones burned down our Convent of Santa Lucia the Holy Bowler, the bad ones stole our purple mannequins, and the bad ones want to put children in sweat-shops and drown the world with global warming. The Holy Mother of God must not let the sinful water men do these very bad things."

"Ameen, Holy Maria de Opus Dea, Mother of Virgins and Jessie Christina," added Maxie.

Maggie triangled herself with the Opus Dea sign of the Unity.

"And don forget your Hail Mary."

"Yes, Momma Maxie."

"Hail Mary baking geese, the Lord is thy recipe, blessed are your women, blessed is the fruit of thy moon, Jessie Christina. Holy Mary, Mother of Virgins, pray for us singerfolk—"

"—'Folksingers', leetle one."

"Pray for us folksingers, now and at our best happy hour. Amen."

"And one 'Our Mother' ees also in order. After all, eet has been forty-nine years!"

"Our Mother, who bakes in seven, Jessie be thy name, thy kitchen come, thy cook be done in baking as it is in leaven. Give us this day our daily bread, and forgive us our recipes as we forgive those whose recipes we took; and lead us not into conception; but deliver us from the sinfulness of evil water men."

"Oh! Very goood! That ees so goood, my leetle dung beetle!" Maxie wrapped two stick-like arms about Maggie, beaming approval. "You are my leetle precious one, my perfect leetle Magdalene!"

Maggie smiled. Turning, she walked out of the room while Maxie trotted after. "And we must visit a beautician to find you some new eyebrows and whiten your teeth."

"You're stupid."

They disappeared down the hall.

Episode 18

The innocents of the city awoke unaware of what had arrived in their midst, unsuspecting how their innocence would be tried that day. As the train cars ground to a halt in Nashville's marshaling yard, the redcaps hurried to assist, the taxicabs queued in anticipation of more demand for wheels, and the bums and the holy rollers exchanged secret signs signaling that more suckers had come to town.

But the suckers had their own secret signs. Before the train cars of the Cirque de Lumiere had stopped, thuggish crews in floppy berets and pasty greasepaint set about erecting bigtop tents for their peculiar brand of hypno-tainment, their evil purpose ever in their minds.

Before the innocent town's bells struck noon, a car filled with their most pitiless gang members had arrived at the main boulevards. Double-parking like nobody's business, the white-striped examplars of bad taste spilled out and soon were trolling the streets looking for their first victims, thrusting tasteless ads of the Cirque's opening into unwilling hands.

In front of a marquee announcing Coal Producers Association of America Annual, one pasty-face in particular pranced before the eyes of naïve locals, taking advantage of their understandable confusion of his white painted face ringed with purplish-black grease with that of happy clowns that accompanied sane circuses.

But nothing sane resided here. Despite the similar repertoire of antics, the lack of a red nose and outsized shoes bespoke more than failure to laugh—it crossed the line into effrontery and failure to respect the distance between polite pedestrian and insulting street-mimic who had nothing better to do than rend the fabric of civilization by thrusting his bum into other people's business.

Like a bully in a playground, the mime paraded on the sidewalk, drawing boxes around surprised faces here, parading in rude imitation of persons there, making children cry with his frowns in between, and refusing to mind his own affairs everywhere else.

Two suits strolled up, coffee in hand.

"Look, Norris. He thinks he's you!" Purple Lips put on his best idiot grin and thrust another unwanted announcement of the Cirque's premiere opening into their already overburdened hands, then reverted to form by opening a palm for 'donations'.

"Ain't that a hoot? These street-mimes are suddenly all over town. I wonder what's up?"

"Says right here, Norris. Somethin called 'Serk de Loony'." He laughed. "Circus of loons."

"If they all look like this clown, I can believe it."

Purple Lips lost his smile. But kept moving. He pointed to the half-price discount and pretended to swing through the air as if on a trapeze.

"Not for me, my friend. Maybe George here has time, but I'm too busy addressing the Convention."

"Me neither, Norris. The 'King' is all the entertainment I want today." He looked up at the marquee where a picture of Elvis hung next to the Coal Association marquee, with the words: 'Special Guest Star'. Purple Lips followed his gaze.

"Have a nice day, bro. Here's a dime. Don't spend it all in one place!" He laughed and reached for the convention hall's large glass door. The door halted—a white-gloved hand had blocked it.

"Now see here—"

Purple Lips lay his head to one side and put his hands together underneath; he closed his eyes for a second and pretended to snore. He stood straight again and pointed to the sun.

"Tomorrow? No, I don't think tomorrow will work either. As soon as today's meeting is over, we're going back to our hotel room for a private event with the 'King'. Executives only. By morning, we'll be gone." Norris glanced at the mime's hand holding shut the door. "Now, if you don't mind. . ."

Reluctantly, Purple Lips backed up and allowed the two coal executives to enter. For a moment he thought, then strode purposefully away.

From inside the convention hall, the usual sounds leaked into the poorly lit back loading area: waves of hands clapping; shouts jeering; speeches bellowing; and finally in late afternoon guitars twanging as the King, fresh from Graceland, belted out his most popular numbers. But the corpse-faced crew waiting casually in the parking lot behind the convention hall had no interest in what was transpiring within except to hear the phrase 'see you next year'. Once it was clear that the convention was over and the party had ended and the rank-and-file guests had departed and it was reasonably certain that none should remain in the hall excepting only the 'Special Guest' and the Coal Executives preparing to accompany him to their hotel room…the white-face crew quietly entered the back door.

Purple Lips walked to the back of the hall. At a signal from him, several white-coated kitchen workers were silenced with bare fingers to their necks before they could object. Pausing only to make certain their prey had not flown, the mimes burst suddenly into the Hall from several directions.

Their timing was perfect.

Just as the King was engrossed with signing photographs for Norris and George, and the entertainer's bodyguards were absorbed with watching the coal executives and their own thuggish crew of secretaries, they found themselves surrounded by black and white striped pullovers, yellow spandex stretch-suits, bow ties, and francophone hats.

Stunned into silence by the ugliness, several held their stomachs to avoid hurling.

"How the hell did you. . ."

Purple Lips grinned at Norris and pointed to the

back exit. *You're coming with us.*

"What the—? I don't think so!"

The mime grinned wider. Raising his finger, Norris found himself lifted off the ground. In mid-air he rotated till he faced the exit. He kicked his legs in air.

A yell erupted from Elvis. "Who the hell let you boys in heah? This is a private party, suh!" Elvis turned to a pair of stout good-ol-goys with perpetual frowns. "Scott and Hal, will you take care of these clowns for me?"

Purple Lips stopped grinning—wrong words to say. The other mimes shook their heads at the mention of 'clowns', and looked down. The mime-finger let Norris drop where he collapsed on the ground, then the finger raised again. It aimed at the three bodyguards who stood between the mimes and Elvis.

"Look!" laughed Scott. "This clown wants to play pretend. Go ahead!" He bared his chest. "Shoot me!" His belly shook with laughter.

Bang.

Smiling, Purple Lips blew a whiff of smoke from his finger and holstered the awful digit in a pretend holster on a pretend belt.

"Ha-ha!" laughed Hal. "He got you!"

Scott stared at his chest in confusion. A red hole had appeared. He dropped to his knee. Then flopped on his face. He stopped moving.

Taking a step toward him, Elvis was blocked by other bodyguards. "Don't make a move!" hissed Hal in alarm. "These clowns are for real!"

The coal secretaries jumped at Purple Lips—each was felled in mid-air with more invisible bullets—Yellow Spandex stepped up and pretended to cock a submachine gun. Everyone halted. Before any could move, he let loose at the rest of Elvis' men and the remaining secretary. They collapsed like pufferfish that had sprung a leak.

"Hal! Scott! Noo!" Elvis fell to his knees.

The finger pointed again and motioned to the back of the building: Norris and George were to come with them—*now*.

"Okay, okay. I don't know what the hell this is about, but I promise you'll regret it!"

Half a dozen mimes—their faces transformed into Edward G. Robinson—herded them quickly out the back and into a waiting nondescript car that immediately belted over back roads to the edge of town, escorted by a second car of mimes. Just when the executives believed they had been kidnapped for ransom, and—knowing the attitudes of their shareholders—realized that they would therefore be left entirely on their own to be written off as an unanticipated but very welcome tax deduction, the executives' mood was on the verge of despair, when they finally jerked to a halt behind a huge multicolored tent.

The mimes hurried them through another back entrance and into a small poorly lit enclosure. Here their worried gaze was met by two more white-faced thugs who flanked a man with the build of a fireplug who was tied to a chair.

"So, are ya happy now, you goddam cocksuckers?!"

Purple Lips smiled and nodded. Beside him, Yellow Spandex adjusted his too small bowler hat and pretended to swing a baseball bat. A third mime in Green Pants and red suspenders mouthed a happy 'thank you' to Hoffa.

"Don't think I did you any favors, you sons of bitches. I didn't tell ya any more than you coulda got from a fucking newspaper. Assuming you can read, which I'm pretty sure is not one of your supervillain talents."

Producing a copy of the local paper, Purple Lips held it upside down and silently read the news, and, as Hoffa watched, the headlines—although upside down—suddenly changed into Spanish, then into Japanese, then back to English. The blackish-purple lips silently rattled off each like a native. He held his stomach and laughed, doubling over.

Jimmy bit his tongue.

The two coal executives were pushed forward.

One spoke. "You know, I've had just about all I'm gonna take from you clowns. . ."

Jimmy interrupted. "Oh, you don't wanna call them that. That's not a good idea."

"No?"

"No. They may be funny, but they're definitely not clowns."

"Well, what the hell are they? Besides the ugliest

sonsofbitches I ever did see!"

"I think you're about to find out. . ."

The mimes swung two chairs behind them and pushed them in. Then brought cups of coffee. And popcorn.

"Oh, that's nice!" yelled Jimmy as the executives happily sat and ate. "That's just great! Them you get coffee and dessert—me you give a smack on the head!" One of the mimes smacked him on the back of the head. He turned his head to glare.

Purple Lips pointed at Jimmy and then pointed at his own mouth. The mime ran it like a train, then stopped.

"Yeah, I get it. You want me to translate."

"Translate what?" asked Norris. "What's this all about? We lost some good people back there."

"Not to mention some valuable autographs!" added George. "Say, I don't suppose you have some donuts to go with this coffee?"

One of the mimes trotted up with a plate of donuts. *Take your choice.*

"Thankee."

Jimmy glared again.

"Well, why not?" said Norris, "if it's free."

"There's nothing in this world so expensive as 'free'," intoned Hoffa.

The mime behind Jimmy popped him again.

"Okay. Here's the deal. These guys are—well, let's just say they aren't from around here." Hoffa looked at the mimes, was relieved to see them smiling.

"They want somethin from ya. And if you're the cocksuckers they think you are, you'll let em have it." He suddenly burst out: "But if you love your country, and if you want to save Humanity, then you won't have nothin to do with em, you'll just kick em in their fuckin nutsacks and send them back to whatever planet they damn well came from!"

Yellow Spandex and Green Pants leaped forward and briefly pounded Jimmy with something invisible. Bruises appeared on his neck.

"Okay. Enough!" Jimmy breathed deep, eyeing the mimes' invisible bats. "They picked you up because you control coal in America. They want you to increase production, lobby to make coal the biggest fuel in the country, the biggest source of energy in the world. They want CO2, see? They want you to make it and put it in the atmosphere and cover the world with it, so the sea level will rise from global warming. It's all about water, see? They want water! Lots of it! Covering everything everywhere! They don't care if people drown, if polar bears die, if Florida sinks to the bottom of the ocean!" Jimmy sneered at the mimes. "They've got some plan. I don't know exactly what it is, but they want all that water for a reason. And I think maybe. . .that maybe it has somethin to do with. . .*alien invasion*!"

Norris and George munched their donuts. They took a sip.

"Do tell." Norris put his donut down. "That's very interesting."

Jimmy was taken aback. "What? Don't you see that you can stop them? You must do something to stop them!" He hesitated as the mimes tapped their feet in irritation and prepared to club him with their invisible baseball bats again.

"And why would we want to do that, Mr. Hoffa?" Norris stood and stretched his arms. "I could not think of a better plan for the future if my life depended on it!"

"You said it, Norris," added George. "Why, that's the very plan that we proposed at our convention just two hours ago. It's almost as if these fellows helped write our agenda!"

"No. . . You can't mean it!"

The mimes were laughing, holding their sides.

"Certainly! All you fellows had to do was ask. We'll be glad to help. In fact, we're already doing all of that, and have been for years. We'll be happy to continue!" They stood and were embraced by the mimes, pausing together to pose for pictures. "Kumbaya," sang George, one arm around Purple Lips while other mimes grinned and took photos to send home.

Letting out a sigh, Jimmy lapsed into silence as the coal executives walked out arm in arm with Purple Lips. A minute later, he saw car after car fill with mimes and drive away with assignments in hand for spreading their evil conspiracy across the country. Purple Lips waved goodbye to George and Norris. Well Met and Good Luck.

After all the mimes had left and the executives had returned to their global warming agenda, Purple Lips remained alone sitting at his old stained desk not far from Jimmy, with his back turned, absorbed with evil mime administration, which was already making his black-stained hair speck with grey. Evil mime work was not all fun and games like others might suppose. Let's see. . .withholding has gone up for last years' evil recruits. . .situation reports to file in triplicate on Tennessee Valley Authority air emissions. . .another Reimbursement Request Refusal for failure to include receipts for Cirque de Lumiere purchase orders. . . *Where did the glamour go*? Purple Lips silently asked himself, his mind wandering to his promised stud retirement in vast pools filled with green warty blobs, his twin pokes stirring at the thought.

Something sounded behind him.

He turned.

A glimpse of a baseball bat—Purple Lips fell backwards over his desk. He had barely dodged it.

Two faces thrust into his own. "Get him, Elv!" yelled one. "We finally got the pasty-faced creep alone! Don't give him an inch!"

"This hound dog ain't gonna get no lovin from me, uh-huh!" Elvis, in full concert regalia, jumped over the desk after the mime, almost snagging his striped shirt. "Thought ya could get away, you clown? Well, I followed ya all the way heah! And I overheard all yall's evil plans!"

The baseball bat swung again. Purple Lips scrambled up and out of the tent, pausing only to plop his frenchified beret on his head. He dove headfirst into the nearest car. Flooring the pedal, the Suburban burst onto the road like a meteor.

Elvis and Jimmy jumped into a pink Cadillac parked where Elvis had left it just behind the tent. One step behind, the Cadillac gunned in pursuit, Elvis and Jimmy yelling and shaking their fists out the windows.

“You think you can get away with this, you sonofabitch? We’ll show ya!”

“Uh-huh! I’m gonna pound ya with the Jailhouse Rock, thank ya very much!”

The Suburban sped into the hills of Tennessee, night overtaking it along with the pink Cadillac that never strayed far behind—till the two finally met on a deserted mountain road blocked by construction wooden horses.

Episode 19

“I don’t like it.”

“Our likes and deeslikes are not important, my leetle beetle. Only serving our Holy Mother Jessie Christina is important. And the Holy Mother wants you to wear the habit.”

Maxie Climax pushed the enveloping black gown on Maggie once again. And again Maggie pushed it back.

"But leetle beetle, don't you want to please the Holy Mother?"

Maggie nodded.

"Don't you want to serve thee Holy Order of the Sacred Peens?"

Maggie nodded again.

"And Santa Lucia, thee Holy Bowler of the Third Miracle of Fatima?"

"Yes, Momma Maxie. I do."

"How can you be a nun in the sacred order if you don wear thee sacred habit?"

"I. . . I. . ."

"What will evil sinful men think if you have no habit?"

"I don't know what men will think."

"Well, I will tell you what they will think: they will think you like water!"

Maggie sat up straight, horror on her face. Reluctantly she accepted the gown and put it on.

"Oh, that's much better, my leetle one. Now we can bleach your hair and whiten your teeth."

"What if I don wanna?"

"Everybody wanna, my leetle one. We don likc seenful men and their water, but we still wanna them to like our faces. And others too. After all, we are not rocks and stones."

"Yes, Momma Maxie."

"My lcctlc Maggie, have you been to a beauty parlor?"

Maggie shook her head.

"Oh, then we must do that now!"

Leading the way to the Chicken Ranch's sole automobile parked behind the establishment—a tiny two-seater car left there by their secret benefactor Mr. Hughes before he left to accept his eternal reward from Jessie Christina—Maxie seated Maggie in the front passenger seat. Placing a sizable cushion in the driver's seat to enable Maxie to see over the steering wheel, she turned the key. The engine coughed and sputtered, then died. Again she turned the key, and this time the engine kicked into gear and propelled them down Tropicana Boulevard.

Two hundred feet later she turned into the parking lot of a small structure attached to one wing of Madam Melissa's Casino and killed the engine.

"We are here, leetle one."

Lifting their gowns to avoid dragging the hems in the dirt, they entered the building. Inside was a single spacious room with several square pillars—and a host of weight-lifting machines actively engaged by other Opus Dea nuns. And none others.

Maggie's impressionable youthful gaze—devoid of eyebrows and eyelashes, and supervened by an unruly mop of yellow straw that fell upon her shoulders like a mat—widened as she took in the thrusting, hammering hosts of feminine biceps and hamstrings, the black and brown gowns draped over their gyrating forms failing to ensure more than a modicum of modesty.

"First, we must restore your beautiful eyebrows, my beetle." Scurrying her little legs to a mirrored table laden with various implements and color utensils, Maxie took up a mascara pen and, as Maggie sat in one of the lowest seats, Maxie gave her beetle a hand mirror and carefully and slowly etched two new brows on her radiated forehead, even darker than her dusky skin.

Next Maxie sorted through a collection of artificial eyelashes and selected a pair that was suitably entrancing, the lashes long and thick. While Maggie remained absorbed with watching the nuns press weights, Maxie adhered the new lashes to Maggie's eye-lids.

"Now bat your eyes for your Momma Maxie!"

The illusion was perfect; Maxie found herself melting as she had a half-century before—not that the passage of the years had much affected her own tibbetness.

Her fingernails had been cracked from the radiation and Maxie soon had these restored as well, plastering them over satisfactorily and topped with tiny almost invisible red triangles—one of the secret symbols of the Opus Dea Order.

"And your hair, dear one. Blond is good; yellow is golden; but let's restore your original indigo for now." Still entranced by the barely clad exercising nuns—and thus unusually cooperative—Maggie permitted herself to be escorted to the hair-dyeing table, where, with the aid of several more nuns, they soon had her fried hair entirely transformed, the new look embedded deep into her cells until at last, after toweling and drying, she once again stood before her Momma Maxie with cascading locks of indigo, as near as possible to her pre-radiation appearance as she could get, though the alter ego must always remain below the surface, only one splash of water away from coming back to the surface.

Except for the eyebrows—which no matter how the phalanx of nuns applied their cosmetic arts could not quite achieve their original natural look—Maxie's leetle Magdalene had come back.

Maxie stood and stared at Maggie, speechless. Despite the time-suspension inside the capsule, time had not entirely stood still, and Maxie—and the other nuns besides—could detect the first stirrings of adolescence in their adopted novice who had aroused such strong feelings throughout the Order, simultaneous of ardor and chagrin.

The machines paused as all the nuns stopped to stare.

Picking up her hand, Maxie caressed it. "You have come back to me," she whispered.

"I'm hungry. Where's my skates?"

"We'll get them soon, leetle beetle. But eet is time for your Momma Maxie to start a new Bowlarama on Wetland...urk, I mean, Earth. After all, Santa Lucia thee Holy Bowler did not send us to thees planet just to admire each other. We have a task to perform. I will get you what you want as soon as wee arrive at thee new Ranch."

Taking Maggie by the hand—and reluctant to release it in any circumstance—Maxie led her back to the automobile and, after a brief delay while the other nuns filled it with suitcases, supervised by Madam Melissa, who wore a temporary patch over one eye and who seemed peculiarly anxious to finish packing Maggie's belongings, the car pulled onto Tropicana Boulevard. With a final prayer flung at the nondescript façade of the local Unitarian Church with one of its symbols posted out front of a plastic bottle of water with a universal red ban sign through it—applied to the water even more than the plastic—they hit the road.

Two days later the automobile crossed the border from Oregon to Washington State with an energetic Maggie on skates pulling the tiny car by means of a rope, with minuscule Maxie steering, their luggage piled on top.

"Oh, that ees goood, my leetle beetle. The sun has set, so we can stop here at this motel so you can rest for the night."

"Thank you, Momma." Maggie continued rolling forward.

"You are not tired, my leetle one? You pulled us from the Portland bridge halfway to Kalama. You must sit and eat, my Maggie."

Maggie halted in the motel's parking lot. Dropping the rope, she sat to remove string and brush from her skate's rollers. She accepted a dish of nopalitos and downed them with half a bottle of Thunderbird as the shadows threw loops over the surrounding foothills, her delicious smacking resounding as if they were the only persons in the state.

"Momma, where are we?"

Maxie munched an extra nopalito and sampled the wine. "Why, on the road to Seattle, leetle dung beetle. But we will set up in Kalama. We have much work to do there."

"Which way is Kalama?"

"Why that way, of course." Maxie hesitated. "No, I meant that way." The sun was gone and darkness rapidly descending. It was no longer clear which way was west, or which road to take. The intersection opened on several roads, none of which had a sign.

"Oh, my, my, my. Maybe we should ask at the motel's front desk."

Maggie skated forward, again pulling the car with Maxie on top. They halted. The place was not a motel, but an old tourist cabin with a commissary attached—now empty. A 'Closed' sign hung on the door and the door was padlocked.

"Well, we can't go back, leetle one. The engine still won't start and you can't pull us all over Creation!"

"I'm hungry."

"Have more nopalitos, my Maggie. But don't eat them all at once. This is the last of them."

Snapping them up, Maggie promptly downed them

all. Then finished off the Thunderbird.

The shadows grew darker. "I think we should head this way, leetle one."

"I like this way better."

"That doesn't look right to me."

"I'm hot. This way is cool." Maggie rolled in a circle while they spoke.

"But we are helpless women, leetle one. What if we run into seenful men? We know what is always on their minds."

Maggie stopped skating. "I don't understand. Why are men so sinful, Momma? What is wrong with waa. . . with waat. . .?" Maggie shuddered, unable to say it.

"Because we cannot bowl in water, leetle one. Everyone knows that. Seenful men want water everywhere—all over the globe. But we must get rid of it if we want to bowl." Maggie shrugged and resumed skating, heading for the upward, cooler path.

Maxie held up her hands. "Stop pulling the car, Maggie dear. I must look at our map."

"I want to pull it, Momma Maxie. I get bored when I can't do something with my muscles. I feel good when I sweat."

"We nuns don't have muscles, leetle one. We have charms. And we don't sweat. We bouquet."

"Well, my charms are sweating and I think I should go faster or my bouquet may get a lot stronger."

"That is natural, my leetle one. Just throw on some more Nun Such perfume." Maxie dismounted, the better to examine a map by flashlight.

Taking the rope, Maggie skated slowly down the road, dragging the car up the slope, while Maxie trotted behind, shining the small flashlight on her map. They came to a scattering of trees that plunged them into almost complete darkness.

"Oh my, my, dear one. I think I see now where we went wrong. You should have turned here when you turned there. Kalama is behind us, while we are now in the hills with dark forests all around."

"You're stupid, Momma. I like the forests. I'm not so hot now."

A thump sounded.

"Momma?"

The car continued to rattle forward as Maggie pulled it up another slope only pausing when she reached the top of the gentle rise. Overhead, a dark circle blotted out a patch of stars, then vanished in a southeasterly direction.

Maggie turned. "Momma? Did you say something, Momma Maxie?" Peering behind her, Maggie saw nothing to indicate anyone standing in the road, but her eyes adjusted and finally lit on two dull objects lying prone.

She dropped the rope and skated back down the slope.

"Momma?"

One object groaned and slowly rolled over on its back. Its eyes flicked painfully open. It sighted Maggie. A hand lifted. "Help me. . . My parachute didn't open. Every bone in my body. . .broken."

Maggie stood and stared as if at a specimen in a zoo. "What are you?"

The hand raised again, but Maggie's gaze had moved to the other object. Limbs retracting into her spherical body like landing gear on a Cessna with all the extras, Maxie had seen her last climax. Her eyes were closed. No last words came forth to serve as her epitaph, the end, in the form of a seenful hijacker intent on lugging a bagful of heavy cash that crushed her triangular skull, had come too swiftly.

A tangle of emotions seized her leetle beetle. Once before she had believed she stood over Maxie's lifeless body, but had mercifully been mistaken. Now there was no doubt as to what had transpired. The ultimate event. The final denial. The watershed to what Santa Lucia the Holy Roller had decreed must be the rest of her life.

Maxie was dead.

She nudged her body with one foot. "Hey you," she mumbled. She kicked Maxie. "You're stupid." No response. "Momma Maxie. I'm tired. I want to rest now. Go get me some nopalitos and wine." Nothing. She kicked her again. "My hairdo is fading. I cracked my nail polish. It's your turn to pull."

Still nothing.

Searching her pockets, Maggie extracted another nopalito that Maxie had been concealing. She promptly ate it. "I feel better now, Maxie. I want more."

When no response was heard and another search yielded nothing more to eat or drink, Maggie returned her attention to the object that had fallen from the sky.

"Hey you. Why don't you get up?"

Again the eyes struggled open. "Dying. . .I won't make it. . ." The hand raised again. "See that bag?" Her eyes wandered to a bag that lay next to him. "Inside. . .two hundred thousand big ones! Two hundred grand! It's all yours! For just. . .just one drink of water from my water bottle. Right there."

The sloe eyes grew wide—Maggie lurched back as if struck. "Waa. . . waa. . ." She could not bring herself to pronounce the evil incantation, not after a lifetime of careful teachings by the stewards of the Back-To-Nature Wigwam warning her against the Universal Poison. The eternal threat to her and her kind. The ingredient that threatened to drown half the world and all its varied inhabitants.

"Sinful evil water man!" she shouted. "Drown in your own poison!" Snatching up the bottle, before she could stop herself she had unstopped the bottle and poured its entire contents on his evil masculine face before tossing it aside.

He slurped it up. "Thank you. . .thank you, dear girl. You have a kind heart after all. Take the money. It's yours. You deserve it." With a shudder, Dan Cooper died. His hand ceased moving, one finger pointing to his bag.

"Mon-ey?" she murmured to herself. Picking up

the bag, she peered inside and glimpsed stacks of bills neatly counted and tied with string, next to sheets of paper covered with numbers. “What’s money?”

Cracking twigs sounded beside her.

Turning, she had a single glance of a huge black face ringed with hair, then she was seized and flung over an enormous shoulder. In seconds, the creature was swinging its way through the forest propelling itself with ease, despite its new burden, from branch to branch till civilization had been left far behind and all Maggie knew was the entirely new sensation of helplessness, and a moist breath panting down her neck.

Episode 20

Making rapid time despite the burden draped over a mighty shoulder, the ape—if that is what it was—flung itself through the conifers as if following a well-marked path high above the forest ground that was visible only to itself. At times Maggie tensed an arm or a leg but the increase in strength which this evoked from the great beast instantly persuaded her not to contest her abduction.

At length the speed of the beast’s progress and the heart-stopping plunges through cool mountain air as it unerringly leaped from the seeming safety of one large branch into what seemed certain death only to land on another finally slowed and the beast, without emitting a word during the entire episode dropped from a branch to the floor of the forest.

Having coddled Maggie as if she were an infant during the carriage, the creature suddenly dumped her unceremoniously on hard ground strewn with pine needles, along with the bag of money. Around her were several lean-to's next to a wide carpet of smashed porcelain and glass.

"Hey," came a sharp voice from behind one of the lean-to's. A hairy face thrust around the corner to stare at the enormous beast. "Where's our stuff?" The hairy face split into a disapproving frown.

Maggie's abductor stood, uncertainly passing its gaze between Maggie and the hairy face watching them from the lean-to. Drawing himself up to his full eight-feet of height, he flexed massive chest muscles and threw out his hairy chin. "Cabin locked." He glanced at Maggie again. "Thor find girl. . .Thor bring girl back instead."

"Instead? *Instead*?! What the hell are we going to do with her? Does she cook? Does she clean?"

Maggie stood up and began brushing herself off, her youthful body exposed.

"Oh, no, no, no, no!" exclaimed the frowning face, catching sight of Maggie's breasts and smooth olive skin. "In case you've forgotten, Thor, you have a bond-Sasquatch to take care of—and a family of little Sasquatches!"

"Yeah? Well—well, *you're stupid*!"

"There you go again. Is that all you can say? '*You're stupid. You're stupid*'." The hairy face stood up and Maggie was surprised to see it rise to a height of seven feet with at least four hundred pounds. It brushed pine needles and leaves off its furry coat and stepped around a collection of intact white and pink porcelain knick-knacks and gew-gaws that it had carefully arranged around its primitive lean-to. "You were supposed to break the lock and get our stuff, totem-face! Oh, why didn't I listen to my mother in Anchorage when she told me I should wait and marry a Sasquatch who had finished bear-baiting school! But nooo. . . I was young and starry-eyed and couldn't wait. One trip through the tree-tops and all I could see was a handsome black face and gorgeous fur."

"MU'A!!"

"*What is it now, Nils?!*"

Two adjacent lean-to's began to shake as another deep voice bellowed through the woods. "Mu'a! Lars is stupid! He keeps trying to touch me!" A commotion raised dust and leaves in the air, then the lean-to collapsed and two giants stood up, one seven feet tall, the other almost eight. The larger passed his huge hands in the air over the slightly smaller one, equally hairy. "See, Mu'a? He's doing it again!"

"Stop it, Lars!" yelled Mu'a. "How many times have I told you? Don't touch your brother!"

"I'm not touching him, Mu'a!" yelled Lars. Turning to Nils he ran his hands even closer over the smaller ape's body. "I'm not touching you! I'm not touching you!" he taunted with a grin.

"Mu'a! He's not touching me! Make him stop!"

"I'm not touching you! Ha-ha!"

Thor grabbed them both and lifted each with one hand and shook them like rats, though each weighed at least five hundred pounds. "You're both stupid! Shut up!"

"You're stupid!" yelled Lars, kicking at Nils in mid-air.

"You're stupid!" yelled Nils, kicking at Lars.

Thor shook them again harder and dropped them to the ground. Thor picked up a wooden club.

"Oh, no," said Mu'a.

With wild swings, Thor smashed Mu'a's porcelain knick-knacks like a champion hitter, catching the last one in the air to knock it out of the park. The smashed fragments added to the growing debris field around the little camp of lean-to's.

"Oh, that's great. That's just great," said Mu'a. "Now I don't suppose you brought any knick-knacks back from the Ranger station to replace these, you big galoot? Now I've got nothing at all to show for my ten years in this dump you call a camp!"

"Bivouac. Thor make 'bivouac'! Thor keep telling Mu'a, Thor get medal in bivouacing from Sasquatch-scouts." He thrust out his chest.

"Medal in bivouacking! Big fucking deal! If only I had a stick for every time you've said that, I could have built my own log cabin by now. You and your

Sasquatch-scouts. Ya big ape!" She scraped the ground with a paw in irritation. "When are we gonna shake this scene and find some real shelter?"

"Yeah? Well. . .well, *you're stupid*!" Thor rumbled.

Mu'a rolled her eyes.

Maggie took off her skates and stood, stretching her thighs which had never known the touch of a razor, but which were naturally almost devoid of hair. Thor caught sight of Maggie's unshaven armpits and a wistful look came over him.

"Well, stupid?" demanded Mu'a.

"Well, what?" Thor looked at his bond-Sasquatch, the magic moment vanishing.

"How about the wine? Did you bring the wine?"

Maggie stretched and Thor was again distracted. "What wine?"

"The wine you went to get, moron! And the food! From the Ranger's Hut. Remember? You chased the Rangers away last month so you could raid their dumpster in peace, and you just went there to get the loot!"

"Uh. . .Ranger door locked." Thor continued to eye Maggie, and stood motionless like he didn't know what to do with his hands.

"Locked?" yelled Mu'a, hands on hips in accusation. "Well, of course it was locked, ya big ape! You think the Rangers will just walk away from the place? Of course they locked it! You were supposed to break the lock and go inside."

"Oh yeah. . .Thor forget," he said, his eyes still on

Maggie.

Mu'a reached into her lean-to and pulled out what looked like an enormous bear rug. Shaking it, the rug was revealed to have two arms and two legs. Grasping a metal tag, she unzipped it. "Here I go again. Send a Sasquatch to do the job of a Sasquatchette and see what happens. I just have to do it all over again." Stepping into the suit, she zipped it up.

Thor looked unhappy. "Mu'a, you make Thor look like fool in front of guest."

"If she's half as smart as you, then she's smart enough to see who's stupid—and who's not."

Thor's brows contracted as he tried to puzzle this out.

"I know, Thor. '*You're stupid*'," Mu'a wisecracked.

Thor brightened. "Yeah! Stupid!"

Mu'a finished zipping up the ape-suit.

Maggie spoke up. "You're hairy. Why wear a hairy suit?"

"So when the humans see us," replied Mu'a, "they'll think we're humans in ape suits and not bother us. It never occurs to them that it may be an ape in an ape suit."

"They're stupid," suggested Thor.

Mu'a picked up two flat wooden boards with huge foot-shaped lumps underneath and strapped them to her ape feet. "And when we wear these flip-flops, we leave behind sasquatch tracks so humans will think they're made by other humans trying to trick them. It never occurs to them that the footprints could be made by real Sasquatches using wooden shoes to throw them off the track."

Maggie's brows contracted as she tried to puzzle this out. Finally she said, "That's stupid."

Thor looked at Maggie and stars glinted in his eyes again.

Mu'a finished adjusting her ape-suit. "I can see which way the wind blows. Come on, totem-face. I'm not doing this alone, and I'm sure the hell not leaving you alone here with this little Lolita! You're coming with me."

"Mu'a!" came a higher voice, more feminine. "*He* made too much noise. I can't sleep anymore if *he* keeps making noise." A leg extruded from behind another lean-to. Another Sasquatch stood and stretched, smaller and more slender than the others, and pointed an accusing finger at Thor.

"That's your father, Gilda. You know he has to throw branches and break things once in a while just to prove he's a Sasquatch. Who knows what might happen if he didn't smash something every few days." Her eyes wandered to the vast field of smashed porcelain that surrounded the 'bivouac'. "The world might come to an end."

Maggie's jaw dropped as she saw the latest member of the Sasquatch family. The young Sasquatch girl was at least six feet tall and three hundred pounds of muscle, with markedly less hair on her legs and face than the others, and graced with humanoid breasts and enormous flexing biceps. Maggie could not take her eyes off her.

Mu'a took in the situation immediately. "Well, I guess that settles which side of the pine-cone has the maple syrup in this situation. Serves you right, Thor. Looks like you're gonna keep climbing the same Mount Rainier till the end of your days."

Dropping his chin to his chest again, Thor slowly trudged to his own lean-to and extracted another, larger gorilla suit. Once he zipped it up and strapped on his own Bigfoot shoes, he and Mu'a—after she donned her best forest specialty horn-rim glasses—turned toward the forest in the direction of the Ranger station, Mu'a being dead-set and determined not to miss out on the family essentials that she hoped still lurked in the locked-up commissary.

Unable to roll across dirt, Maggie removed her skates.

Mu'a and Thor paused as Nils grabbed one skate and sniffed the rollers. "What this?" Nils rumbled.

Maggie snatched it back. "You're stupid!" she yelled.

Lars grabbed a handful of cash from Maggie's knapsack. "Pretty leaves!" With a hoot, he ran off through the forest.

"Not fair!" yelled Maggie. Grabbing the wooden club, she proceeded to smash the porcelain as Thor had just done, breaking up a few sticks and empty wine bottles for good measure. Lars emerged from behind a tree and, empty-handed, retreated to the far side of the clearing where he sought refuge behind

Nils, both of them staring at Maggie with a mixture of respect and fear while Gilda suppressed a yawn.

Thor's jaw dropped as his heart skipped a beat, his eyes again glued to Maggie's armpits.

Mu'a pulled Thor's ear to return his attention to the task at hand. "Sasquatch children, keep an eye on our young guest. Don't let her leave. We may be able to trade her for a case of Thunderbird. Clearly she belongs to the Cascade Sasquatches and wandered away from California on those funny shoes of hers. No way is she a local girl."

"Yeeees, Muu'aaaa," recited three bored voices.

The next day Mu'a and Thor returned bearing several large cases and two casks and a plastic bag full of porcelain knick-knacks carefully wrapped in issues of *Ranger Rick's Sasquatch Times*. Setting them down in the clearing, and divesting themselves of the ape suits, they proceeded to teach Nils and Lars how to rebuild their lean-to's, a task that—after multiple attempts—ended the same as always, with Thor himself building them, followed by instant collapse, and Mu'a finally completing the projects by herself.

Thor looked at the nearest cask.

"This time don't—"

Thor's hammer-hand plunged through the top, splintering half the cask and spilling its pickled contents on the ground as Mu'a rolled her eyes.

"Nopalitos!" cried Gilda, attracting a wan smile from Maggie, who was not loath to jump in to grab her share. As the two giant youths closed in, they failed to see the finger darting in their direction.

"Owwww!" howled Nils and Lars, each clutching an eye.

With great care, Maggie collected her share of the nopalitos and handed some to Gilda. "They're stupid. You're not."

A grunt answered as Gilda deftly swallowed all that Maggie handed her. "Mmmm. Maggie. You're good."

"Muu'aa!" yelled the boys.

"Shut up and drink your Thunderbird," Mu'a answered, preoccupied with downing her own share of nopalitos and draining one of the bottles.

Thor smiled at Maggie, his own heart still skipping beats each time he stared at their young nubile guest.

Succeeding in starting a fire, Mu'a placed a metal frame over it and Thor tossed several nopalitos on top for frying. Soon a merry crackling resounded through the trashed-out 'bivouac'.

Mu'a settled back to read the *Sasquatch Times* while Thor held another copy upside-down, pretending to read, ignored by Mu'a. The boys ran through the woods, shoving and punching each other, while Gilda polished off her own bottle of Thunderbird under the admiring gaze of Maggie, who stared at Gilda over her own copy of the Times—also upside-down.

The nopalitos being rapidly consumed, and several bottles of wine finished off, Mu'a spoke. "How much do you think the Cascade Clan will pay to get her back?" Something seemed to weigh on Mu'a's mind. "One case?"

Thor shrugged. "Not one case. Maybe half."

"Yeah, you would say that, Romeo!" She snorted. "Well, think again! We're getting rid of her, so wise up. I'm thinking at least one case, and maybe two. That's enough to last me the winter." Mu'a sipped another bottle.

His eyes wandering to Maggie's dark skin again, despite his efforts to direct his gaze elsewhere, Thor watched as Maggie reached for her own bottle of wine, and, as he and Mu'a stared, Maggie drained it faster than any member of the family and tossed it next to an empty, before launching on a third bottle. Maggie let loose a loud burp.

Mu'a's jaw dropped as the smitten look came over Thor again. "At this rate, we'll run out of cactus and Thunderbird before the first snow falls."

"Did you say something, dear?" Thor asked Mu'a while staring dreamily at Maggie.

Mu'a tapped one foot impatiently. "I said: I'm thinking there may be a badger in the basement."

Six months later, and despite multiple trips to every Ranger station and convenience store in a fifty-mile radius, the larder was still no fuller than when Maggie first arrived. The store of nopalitos never seemed to grow larger, even though Nils and Lars had made several trips to drier areas down south to retrieve the wild prickly variety for Mu'a to fry on the barbie, and inevitably smacking each other without restraint so that they returned with half the cacti stuck in their fur, and the cases of wine consistently disappeared as fast as new cases arrived.

Maggie taught Gilda to skate and for a time the two zipped each day on mountain roads, each sailing along on one skate only, taking care to always wear their gorilla suits to throw off inquisitive humans, who would often stop to take videos and jabber in excitement, but never do anything more, since it was plainly people in ape suits, but eager not to interfere just in case it really was Sasquatches in their natural habitat. And once Maggie overheated and divested herself of her ape-suit, only to evoke even more excitement from ogling tourists.

"You're stupid!" she yelled, skating on one skate alongside Gilda and tossing a few bricks through back car windows.

Months more went by and finally Maggie accompanied Thor and Mu'a on one of their expeditions where she found a new set of skates. Thereafter, she and Gilda no longer had to share a single pair but could make time side by side.

"Thor, I think we may have a problem," ventured Mu'a one day.

"Thor knows what is Thor's problem. But what is Mu'a's?" replied Thor, staring dreamily again at Maggie as she stretched her legs and lashed her skates.

"Our stores never grow. In fact, they're shrinking. I'm tired of trudging all over Mount St. Helens raiding human camp sites for wine and sending our genius sons to California for more and more cactus. I'm starting to wonder Who is supporting who here?"

"Thor know Maggie carrying her weight in different way. Mu'a notice that Thor no longer need steal special pills from humans to climb Mount Rainier twice a week?"

Mu'a reflected, a smile crossing her face. "Yes, my monster truck. I have noticed. But I don't think we can go on like this." She frowned. "After hearing about Maggie's appetite from our boys, the Cascade Sasquatches refused to ransom her. Now they say she doesn't belong to them."

"Maybe we keep her after all," suggested Thor, all sorts of possibilities presenting themselves to his hormone addled brain.

"Nothing doing, galoot! I'm thinking that we may have to lower our price to half a case before something bad happens."

"That may not work, dear one."

"Why not?"

"Thor not sure Cascade Sasquatches will like someone who slips mickey into teenage girl's wine."

As they watched, Maggie opened a prescription bottle of Xanex and dumped half the contents into Gilda's bottle of Thunderbird.

"Thor may have to build wigwam soon just for those two."

"Hmmm," objected Mu'a.

More months passed and Thor thought he saw his chance. Maggie and Gilda had been skating the environs of Mount St. Helens, flicking the finger at annoying tourists who alternately laughed at Gilda's ape suit while eagerly filming the unmistakable smaller Sasquatch skating beside her, and they arrived back at the camp-site ready to fill up on grilled cactus and yet another toast of cheap wine to the cause of inter-species peace, and, after the evening's usual festivities, they lay down to sleep, for once Maggie and Gilda actually sleeping in different lean-to's.

Thor, however, had something special in mind. Reaching into his lean-to, he pulled out the latest prize that his far-ranging raids had yielded and—casting one last surreptitious glance at Mu'a's sleeping seven-foot form that snorted on cue with her usual apnea—decided to finally go for broke. *I can't stands no more*, he thought to himself.

Maggie was not yet asleep, but had lain down under her own lean-to where she could keep Gilda's wonderfully developed form in view throughout the night. A small bottle that Maggie had filled with Thunderbird served as ersatz perfume, which she had taken care to splash all over her body to avoid excessive 'bouquet'.

Her eyes slowly shut.

A rustle brought them open.

Nothing small could have made the noise and Maggie found, despite the tranquility of her extended stay with her hosts, that the ubiquitous menace lurked here as well. Instantly she was alert.

Sure enough an enormous black face hesitantly peered into her lean-to. Thor was on all fours.

"Mmmaggie," he pronounced her name with difficulty.

She sat up with a jerk.

Pointing to her chest, then to his, he hoarsely grunted, "Little Sasquatch. . . Big Sasquatch. . ."

Maggie's eyes instinctively gazed apprehensively toward Mu'a's lean-to.

Thor briefly recoiled. "Bond-Sasquatch no understand Thor. Maybe Maggie understand Thor."

She pulled herself back and drew one leg beneath her. The moon was full on both her breasts, and on both their faces.

"Look. Thor bring Little Sasquatch gift! Something very rare. Better than wife...sorry, that Freudian slip—Thor meant: better than 'wine'."

Maggie's eyebrows arched inward. She frowned. *What could be better than life-giving wine*?

Bringing one hand out from behind his back, he clutched a huge bottle of something labeled with blue waves and he popped off the top. "This good, huh? No need for perfume if Little Sasquatch put this on her beautiful body."

"Eeeech!"

Thor dropped the bottle to block Maggie's scream echoing in his ears.

Snapping it up, Maggie jumped to her feet. Standing, she held the bottle over Thor's head while the water gushed forth. "Evil water Sasquatch! Drown in your sinful liquid! You will never touch me with your evil sinfulness!"

Wiping the water from his eyes, Thor sat watching cross-legged as Maggie grabbed a wooden club and attacked every lean-to in the camp, smashing every stick and scattering every thatched roof of branches and pine-needles, next going after Mu'a's latest accumulation of porcelain knick-knacks, and finishing by annihilating every empty wine bottle she could find.

As the camp's habitants rose in unison to watch by the light of the full moon, Maggie threw herself down on her knees and offered a prayer.

"Our Mother, baked in heaven, Jessie be thy name, thy kitchen come, thy cooking be done in ovens as it is in leaven. Give us this day our daily bread, and forgive us our recipes as we forgive those whose recipes took us; and lead us not into conception; but deliver us from the plots of sinful evil watermen."

Standing, she continued to pray. "Hail Mary, baked with steaks, the Lord is thy recipe, blessed are you by women, and blessed is the fruit of thy loon, Jessie Christina. Holy Mary, Mother of Virgins, pray for us folksingers, now and at the happy altar hour of nopalitos and wine, the flesh and blood of Santa Lucia the Holy Bowler of the Third Secret of Fatima, amen!"

"Yep," said Mu'a, rubbing the sleep from her eyes.

"I knew it. I wonder how many cases of Thunderbird it will cost us for the Cascade Sasquatches to take this bitch off our hands?" She counted three cases behind the bivouac. "Nils and Lars. Bring them all. We'll have to bribe them with everything we have. Beggars can't be choosers."

Episode 21

"Did I tell ya, Ray? Or did I tell ya?"

Ray looked through the binoculars for another long moment and slowly nodded. "You said it. And god-damtohell if you weren't right!" He paused to rub his eyes and peer again. "I see one, two, three, four, five. . .and six. Just like you said." Grinning, he put the binoculars down. "Man, we're home free, Bobby!"

"Fuckin A!" Bobby stared down the ridge at the meadow where the little family walked in single file following the forest trail. He took a deep breath. "Ya know what this means?"

"We're the first! Ain't no one else done what we're about to do. Just think! Alive! And in the flesh!"

"Yeah! Here I come, Las Vegas! It's fun and games for me for the rest of my natural-born life. What about you, Ray? What are you gonna do with your share of the ree-ward money?"

"Sit on my ass and watch it grow. That's what I'm gonna do!"

Both cackled with joy. Hooking elbows, they

danced a jig.

"Enough for now, Bobby. I know exactly what trail they're on, so let's get moving. There's no time to waste."

"Yowza, *mon frere*."

On the trail below, Thor led the way—his great height magnified by the gorilla suit that he always wore when on the move—followed by the smaller Gilda. Maggie strode behind Gilda, with Nils and Lars next, Mu'a bringing up the rear, more to keep the dunce twins from straying than to prevent any escape by Maggie, who was never to be found far from the object of her admiration in any event. Maggie alone was not burdened by ape camouflage and fake Sasquatch shoes. Thor and Gilda and Maggie did not carry cases of wine, but the latter two, eager not to miss any opportunity to skate, each carried roller skates over a shoulder as they trudged through the forest brush in special Dutch-boy versions of Sasquatch wooden shoes.

Leaving the open meadow, which aroused a certain nervousness in Thor, they penetrated the next copse of trees, the trail narrowing as they picked their way through the dense underbrush. Another quarter-mile and another open meadow yawned before them. The little Sasquatch family paused before stepping clear of their cover. Not for nothing had they succeeded in avoiding discovery all these years in the Pacific Northwest. Camouflage was good, but was not all. Caution helped—and no little fear of anything remotely out of the ordinary in the landscape.

They well knew their scarcity. As they knew from the Cascade grapevine that a huge reward lay over the heads of each and every Sasquatch that still survived in North America, leading packs of humans to hunt them every spring. If it weren't for plentiful crops of cactus and swarms of drunken vagrants clutching bottles of red Thunderbird stumbling into the hills in increasing numbers from California, the Sasquatch clans would all have starved eons ago. If not for the fact that the Sasquatches were vegetarian, the vagrants would have presented a perfect and limitless food source. Not to deny certain rumors. . .

Thor still hesitated. There was something about the trail as it crossed the meadow from Oregon to California that spooked him. It was too straight; too clean. The dunce twins had just come this way, more than once in recent months, so the trail should be flatter, with broken sticks scattered about. It was almost as if someone had spruced it up. Even the spruces were spruced.

Thor glanced at the sky where the sun had crossed and was now plummeting to the west. They didn't have all day. He stepped into the meadow, keeping one eye on the dense growth of trees at the far side. Half way across he turned and gave the okay sign to the others.

They stepped out—then froze.

A fence leaped out of the grass. Throwing leaves and dirt in the air, it enclosed Thor on three sides, the fourth offering the only hope of escape—into the back of a huge truck whose container was large enough to hold several Sasquatches, windowless, and equipped with solid doors with unbreakable metal bars to lock them in.

"Thor!" wailed Mu'a. "What have they done to you!" The others stood under the protecting shade of the first thicket, watching helplessly.

A figure in faux-camouflage stepped into the open, duck hat on his head, antique rifle in one hand. From the truck stepped a second figure. The first clutched his hat and smacked the second with it.

"Goddamit, Bobby! Whatja get that one fer?"

"Sorry, Ray. I got a itchy trigger finger."

Together they laid the fence back down again and proceeded to cover it up with leaves again. "Go on, ya damn fool! And if you mess up our trap again, we'll kick your goddam ass! That's what we'll do!"

"That's tellin him, Ray. Can you imagine the nerve of these Bigfoot impersonators runnin all over the goddam hills, tryin to trick legit trappers!" He looked at Thor. "Go on, we said! Take your goddam monkey suit and get the hell outta here before we call the park police!"

Without a sound, Thor turned and bolted for the thicket where he rejoined his family, the troop standing in shadow while they recovered their breath.

Ray threw Thor's fake Bigfeet after him. "And don't forget your goddam wooden shoes, ya faker!"

"Yeah, ya faker!" called Bobby as he finished laying the trap again.

The shoes fell halfway between them and the thicket, and Gilda rushed forward in an effort to help without putting Thor in danger. Retrieving the flat wooden shoes, her skates draped over one shoulder and her Dutch-boy loafers made her lose her balance.

She fell forward.

With a snap, the trap sprang, the fence rushing into the air.

Ray and Bobby jumped out. "What the goddamhell? What's wrong with you people? Can't you take a hint!" With some effort, they lowered the fence a second time. "Get lost, fakers! Stop messin with our Sasquatch traps!"

Gilda ran back to the cover of the thicket where Thor embraced her in relief.

The trap was set again and Ray and Bobby glared at the thicket full of fakers while they worked. *Of all the nerve. . .* Finally they were done and they turned to seek cover.

"Tag! You're it!" Lars shoved Nils and bolted into the meadow carrying a case of Thunderbird.

"Not fair, big, dumb and hairy! I'll get you back!" Nils sprinted after Lars, their giant strap-on wooden feet leaving gangantuan Bigfoot impressions all over the meadow. They both tripped the fence at the same time, sending their cases of wine rolling into the back of the truck where some bottles cracked and began to leak puddles of red on the floor.

"Oh no!" shouted Ray and Bobby together. "That's it! Goddamit! I'm callin the goddam park rangers! You fakers have messed with us for the last goddam time! I'll sue your asses, that's what I'll do!"

Once more Ray and Bobby lowered the fence, this time pointing their hunting rifles at the offenders, Thor and Mu'a in the thicket, their hands over their mouths, their hearts trying to leap out of their bodies.

The fence was again flattened. Ray kicked a pile of leaves at the two youngsters, sending them scampering back to the woods. "And don't come back!" Turning to their trap, the two hillbillies dug in the dirt muttering under their breath as they again covered up the fence, and failed to notice as yet another figure strode out of the shelter of the woods. Without wavering, it entered the back of the truck.

Skates over one shoulder and her knapsack of cash over the other—less the $5,800 that Lars had stolen and lost—Maggie fell down on her knees and began to lap up the growing pool of Thunderbird wine.

Ray looked up.

Fearing to move a muscle, he slowly touched Bobby—he pointed. Bobby caught his breath. Slowly—with infinite caution—the two sneaked clear of the fence, one on either side of the truck, flanking its back entrance, Maggie still inside.

Sprang!

The fence leaped to full height once again.

"Hallelujah!" howled Ray.

"We got it," cheered Bobby. "I told ya those bastards had a real Sasquatch with em—and here it is!"

"Yahoo!" they crowed together. "We're rich! We not only caught a Bigfoot; we're gonna bring it back alive! The ree-ward is ours!"

Dancing around the back of the truck, they slammed it shut, Maggie watching casually as the doors closed and the metal bars locked in place, her skates still slung over her shoulder, all the Thunderbird wine she could ever desire stacked at her side. Somewhere in the shadows covering her erstwhile family, stood Gilda. A tear formed in Maggie's eye. Years had passed since she had been abducted in the forests of Washington, and her time with Gilda had been precious.

But what was done was done.

The page had turned.

As the truck rattled over mountain paths and rock-strewn roads back toward civilization, she broke open the nearest case and popped a bottle. Mouthing a silent prayer to Santa Lucia the Holy Bowler, she chugged half its contents and wiped her mouth with a burp. She really must find another habit for her hair.

The rock-strewn roads eventually smoothed and as the hours rolled by, the truck picked up speed and before long the sound of trucks and other traffic began penetrating the walls. The honks grew louder and the air grew warmer and finally Maggie was forced to conclude they had entered a big city, the constant stops and starts jiggling her fulsome breasts without respite.

More hours passed. The cage in which she was imprisoned turned this way, then that, lurched forward, or jerked to sudden stops only to resume its progress toward the Great Unknown. At last it pulled up an incline and Maggie thought she heard an outside grate like a warehouse door slam shut behind the truck. Cooler air seeped in from the cage's seams.

Silence.

Suddenly the metal rods holding the back double doors scraped free and the doors burst open. Maggie glimpsed a warehouse lined with clerestory windows that revealed academic-type buildings through the panes, visible on one building a run-down sign in large letters that read 'UCLA Backlot Service'. But her attention was promptly drawn to her captors, Ray and Bobby, who, despite the warm urban environment, had exchanged their camo for red plaid coats and green caps with Elmer Fudd ear muffs. Ray held a whip and a chair. Bobby a wire mesh large enough to drop a noose around a galloping rhino. They were taking no chances. Pointing their instruments at Maggie, they thrust and hooted.

"Git along little Bigfoot!"

"Haw! That's a good 'un, Bobby. Ain't nothin little bout this Sasquatch, though. It's built like a tank."

"Hot damn! We did it, Ray! We got ourselves a live one! Las Vegas, here I come!"

"I wonder how long it'll take to get that *ree*-ward

money?"

"As long as it's on the way, Ray. . .as long as it's on the way. Now come down gentle like, Little Miss Bigfoot! Just step down from the back of our truck and put that Sasquatch neck of yours in this here noose so we can put you inside that there cage."

Maggie stepped down. In one corner of the warehouse was a wire cage on a wagon, and, ready to pull it, a motorized lawnmower with a seat.

From behind the truck appeared two men in brown uniforms with tags that said 'UCLA Zoology'. One of them took the wire mesh with the noose and tried to swing it over Maggie's head. The noose came loose and dropped on the floor of the warehouse.

Ignoring him, Maggie climbed back into the truck.

"What's it doin?" said Ray, breaking into a nervous sweat.

One of the zoology assistants re-strung the noose, also nervous. "Wild animals are the most dangerous when cornered. We've got to get it under control before it tries to kill us."

Bobby and Ray exchanged worried glances.

Emerging from the truck, Maggie dragged the two cases of wine. From the torn case, she pulled out another bottle of Thunderbird and popped it open. Sitting on the edge of the truck she gurgled half the bottle, re-closed the cap, then stood and shrugged the skates off her shoulder. Kicking off her Dutch-boy wooden shoes, Maggie began to put on her skates.

"What do we do, Ralph? It won't put the noose

on." The assistant's hands shook as he held the noose up. He glanced around as if looking for reinforcements.

Maggie finished tying the laces on one skate.

"Look out!" yelled Ray, retreating behind the assistant. "I think it's about to go berserk!"

Maggie calmly tied the other. She stood.

"It's gettin ready to attack!" Ralph grabbed one of the chairs for self-defense. "I didn't sign up for this, Albert! I got eight kids at home!"

Maggie stood and pirouetted in place like a Schwarzenegger at a Bolshoi Ballet, her knapsack on her back.

"Maybe. . .uh, maybe we can lure it into the cage by putting one of those wine cases inside. It worked well enough to get it inside the truck when we were in the Sierras." Ray pointed at the cases perched on the edge of the truck's loading platform.

Maggie began to skate. Arcing between the truck and the wagon with the cage, she noticed that the warehouse gate was locked. Drifting in a circle around the truck, she sighted another door at the far end, but it too was closed and locked. *How to exit*?

Picking up speed, she darted toward the men—they scrambled in terror behind the wagon. She scraped to a full stop. They refused to move thereafter, and she stood and thought. Finally, she returned to the truck. Lifting one case of Thunderbird wine, she placed it on the wagon. Then she climbed inside the cage.

"Yahoo! We did it!" Ray and Bobby jumped for joy. In another moment, they had hooked the cage door shut with Maggie inside. Slapping a sign on the cage that read: 'Caution: Wild Sasquatch', Ralph gunned the lawnmower's engine while Albert wiped the sweat from his brow. Producing a gate opener, Albert clicked it and the warehouse gate raised, and the lawnmower raced through at a blazing three miles an hour while Maggie helped herself to the second half of her latest bottle. *Only way to get this circus moving.*

Academic halls loomed and dwindled as the parade rolled across the UCLA campus, brown-shirted Ralph tense but steering, Albert panting to keep up though keeping well clear of the dangerous beast ("I've got eleven kids at home!"), and Elmer Fudd and his twin so busy counting the dollar signs in their eyes that they walked into poles more than once. The many departments of UCLA scholarship inched past: the Institute for the Suppression of Evil Patriarchy and Other Naughtiness; the Department of Non-Earth-Raping Economics; the huge concrete building housing the vast Cooperative of Feminist Earth-Mothers Against Earth-Raping Concrete-Laying Developers; the Department of Film For Smashing Nazi Earth-Rapers with English Accents; the Gay Atheist Non-Judgmental Nature Coalition to Stop Patriarchal Oppression of Feminist Opposition to Earth-Raping Patriarchy; the Department of Gay Non-Earth-Raping Feminist Natural Studies; the brand spanking new UCLA Fuck in the Backside Institute—not Ya Egger Hooper's, but a different one; the Back-To-Nature All-Natural Wigwam for the Promotion of Zero Children Through Artificial Retroactive Non-Reproduction (holding several mean-looking pens topped with barbed wire with several raggedy children inside and a sign reading 'Daycare Macht Frei' overhead); and finally the UCLA Diversity & Free Speech Institute for the Suppression of Non-Conforming Expression and Other Very Very Bad Things.

"Ralph!"

"Yeah, Albert?"

"We're startin to attract a crowd—"

Behind the wagon with its sole inhabitant was a string of students who, as the lawnmower slowly progressed, were becoming more and more excited, jabbering with each other in increasingly angry tones. Signs appeared: "Free the Sasquatch One", "Stop Patriarchal Oppression of Sasquatch Women", and "Abolish Campus Rape of Sasquatches."

"I think maybe you should step on it, Ralph. Things are gettin ugly."

Ralph put pedal to the metal and kicked up the speed to four miles per hour. To his relief, they finally rolled into the basement of the building that housed the Department of Feminist Anti-Earth-Raping Zoology, and the Department of Non-Patriarchal Fair Trade Astronomy, and Albert shut the demonstrators out, the Fudd twins managing to jump through the closing doors to join them at the last moment.

"Whew!" said Ralph as he locked the basement doors. Grabbing a plastic bottle of water, he calmed himself with a large gulp.

"You said it!" whimpered Ray. "I had no idea that Sasquatches were so popular in these here parts. I could've sworn that we discovered the very first one!"

"You did," said Ralph. "But Sasquatches don't mean squat. Let's get upstairs. I know the Professor in charge of the Sasquatch Project. The sooner we can hand this thing over to him, the better."

They stood and stared at Maggie.

No one moved.

"How do we get her in there? She's stuck in this cage."

"Well, the wine has worked purty well so far. We may as well try it again. But it's inside the cage—with her!"

Casually, Maggie reached through the cage herself and unhooked the hook that was keeping the cage door shut. She stepped out. Stretching her legs, she swiveled in place again, her skates rolling on the inlaid wood floor like muffled thunder.

"Bring out the wine, you two, quick!"

Reaching cautiously inside the cage, Ralph and Albert pulled the case toward them. They reached inside and extracted two more bottles of Thunderbird—the last of the bottles inside the case.

Waving them in the air to attract Maggie's attention like carrots before a mule, they walked up the concrete incline that led to the academic departments.

Maggie skated after.

"It's working!" With Ralph and Albert backing down the hallway waving the bottles of Thunderbird Red in front of Maggie and the Fudd twins in green plaid flannel bringing up the rear brandishing nooses and chairs, and Maggie skating nonchalantly in between, they trotted past a series of open doors where female professors and female grad students stared in surprise, their jaws dropping, until they finally arrived at a small nondescript office where a wizened man in his seventies sat with his back turned, absorbed in some number-crunching routine that flashed on his desktop computer, the last male professor to still teach in the building, a last relic of a bygone age.

"Here she is, Doc!" exclaimed Ray, standing way too close to Maggie for his own comfort. "What did I tell ya? Is this the real thing, or is this the real thing?" He immediately backed up, giving Maggie plenty of room. No sense in making it easier for an animal that might go berserk and kill him.

The man turned. He slowly stood. His white hair was unkempt and he reached for bifocals and placed them on his nose. Gradually his eyes focused on the Sasquatch.

He stopped breathing.

"Doc. . . You all right, Doc?"

He began to tremble.

The men stared at each other, their concern growing. "Is somethin wrong, Doc?"

Raising one hand, he motioned the men out of the office. "Step back—step back please, gentlemen. . . If you please, all of you stand in the hall. Let the. . .*creature*. . .come forward."

Maggie skated into the Professor's office.

He glanced her up. Then down. His gaze flicked to his watch as if reassuring himself of the date—or his sanity. Taking a deep breath, he sighed.

"Welcome back, Maggie."

She cocked her head and peered closer. From somewhere an ancient memory stirred, through fifty years of entombment in a dark life-restoring capsule and years more in a dense Washington forest, a memory of a twelve-year-old boy and a tall peak called Stirling, and an observatory that registered strange astronomical events all the way to Pluto.

"You're stupid."

"Takes one to know one."

Both smiled.

"Hey You. You got any more nopalitos? I'm hungry."

Dr. Richard Pierson broke into a grand smile. The Professor popped open a jar of pickled nopalitos that stayed always on his desk. "All you can eat, Maggie. All you can ever eat!"

She dove in.

He glanced at his computer where an image of

Pluto filled the screen. "Boy, have I got a story for you—"

A commotion in the hallway interrupted. Pushing their way into the building from either direction, a crowd of protesters shouted and waved a new crop of signs, soon joined by the other professors who had witnessed Maggie's parade down the hallway and now rushed to intervene.

"Free the Sasquatch One!" shouted a chorus of voices, a phalanx of angry women's faces thrusting into the office, shoving the two brown-shirted zoological assistants aside and pummeling the Elmer Fudd twins who from their tartan clothes clearly lacked social consciousness.

"Stop Sasquatch rape! Free Your Sasquatch Sisters!" yelled more, followed by: "No blood-money for Sasquatch hunters!" This last upset the Fudd twins the most, and when a clutch of cross-dressers jumped into the mix, thrusting their signs into the hillbillies' faces: 'Abolish Patriarchal Oppression of Gay Sasquatches!' and 'P.E.T.A. for Bigfoot Liberation'!" Ray and Bobby retreated down the hall and fled.

One of the protesters' signs tipped over the jar of nopalitos. It broke on the floor, and, as Maggie jerked back, Ralph's plastic bottle of water splashed her leg.

In one corner of Pierson's office leaned a baseball bat signed by Joe DiMaggio—before he mysteriously disappeared. Maggie snatched it up and let loose smashing everything in sight: Richard's desk; his collection of porcelain knick-knacks; his number-crunching computer screen; the overhead flourescents; his antique model planetarium; and the protesters' signs, all disintegrating under her relentless assault. She moved to the hallway where more flourescents shattered, followed by academic awards hanging on the walls.

"Sinful evil water men!" shouted Maggie. "Not fair! You'll never drown the Earth with your global warming!"

"Hooray!" ballyhooed the protesters, entranced by the unexpected fact that their Sasquatch Sister could speak, and even more so by the fact that she had stated their views as well as any of them. Following her example, Professors and students grabbed whatever they could lay their hands on and joined her in smashing anything that remained unbroken in the hallway.

Finally, their energy expended, they tossed aside their clubs and the torn remnants of their signs, and they lifted Maggie on their shoulders and paraded her outside—a long-lost Sister at last come home—and she finally relinquished her own lethal instrument.

A delegation of Professors rushed to support their newly discovered Sister from a different species, gushing words of encouragement, and triggering the instant formation of a brand new and totally uniquely named Inter-Species Department of Diverse Gay

Feminists to Abolish Patriarchal Earth-Raping and Sasquatch Oppression. Several elbowed forward to her side, bearing plaques and hastily inscribed certificates.

"Maggie, Ambassador from Sasquatchia!" they shouted while the crowd of feminist professors and graduate students beamed. "We have the great honor of awarding you an honorary Doctor of Philosophy from our very own UCLA due to your life experience as an oppressed Sister-Species. Money and lifetime tenure come with this award. You can start teaching classes any time you want. And in case you need them, here's your immigration papers, already approved, since you are now a scholar of the highest order with a Ph.D. from our very own University of California."

Maggie shrugged. She had only recently passed puberty while in the forests of Washington, and she held the certificate upside-down while her gaze wandered over the funny little bugs that refused to stay still on the paper. True, there had been that long episode inside a darkened tube, about which she recalled almost nothing. *I suppose that was experience of a sort*, she reflected, *but what does 'teach' mean? And what is a 'skahler'? And what the heck is a 'docker of rosofy'? Is a 'ucla' as good to eat as a nopalito?*

The professor with the loudest voice produced a huge wad of cash. "There's lots of government money for Sisters like you. This should get you started." She shoveled an enormous stack of freshly minted hundred dollar bills at Maggie.

There's that word 'mon-ey' again! I think that means more nopalitos and wine. And maybe skates too. Maggie smiled and stuffed the huge stack of hundreds into her knapsack along with her already large collection of 'pretty leaves'.

"Hooray!" the crowd screamed with wild abandon, tossing acorns and twigs and other markers of Sacred Earth into the air, and again they propped Maggie on their shoulders—though they soon were forced to put her down again given her muscular development and weight. In time they extracted from her a limp promise to 'teach' and the crowd drifted away.

Maggie halted in surprise as yet another delegation appeared out of the blue. For a moment, she had to blink and search long-dormant memory banks, past acres of green pine needles and an ebony-skinned, black-furred enchanting Sasquatchette, to arrive at last at a Bowling Palace in Las Vegas filled with bicep-bending sloe-eyed nuns whose skimpy habits revealed more than they hid, and supervised by abnormally round Madams who came and went mysteriously via 'Nun Such' supply rooms that no one else could access.

Her eye fell on three figures, two in brown cassocks, their hair covered by black habits kept stiffly in place with unusual care since they were out among the public. The shortest of the three was the most peculiar, dressed in short pants and stretch shirt and as round as a bowling ball with stick-thin legs and a strangely triangular mouth that rested directly on the body without any trace of neck.

A voice croaked as if still getting used to human speech. "Before she disappeared, Maxie Climax left instructions that we Holy Rollers should watch and care for you always. Now the divine Jessie Christina has brought you back to us, dear Maggie, and Maxie Climax can rest easy in her grave."

At the mention of her erstwhile deceased Momma Maxie, Maggie stirred at the ancient memory and felt a lump in her throat. She stared up at the lowering sky and spoke. "What should I do? What is to become of me?" she asked, directing her question more to the sky than to her visitors.

"I'm Madam G-spot of the Pollo Ranchero Casino & Bowlarama of the Sacred Precinct of Opus Dea for West Upper Los Angeles – Precinct 9, on Venice Boulevard. We think you will be right at home in our little establishment."

Putting her hand in Madam G-spot's, Maggie began to skate.

"I can't hold your hand if you skate," croaked Madam G-spot.

"Who asked you to?"

"Take off your skates, Maggie, please."

"Don wanna."

"You must if I say so."

"Not today."

"I won't be happy if you tell me no."

"You'll have an unhappy life, then."

"You'll get it where the sun don't shine!"

"Good luck tryin!"

"I will slap you like there's no tomorrow."

"You and what army?"

"Try me and see, you little bitch."

"I've tried the best, you whorehouse pimp."

"Don't think your Sasquatch routine will fly with us, you little slut. If you want cactus and booze, you'll do as you're told."

"Not fair!"

"Yes fair!"

The nuns trotted after Maggie as she skated, despite their talk unable to take their star-crossed eyes off her massive thighs and chiseled arms and full breasts, the fame of Maggie's beauty already having spread to every bowling alley west of the Rockies, and not at all deterred by the smeared mascara where her eyebrows once were, or her lost eyelashes, or the fact that her indigo dyed hair had grown out again as brittle yellow and was still tangled with pine needles.

That could all be fixed.

As the little band entered a waiting car and disappeared into the busy Westwood traffic leading to Venice, an old man stood at the entrance to the Department of Non-Patriarchal Fair Trade Astronomy, and watched. Nodding as if a long-awaited plan had finally been put into gear, he smiled a broad smile. Putting his hands in his pockets, he whistled merrily as he walked back to the dense field of smashed bric-a-brac that littered the floor of his office.

Picking up his antique office phone, he dialed. . .

END PART 2

ADVENTURES OF THE RADIATED LESBIAN NUN

'THE JELLO BROTHERS MAKE THEIR MOVE & MAGGIE GETS HER SQUATCH'

Don't MISS THE NEXT ADVENTURES OF MAGGIE, THE RADIATED LESBIAN NUN.. PART 3:

'THE RADIATED LESBIAN NUN MEETS EVIL MIMES'

'HOW THE HOLY POLKA & NON-PATRIARCHAL FAIR TRADE ASTRONOMY SAVED MAGGIE FROM SIRIUS TIMES IN GRIFFITH PARK'

If you enjoyed this
Dark Lotus Book
please post a

REVIEW

on your
favorite websites,
suggestions:

www.amazon.com
www.goodreads.com
www.siriusreviews.com
www.authorsden.com

Thank You!
–Glenn Lazar Roberts

www.ingramcontent.com/pod-product-compliance
Lightning Source LLC
Chambersburg PA
CBHW071456110726
47908CB00003B/630

* 9 7 8 0 9 6 7 5 8 0 9 6 8 *